To Isabel with much love.

Christmas, 1972

Mimé.

COLD GRADATIONS

STANLEY MIDDLETON

COLD GRADATIONS

HUTCHINSON OF LONDON

HUTCHINSON & CO (*Publishers*) LTD
3 Fitzroy Square, London W1

London Melbourne Sydney Auckland
Wellington Johannesburg Cape Town
and agencies throughout the world

First published 1972

*This book has been set in Plantin type, printed in Great Britain
on antique wove paper by Anchor Press, and
bound by Wm. Brendon, both of Tiptree, Essex*

ISBN 0 09 110430 0

'And with no fiery throbbing pain
No cold gradations of decay.
Death broke at once the vital chain
And freed his soul the nearest way.'

Dr. Johnson

I

The old man stood in a garden.

On this spring night, the sky stretched luminously chilly as the wind moved twigs, fidgeted. In the paddock beyond the five-barred gate where James Mansfield leaned, the ground spread dark, in hummocks of shadow, but trees on the far side were outlined, thick tracery, against faint blue now that his eyes became used to the light. Rustling, scraping, the branches massed, above his head, in the next hedgerow, in the far woods, as if to the forests that once coated this land.

Mansfield fingered his dental plate at his fancy. Forest on forest, gnarling in front of him, like massive statuary, but with small activity round each unmoving, rooted bole.

A car's headlamps split the sky as it took the hill, raked the lane, flashed arrogantly into the drive. He scowled, not looking round, gloved hands hard on the top bar. The bell pealed, an outside door opened, smooth in lantern light, voices crackled, a latch clicked, and Hampshire resumed its mild nocturnal chaos.

He turned, cheerfully, to whistle. A Labrador lolloped across, nuzzled him, pawed upright, then dashed in a ring as he let her through the gate. Round, heavily round, with fierce pace and then to stand gasping.

'Good girl.'

The wild motion pleased him, seemed suitable, fitted the cold sky and the nudging branches. It was as if the small movements above had been collected, swept in and released compact into the bounding thump of the animal's mad caper.

'You shouldn't be out, girl.'

His gloved hand felt down to stroke the head. He oughtn't to be there either, but unlike the bitch who'd shot skedaddling for freedom, he'd scarfed himself, found his heaviest overcoat, pulled his golfer's cap on. Slowly, arguing merits, he moved to open the gate and let himself into the paddock. The gate, new, weighty, fresh with white paint, clanged efficiently shut.

Mansfield bent, picked up a cylinder of rotting wood, tossed it.

'Fetch it, Jet.'

She plunged out into the darkness, thumped in circles, burst back panting but without the stick. Gently he massaged her chops.

'You haven't got it, girl.'

At the sound of his voice, she wheeled, stood ready, he could feel her muscular preparation, for another dash. Now he saw more clearly clumps of grass, the dark litter of a mole-hill. He breathed heavily, regretted his polished shoes as he began to cross the soft ground of the field.

'Muddy, my lass. We'll be for it.'

They climbed a stile, into a lane hedged with untidy hawthorn. He fingered down for the dog's neck and she bounded away.

'Here, m'lady.'

In her own time she slithered back, and he touched her, shoving fingers under her collar, before he made a short leash with his handkerchief.

'Steady now; you'll have me over.'

She walked gently at that, though the pull on his hand was strong. High up twigs whisked, and once a sudden rush of wind like a flight of heavy birds caught the tree tops above the sheltered hollow where he walked. The whole night moved minutely alive, nipping the blood, stirred like the boiling of water.

Mansfield turned out of the lane into the tar macadam road with its broad grass verges and arching trees in the hedgerows. He was not sorry to be back and completing the circle let Jet loose as he turned into the broad gravelled drive of Stansmore House, some thirty yards back from the gates. Now he stood, one hand on ornate wrought-iron as the dog snuffled round under the tall lights of the drive.

The house, his son's, was modestly Georgian, four-square from this angle but, he knew, with a bowed west end, wide windowed, to the right. The wall gleamed whitely spick and span while coach-lamps lit the space under the pillared portico with its unassuming three steps. The place was satisfying, well-constructed, modernised, some comfortable farmer's place or curate's or maiden lady's when it was built; but now to the left, unnoticed because curtains were drawn, stood a long, one-storey hall built by an Edwardian squireling, and at the back, bigger than the original block, a wing at right angles where the guests were accommodated and work went on.

Money.

This was a rich man's house, and the cars of affluent friends were ranged in the drive. From the hall on the left music bumped, drably enclosed. James Mansfield massaged his smoothly-shaven face, smiled, straightened his shoulders in a flush of well-being. At seventy-two, on a cold night, he felt healthy, vigorous, ready for labour. His fingers tap-tapped his mouth, smothering no yawn, covering no indecision because he knew what he must do. When he had returned dog and coat to the back-wing he'd walk down to the hall, watch the dancing, drink a small whisky, perhaps push his daughter-in-law through a few steps of a slow fox-trot.

He rounded the house, let himself in at the back through a stone-flagged kitchen, and upstairs to his room. Obediently Jet stayed below, comically, with a rubber doll between her front paws. In his own room, lined with books, he dragged his coat off and walked out to examine himself in the mirror of his dressing room.

'Evening wear,' he said out loud.

Face red under the short white hair, he stroked the lapels of this, his first evening suit, laughing, but ironically pleased. To do the heavy at the age of seventy-odd amused him, but gave him a sense of power, of opportunity, of the available variety of his life. An ex-schoolmaster, he had suffered a coronary thrombosis some months ago, and on his convalescence had come down from his Nottingham-shire bungalow to stay with his son in Hampshire, and there Eleanor, his daughter-in-law, had insisted, very beautifully, that he be measured by her husband's tailor for this finery.

'I don't want togging up at my time of life,' he'd said. She liked this blunt man with his exaggeration of a Midlands accent.

'It's the uniform,' she'd said. 'And it will make David spend some money on you. He never gives you presents.'

'I don't want . . .'

'Father, ' she said, grave grey eyes, mouth superb. 'This time you'll please me.' Softening. 'Won't you?'

He could not resist her, and she knew it. Eleanor, David's wife. Dr. and the Hon. Mrs. D. E. Mansfield.

As he took a brush and duster to his shoes he re-membered his son. A state scholar, first-class honours at Imperial College, doctor of philosophy; time had been when he hoped to see his boy established in a university chair, a scholar. But while David had still been an under-graduate he'd gone to the laboratories of an engineering concern where he'd lasted two years, leaving to join the Mattison-Foort group on the management side.

His father had been shocked.

'Are you wise, David?'

The boy shrugged, grinned, rubbed his handsome jowl. 'I think so.'

'But what about your research?'

He hitched his elegant trousers from his gleaming shoes, smiling thoughtfully as if considering his father's objec-tion seriously. In his mother's rocking-chair he seemed enormous, powerfully ballooning, perfumed, with huge manicured hands whitely mastering the air.

'I've come back home,' David said, ironically. 'To your side. The arts. Back to men and government.'

'Climates, cities, governments.' The quotation masked fear.

'Of man, the heart of man, and human life.'

The boy was clever, read books still, but had outleapt his father. Now he sat, legs crossed, ruthless, efficient, sympathetically eyeing his father because he recognised no rivalry there.

A year later he'd married Sir Robert Mattison's daughter and had duly joined the board. He hardly visited his home town, flew to America, was seen briefly and anonymously on television at take-over considerations, made the business sections of the great newspapers regularly.

To his father there seemed something unsatisfactory about this; his boy was not called 'Minister' or 'Professor', did not appear on discussion panels. When the father-in-law, Sir Robert, succeeded after two deaths to an uncle's title, and Eleanor became the Hon. Mrs. Mansfield, David answered his father's query whether to write to congratulate his lordship: 'Please yourself. I expect everybody else will. But it's a bit of an embarrassment to him really. He doesn't want it. But you write if you want to, dad. I believe in people pleasing themselves and besides you might think of something sensible to say.'

That was typical. Father was now a licensed jester, an intellectual eccentric who might amuse tycoons between ingestions.

Shoes shining, James Mansfield washed his hands, parted his hair again, made his way downstairs, along the windowed corridor, into the foyer with its spacious new oak stairway, and through into the hall. For a moment he stood at the top of the steps, under the gallery, to watch, a servant deferentially at his side.

'Let joy be unconfin'd,' he said drily.

The flunkey gravely nodded, said, 'Yes, sir,' without a smile, and moved some paces distant. A stranger, an employee of the catering firm, in his wine-dark livery, he knew nobody, palmed glasses about on salvers, recognised the host and one duke, added, with others, distinction at enormous expense. Even now he was signalling unobtrusively to a subordinate, who sidling up to Mansfield enquired after his needs.

'Nothing, thank you.'

The man moved away, offended perhaps. Mansfield looked down the hall to where David stood, big, blond, the great left hand sawing the air among respectful cronies. That voice, without taint of a Midlands accent, would comment on local affairs, but uncontradicted; wherever he went yes-men lined his route.

'Hello, grandfather.'

Mansfield started. 'Sarah.'

She'd come quietly behind him, a big girl for her fifteen years, fair like her father and with a touch of her mother's beauty, but more heavily moulded, more human.

'I thought you'd gone out.'

'I did. Jet and I had five minutes' fresh air.'

'She's beautiful.'

'I believe she is.' He loved this child. 'But pretty stupid. Are you enjoying yourself?'

'Not really. Well, yes, I suppose I am in a way. I'd looked forward to it so much. This is the first weekend they've let me off from school. You don't know what it's like.'

'I spent forty years in schools.'

'Not like ours.' She laughed, in contralto depths. If one couldn't have seen her, one would have guessed her age at a mature thirty-five. 'Yours was a school. They learnt things and went home, then.'

'A boarding school's different?'

'It ought to be more efficient. They've got us at beck and call for twenty-four hours a day. And daddy pays the earth. But they're hopeless.'

12

'Martinets, you mean?'

'No. Drips. Wets. They aren't even interested in what they're teaching us. As for occupying us . . .' She laughed again.

'Does your father know all this?'

She turned, so that the flash of full face seemed momentarily dazzling; fair straight hair, bright teeth, blue silk of her dress caught him and he gasped, physically winded at youth's perfection.

'I talk to him sometimes.'

'And?'

'I don't know whether I ought to tell you this, grandpa, but he doesn't think highly of schoolteachers.'

'Merely pays considerably?'

'I expect he sets it off against some sort of tax or other.'

'I see.'

He wanted to put his arm through hers, but daren't because he'd little notion of how she'd take it.

'What d'you see?' she said. The voice swelled southern-standard, country, hunting-haughty. His wife would have enjoyed hearing her grand-daughter with a grande-dame's vocal habits.

'Your father makes poor tax-payers subsidise you at an inefficient educational establishment where the money is wasted?'

'Probably.'

'You'd do just as well at Edge Park Grammar?'

'Education-wise? Yes. Otherwise . . .' She spread her arms, hands splayed, a gesture from her father.

'Aren't you dancing?' he asked. The girl spoke frankly to him, and the impact of her turning full-face affected him still.

'When they ask me.'

'There must be plenty of good-looking boys here.'

'Where?'

The word dropped in ironical despair, a child's sound, from a world of minor tragedy. Sarah's mother approached, without hurry, in beauty, tall, mouth poised, curved in a smile, utterly fetching.

'Have you had your evening whisky, father?'

'Not yet.'

A footman stood at her elbow; graciously she issued instructions.

'I wouldn't stand up there, Sarah.'

'I was talking to grandfather.'

'Yes.'

The monosyllable fell, finally, damning the child for indifference or impropriety. It slit her throat, softly.

'I saw James and Clare in the bar. And Angélique quite on her own.'

'I'm not wanted?' Sarah's voice flared, uncertainly. No annoyance showed itself in her mother's smooth face, but the girl touched her grandfather's sleeve, a blind, searching movement, before she moved off. The two watched her as she avoided the dancers, walked between tables.

'Poor Sarah.' No pity there.

'Rough grub,' Mansfield said.

'What does that mean?'

'Just what you said. Awkward age.'

'Was David?' He never understood why she took trouble, displaying such virtuosity of animation. He was unimportant.

'He was a hefty lad. Good at rugby, cricket. And working hard.'

'A paragon?'

'If you like.' He did not approve. 'Is he now?'

'You belong to the generation which doesn't believe in criticising spouses. Spice.' She laughed, moderately, to attract. 'If I said something, you'd read more into it than I meant.'

'That's naive,' he said.

'Of course. I'm sorry.'

She nodded her head, and was gone, gently. Before she'd progressed six steps, she'd collected a knot of men. He didn't understand her, that was a certainty. An excellent hostess, she seemed to care little for her four children, by whom she did her duty, employing expensive nannies, sending them off, later, to schools for the rich, providing clothes and presents and holidays. She was beautiful, almost perfectly so, knew exactly what to say, never appeared to scheme, made no errors either with her husband's business acquaintances nor when she sat on the local magistrates' bench. Mansfield wondered what she made of him.

He, by a fluke, had produced David, the one person she seemed to admire. Her father-in-law's interest in books and music and the radio meant nothing to her; she inquired every day after his comfort while he stayed there, made a point of sitting with him for at least half-an-hour so that he was flattered. All this was done without ostentation; when he tried to talk to her about a novel he was reading she neither made faces, nor sharpened her voice in feigned interest. She listened, she replied, mainly from ignorance as she admitted, but sometimes surprising him with a titbit of knowledge. Nothing overdone, she played her ravishing part, mystified the old man.

'Has El been looking after you?' David would shout, looking in at the weekend.

'She sat with me this afternoon.'

'Good. That's the way.'

The door would close, and his son would exchange a dozen further words with his youngest children, if they were still up.

Modern love.

James Mansfield moved along the dance-floor, passing Eleanor who, surrounded by men, was listening peaceably to an anecdote from the local M.P. He made for the bar, where he watered the small whisky and parked himself. David danced past with the Duchess of Belvoir, a severe young woman with shining black hair parted down the middle. As he receded he winked at his father who smiled sourly.

The old man had nothing against his son's grimaces, but that morning he and David had talked together, so that James felt he had been bullied, drilled, treated as a fool, and had sat an hour, resenting it, unable to read or listen. David, who had been at home all day because of the dinner-dance for the Conservative Party funds, had knocked, sharply, but had waited. He asked permission to sit down, wasted no time.

'Eleanor tells me, dad, that you're talking of going back home.'

'Yes. I am.' His son's reasonable approach always caused him to answer sulkily.

'Well, now, is that wise? You're a lot better, I know, and you must please yourself.'

'And if I go back I shall start to overdo it and have another heart attack.'

'You know the story better than I do.'

'No, thank you, David. I'm very grateful.'

'We don't like to think,' the deep voice purred, a machine, 'of you on your own up there. If anything happens . . .'

'There are doctors. There are neighbours.'

'We could get preferential treatment here. A doctor inside five minutes . . .' The huge hands spread indicating the consultations, the private wards, the medical expertise to be purchased.

'They don't purvey immortality, David.'

'No, but I want you to die in comfort.'

A warning, a polite thrust. Mansfield could not help admiring his son, who matched the exact word to the situation.

'Thank you all the same, but I want to go back.'

It sounded childish, mardy.

'You're no trouble. Eleanor and the children enjoy having you. And I think you keep your eye on us all.'

'What does that mean?'

'I look at you, and I think, "That fellow shoved me

16

round in a pram. And it doesn't seem five minutes ago to him, either." '

'Well?'

'I'm human again.' A boyish smile twisted the mouth. 'I push people about. I make things work. It's fascinating. It gives me no spare time. Power is a full-time occupation.'

'That doesn't recommend it to me.'

'Because you've never had it.' Again the smile. 'I'm the type. But it does me no harm to think, in a two-minute let-up, that somebody exists who can remember the first word I said, the first step I took.'

Mansfield said nothing, uncomfortably, for they could not sit easily in silence together.

'What happens,' as the father began, the son's eyes squinted warily, 'when you come up against an even bigger, more ruthless power-hog?'

'Easy. I join him.'

'And if you can't?'

'I run away when I have to. That's called intelligence.' David examined, scratched his right palm. 'I don't advertise it in the papers. I wish you'd stop, dad; just for a few more weeks at least.'

'Has Eleanor been at you?'

'It so happens, you silly old sod,' a long finger prodded the third button down on his father's cardigan, 'that I'm fond of you.'

Both laughed, the older gratefully, and then the son towered, waved, backed out, his wife's instruction complied with. If Mansfield left now, it would be guiltily.

Now, this evening, as James Mansfield watched, the Duke of Belvoir stood alongside. A man of forty, with a heavily lined face, and thick, untidy curls, deeply grey, he stroked his cheek with stained hands, breathing audibly. As David sailed past with the duchess, faces serious, he pushed his lips out, but wasted no glance, with feet wide apart and fists doubled now in pockets. There was nothing aristocratic about the man, nothing of the years of lording it; he looked and dressed like a night-club owner.

Mansfield grinned at his observation. Not a yard divided them.

Eleanor's father edged up to the duke, spoke in a low voice. Belvoir, straightening slightly, said loudly, 'Really?' and lit a long cigarette. The two men squared shoulder to shoulder, of a height, in awkward silence until Robert Mattison, Lord Charnborough, blurted out:

'You know David's father, don't you?'

Belvoir turned towards Mansfield. His eyes were large, darkly liquid, under hooded lids.

'Good evening,' he said, coughed.

Mansfield nodded, not wanting to talk to the man, merely to watch him, closely, and if the truth be known to play round him in imagination.

'I was brought up on your estate,' Mansfield said.

'Really.'

'In Welstow.'

'Oh, yes. It's quite a pretty village, or it was.'

'Do you never go there?'

'No. I don't live in the Abbey now. I've no interest in country life. We live abroad, and in South Africa.'

'You've no feeling for the place?'

Belvoir blew smoke, but tiredly. That question should not have been put, in that Midlands accent.

'I wasn't brought up there, you know.'

He shrugged into himself, like a man wrapping, whirling a cloak around.

The three peered, silent, shy until James Mansfield made his effort.

'Excuse me,' he said.

The other two lifted heads, comically together as the third pushed away across the floor, towards bed.

J ames Mansfield, legs out, basked behind glass in the
spring sunshine. Clouds flew but without menace, their
shadows sweeping the landscape. In his arm-chair, at home,
he stirred uncomfortably as the garden darkened for brief
seconds, burst back into the fickle brightness of sun.
Blowing aloud, he reperched the writing pad on his knee,
and began again on the letter of thanks to Eleanor.

He did not write easily.

First, he had not enjoyed the visit, nor the leave-taking.
This he blamed on himself, on his independence, on his
inability to feel grateful. He wished to give, not receive.
Ungraciously he finished, wrote a post-script: 'I don't
deserve such good children. I know that.' Hypocrite.

The ringing of the door-bell surprised him, for he'd
noticed nobody come across the garden. Alfred Hapgood.

'Come in,' Mansfield almost shouted.

'Are you not busy, then?'

'No.'

'Are you sure?' Hapgood had not budged.

'Come on in, man. I'm glad to see you.'

He showed his visitor into the lounge, before putting
the kettle on. When he returned, he found the newcomer
standing by the plate-glass window, looking over the daf-
fodil clumps and down into the valley.

'Beautiful view.'

'Yes.' This was the end bungalow of the row, much
bigger than any other, built in an old cottage garden with a
view over the dipping fields, two railway embankments,
the gorse of the common land, and then smoke-smudged
streets, chapels, factories low by the river. Behind, for his
place formed a corner, sprawled a new private housing
estate, avenue after crescent of bijou housing for the young

middle-classes, bright in Scandinavian wood without garden walls, Escorts and Avengers in the drives, shrill with the calls of tricycling children. But here, from the front with its apple-trees, its beech hedges, Mansfield's home seemed placed in the country, hung on a hillside.

'Beautiful.'

Grey, silver to leaden, under the clouds; sunshine and shadows shifting, clear-edged over the distant houses, the rising hills beyond, with fringes of trees and lower the straight prim rows of new corporation flats. The two men stood together, hands over the radiator.

'I wanted to see you, Mr. Mansfield.'

Hapgood was nearly his host's age, a stocky man, with big, crumpled hands, an ugly, deep-lined face. Two of his sons had been pupils of Mansfield's at the Grammar School; both held administrative posts abroad.

'It's about our Tom's child.'

Tom was the youngest son, an awkward lout, who'd fooled and failed the eleven-plus, had worked in the mines, in a garage, on building sites. The child of his parents' maturity he'd been accident-prone, trouble-courting. At eighteen he'd put a girl seven years his senior in the family way, had married her, and then stupidly watched their child die. He deserted his wife to work away, leaving the Hapgoods, who despised the woman, to look after her as far as her filthy habits allowed in the terrace house where she lethargically eyed the cobwebs or stamped on the silver fishes scuttling across her hearth. She never returned visits, merely thanked them passively for the money she wasted the same evening on beer with men in the nearest, dirtiest pub. While the other two boys, a doctor and a college principal, were promoted, travelled, married suitable wives, Tom drank, drifted, did not care.

Seven years back, suddenly, his wife had been taken into hospital with cancer and had died within days.

The husband returned, slept in his old bedroom, got a labouring job, and within six months had married again, a young whey-faced girl with limp flaxen hair from one of the hosiery factories.

They'd lived, in spite of the Hapgoods' offer of money, with Enid's people. Almost immediately, on the way to a seaside holiday, the four had been involved in a car accident; the parents had never regained consciousness while Tom, who had been driving, was unmarked. When a child was born he was found to be sub-normal, dull and ailing, so that neither parent took an interest in him. Enid found herself a job, parked the boy with the Hapgoods, collected him reluctantly each evening from his exhausted grandmother.

Then, four months back, Tom and his wife had flitted without warning, leaving the child with the grandparents and not writing until six weeks later. Could they hang on to Clive a bit until they'd got a proper home? It wouldn't be long. Since that, they'd received one more letter, written from a different address, announcing both had jobs, but that Tom was coming down as soon as he could. Love to Clive. They hoped he was all right.

Mansfield knew this.

As he stood, he considered his visitor. No, Hapgood wasn't quite his age; perhaps he was sixty-five or six and still efficiently supervising his hardware shop on the main street. A clever man, with opportunity he would have made a barrister, a popular clergyman, an actor: he never publicly regretted his status, lived through his elder sons.

'It's killing my wife.'

The voice was deep, beautifully controlled, and though the accent twanged local, its power and resonance impressed the listener.

'Well then, Mr. Hapgood?'

'I don't know. I don't know.'

A week ago he'd been shoulder to shoulder with a duke, today with an ironmonger, and the latter was impressively superior. Hapgood swung round.

'He'll have to assume his responsibilities. But I can't get

him to see it. He lives up there in two rooms in Bradford. I drove over this day week. I put it to him as I'm putting it to you. "Tom," I said, "it's killing your mother," and all he could utter was something about putting him in the care of the local authority. "It's your child, and your responsibility," I said. "You brought him into the world," but I might as well have talked to a brick wall.'

The two settled to their tea.

Hapgood called on this, his early closing day, and the two would sit until four-thirty when they'd shake hands solemnly. The friendship was formal; no christian names. Mansfield, both assumed, knew the way of the world better for they had first met when Hapgood, greatly daring, had knocked to ask about a sixth form course for his eldest son. The schoolmaster had been attracted by the great voice, the lined ugly face that had changed little in the last twenty-five years, and saw in young Stephen something of his own hopes for David now scoring inevitable alphas at the County High School. This lad would be the forerunner, the John the Baptist for his own boy.

Friendship developed slowly, with a few words in the street or at some school function. When, just after David took his brilliant first, Mrs. Mansfield had died, the Hapgoods sent a wreath, and a few days later presented themselves at the front door. It had comforted Mansfield, against his judgement, to see this couple with straight faces, in their Sunday best, making gestures, saying words, accepting tea, staying just too long, acting like chapel stewards.

'I wanted your advice, Mr. Mansfield.'

The older man tugged at the sleeves of his cardigan, admired the white woodwork of his windows and the shifting sky beyond.

'It's killing Clara. She can't stand much more, that I can tell you.'

'What do you suggest, then?'

'I'll go see him, face him with it.'

That's it, take the child, dump him on them, and watch them abandon him, bash, starve, neglect him to death. Reason had nothing for Tom Hapgood. Who'd burden himself with a cross-eyed brat squawking himself and you daft all day and half the night? Put him in somewhere. Let them see to him.

'Will it make any difference?'

'Even him and that fly-by-night wife of his will know what I mean when I say that their mother's had enough.'

'What will he do?'

'I don't know, Mr. Mansfield.' The voice drooped with a great harmony of sound, should have been at some climax of poetry, some tragic resignation of resonance. *O noisy bells, be dumb. I hear you.* 'But there I go, and I don't come back until I've seen him. It'll mean staying overnight. Mr. Mansfield, there's something I want to ask. That's why I come. Will you go up with me? In the van?'

'Of course.' The still, small voice followed the earthquake. Mansfield rose to the table, poured again, stood sipping. This acquiescence was quixotic; he'd be no help; he could not keep his temper.

The other day he and David had argued, in one of their five minutes together, and this had driven the father spare.

'Where'll you retire to, David?' The old man enjoyed springing surprises, a schoolmaster's trick.

'The Bahamas.' Immediate.

'Why there?'

'Weather, principally. None of your coughs and bronchitis. No rheumatism. No servant problem. Plenty of drink and company.'

'There won't be any libraries, or concerts, or theatres.'

'You can't have everything.'

'Aren't they important to you, then?'

'How many times a year do you see me at a concert now? When do I have time to read a book?'

'Music, reading, don't mean anything?'

David thought; the eyebrows lifted over the clever eyes.

'No. You lose the habit.'

A spasm of temper shook the old man so that he crouched in his chair, weak, breathless with rage. This, this prize-winning, starred-first doctor of philosophy would not, could not, on his own admission, open a book with enjoyment. Tears flooded his eyes. The son considered, turned the tap of a radiator, immersed elsewhere.

'That's not an admission I'd care to make.'

'I see that,' David said.

'But what will you do when you control nobody, when your companies have gone, when you've twenty-four hours a day to yourself?'

'Sit it out in the sun. Drink my liver stiff. Eye the dollies. Play the market. Bore the world telling 'em how I did it.'

'Culture . . .' What could he say? Heart-broken he blew his nose.

'I know what you mean, dad,' David said. 'You're probably right. I'll leave you. You haven't got far with *The Bostonians* there.'

On target. His father saw that. He'd been three weeks with them and hadn't read a hundred pages. Culture. A played game. Not reading a classic, you pretended you were.

Alone, he sniffed in weakness.

Now he'd promised to accompany this other old failure to Yorkshire, two of them in a shaking van, testing their hearts out. Not hurrying themselves, they now made provisional arrangements, one of which was that Mansfield should visit the Hapgoods next day to see the child.

The shop was closed, and the boy, freshly bathed, sat in pyjamas and dressing-gown in front of the living room fire. He'd just been scrubbed, but his hair stood upright in spikes, a gutter-urchin's total quiff; when he turned, his right eye had a cast so violent that it hurt, like looking at an open wound. Now he hardly stirred, picked at his toes, half-heartedly rested his hand on the cab of a wooden yellow lorry on the hearth-rug. He seemed lethargic, ill coordinated, slow, until the gash of boss-eye, the open mouth forced the spectator to turn his head.

Mrs. Hapgood pulled him on to her knee, not tenderly, where he lolled, tongue thick.

'It's your bed-time, young man,' she said.

The boy made a noise, stretched, broke wind.

'Do you want to go to the toilet?'

Again a whine, discomfortable only, in tone.

'Are you sure?'

The face lurched round to Mansfield, who drilled himself to look. The features apart from the eye and mouth were good; a straight, delicate nose, square forehead, neat chin, but the cast and the dribble of saliva marked idiocy only too plainly. One could not tell where he looked, if he saw, even.

Mrs. Hapgood stood.

'Say good-night then, Clive. Nightie-night.'

He made a sound that was almost recognisable. She took his hand, led him from the room. From the back, he appeared normal, a three-year-old going up to bed, not hurrying.

'He's tired, now,' Hapgood said. 'Sometimes in the day he's like a devil for energy, thrashing about. You just can't hold him.'

'Can't they do anything for his eye?'

'They'll operate, they say.'

'Oughtn't it to be done already? I mean he can't have binocular vision with his eye like that.' The words soothed Mansfield; he forgot the hideous effect.

'He's very delicate.'

'He doesn't look it.'

'No? That's half the trouble.'

The two men talked until Mrs. Hapgood returned. She joined the conversation, but withing five minutes was in tears, clasped hands shaking. 'I can't go on,' she squealed. 'I can't go on. It isn't fair to ask me.'

Mansfield, embarrassed, looked away as his friend

slouched across the floor, pulled out his handkerchief, held it to his wife's face.

'Blow,' he ordered, as if to a child.

She obeyed; it did her good, and patting at her hair, rearranging her spectacles, she sat straighter.

'I don't know what you'll think of me, Mr. Mansfield.'

He made noises, no words. For the last few moments nobody had observed propriety; the woman's shaking limbs had done for them all. It reminded him of war; grown men vulnerable as children, brash, cowering, pulling themselves together, drawing desperately on a fag before shrapnel ripped them to shreds.

'You must do something,' he said. It sounded sane.

'He's got to take his responsibility.' The husband.

Mrs. Hapgood looked hopelessly from one man to the other, in comical resignation.

'He'll none do a stroke unless he's forced.'

'Then we'll force him.'

'How can you? That's soft talk. I don't know how we could have got such a son, Mr. Mansfield. He's no more thought than that child upstairs. Feckless and wild; married that girl with nothing to her. But then to have that Clive. He might be cursed by God.'

She wept, not much, unobtrusively in a comfortable armchair. After ten minutes the men began to speak more freely, about a book, Leonard Woolf's last volume of autobiography, and the woman intervened though in a shaky whisper. They enjoyed themselves on his arithmetic of service, the hours he'd spent on committees, on good causes.

'I can't make up my mind if it was wasted,' Mansfield said.

'In a way. In a way.'

'But how could he, being who he was, have spent it otherwise?'

'He's got his book out of it, any road.'

'It'll be forgotten. It's good, but it won't last.'

'However long he spent,' Mrs. Hapgood looked up, handkerchief ready, 'if it only did one person five minutes' good, just once, that's something.'

'Isn't the price high?'

They didn't answer, three in front of a coal fire, aging.

When he left, saddened, he could not shake off depression. The woman's misery had been too open, too blatant. That she had made no attempt to hide her state appalled him because he saw utter change in her character. Perhaps that was wrong; she was built for success only, to live healthily, making her shop pay, her husband content, proud in the achievement of her family. In that environment she appeared bluntly good, with independence of mind; now, under physical exhaustion, she crumpled: a nobody, a cry-baby, untrained in the sourness of failure.

Mansfield hated this.

As a schoolmaster he knew he remembered his successes, but, in fact, the majority of his pupils turned out mediocrities if not outright disappointments. It was not perhaps his fault, but if he took no blame for their unsuccess, their commonplace dullness, then he deserved no credit for the bright stars. They would have done as well, better, under other teachers. Mere chance had included him. Hating this conclusion, he stumped about the house, fingering books, tinkering at the piano, and finally in despair polishing already gleaming furniture. The mood would pass. He who is down needs fear no fall.

Next morning he received a reply to his letter of thanks from his daughter-in-law. She always wrote well, with care, almost as if she'd dictated first, then revised the type-script to re-write it in her own large handwriting. It was a privilege, he believed, to be allowed to read her missives, on the huge square pieces of paper with an equal margin at all four edges.

Today, she did nothing for him.

First, she said they were sorry he'd felt he had to go home, but they were pleased he'd enjoyed himself. As long as he hadn't felt neglected while they organised their dinner-dance she was satisfied. However, she had unfortunately something to tell him, and she wished she hadn't to write it.

'The fact is David and I aren't getting on well together.

'I don't know whether you noticed this while you were here. I guess it's fairly obvious.' God. He had not. He thought back. Nothing. While these two ruined their lives, he'd sat there talking to the dog.

'David says I should have told you, on the grounds that if anything rotten comes of it, you ought to be prepared. He wanted me, though, to do the talking, because he says he'd make his own side right, he couldn't help it. I don't know if that's true or not. I think perhaps he's a bit afraid of you still, as I am of my father. But I said, "As soon as I let it out, he'll face you with it, if I know him." And he replied, "Yes, but he'll have heard your side first."

'I don't want you to make too much of this, because perhaps nothing will happen. We've got a young family and David won't do anything precipitate there. Of course we don't know. When once we faced the facts, not that we're not in love, but that we've pretty well nothing in common except the children and the furniture and the years we've lived together, one or the other of us might decide on something, somebody new. One doesn't know.

'Oddly enough Sarah noticed.

'She asked me why we didn't talk so much to each other. I denied it. She just said, "Well, you don't." I told David, and he snapped, "It's true, isn't it?" That's how he is. I could hate him without too much encouragement.'

Mansfield took the letter out into the garden.

Sunshine spread warmly and in the distance a great cloud of birds chirped and clamoured. He retained the letter in its envelope as he stumbled from new growth to flower, in the green and yellow riot of nature. While he had been in Hampshire, Eleanor had driven him up to London to see Shakespeare's *Twelfth Night*.

28

That was the play he'd studied for the London Matriculation fifty-odd years ago, and he remembered it still, was caught again by its young fire.

> 'If I did love you with my master's flame
> With such a suffering, such a deadly life,
> In your denial I would find no sense;
> I would not understand it.'

He recalled old Percy Hardy spouting the words in front of the class, his nonconformist conscience, his ulcer, his lay preaching forgotten. Or Dorothy Drew in their college production, hair short-golden, womanly boyish. And in the box, from his carping soul, as he revelled in this bursting language of spring, he had suddenly thought that he'd probably never hear these words, fresh and familiar, again in the theatre. Cold horror touched. Ice of death. A blank, my lord. She never told her love. That. That.

Now with equivalent chill he faced the morning.

Who was he to bask, to snatch at the scents, while the world disintegrated round him? Why should he stand in his own ground, healthy, happy, while Eleanor broke her heart or Clara Hapgood dragged mad? He'd be next. His star-card marked, he'd be tested. God be merciful.

He turned indoors.

Four days later Eleanor phoned.

She usually kept in touch only by letter, so that he knew something had gone amiss.

29

'Have you seen Sarah?'

'No.'

'She's run away from school. The day before yesterday.' Eleanor's voice sounded tiredly rational, but composed. 'We thought she might have come to you.'

'No.' Speak, man. 'Is this unexpected, Eleanor?'

'Oh, yes. Both to the school and to us. They say, as I would, that she's both clever and conventional. She played for the teams, took a big part in producing her form play, seemed perfectly happy. Then she and her friend just disappeared.'

'Where?'

'They took a bus into Oxford. That's all we know.'

'Money?'

'They'll have some. A pound or two.'

'I see,' he said. 'And the other girl? Is she likely to have influenced Sarah? To do something daft?'

'I've no idea. I've not met her, but the school didn't suggest anything.'

'What does David say?'

'He's upset. He's in London, but he offered to go up. Oddly enough the school didn't seem unduly put out. All in a day's work to them. Seems quite common these days to pack your bags.'

'Eleanor,' he asked, slowly, 'it's nothing to do with this other business, is it? Between you and David?'

She did not think so; nothing further had happened there, or was likely to. He was not to make mountains out of molehills. For the next five minutes she talked to him as calmly as to her butcher. In the end she said:

'Basically, I don't think Sarah's capable of anything really silly. That's where I could be wrong. In that case, I don't know what I'll do. Or David.'

'Well, don't forget to look after yourself.'

Outside the window the swirl of spring, flying clouds, windy sun, danced festival.

Not a quarter of an hour after Eleanor had finished,

Hapgood rang to ask him for company tomorrow on his Yorkshire trip.

In the plain van, the old men talked, this time about science. Both believed that the human race could pollute the world, so that only those inside the domes of cities would be able to breathe and live, but while Hapgood relished the idea, grumbled but felt it a just reward, Mansfield's optimism looked for some saving miracle. They spoke between silences; sentences were interspersed along the whine of wind and tyres. Neither convinced the other; both boasted of their reading and listening, though the older man felt the exercise useless, because whatever they decided the earth would sprawl on, poison or redeem itself without their leave. And yet, warm in the cab, they enjoyed each other's company, the release from the humdrum, even in the dread of what was to come.

They ate a snack in the car, bought themselves a cup of tea at a lorry-driver's café where they watched the long-distance men calling out, in a hotch-potch of accents, bits of incomprehensible, dull news.

'This is one thing,' Mansfield said, 'that the car does for you. It pitchforks you fast into other people's lives. You stand in a village post office waiting to buy a bar of chocolate and listening to some stranger's tale of woe.'

'It would happen if you were on a walking-tour.'

'Not so often. And how many of us did hike, in fact?'

'No. We saw railway stations.'

By five o'clock a policeman had explained how to reach Mount Street, and they had looked at, commented on the black stone of public buildings, had visited the public lavatories and were ready.

'We'll get there just before six,' Hapgood said. 'That gives 'em time to get home. I wrote. I don't know whether I did right there. I wouldn't put it past him to be out.'

Mount Street was squat and Victorian, terraces of five houses between entries, all with bow-windows and cramped front gardens trampled to earth and littered with coal-lumps or filled darkly by a privet hedge. Curtains varied from window to window, all garish, most dirty, and any new painting work was daubed, with splashes and unwiped drips, over unprepared wood. The house next to Tom's was pink, the colour of a primer. Hapgood drew his lips in.

'Done by a drunkard on a dark night,' he said.

Nobody answered his sharp rap. He knocked louder.

'They're in no hurry,' he said, banging again. Two piccaninnies stared from the street. The door creaked open so that Enid greeted them from the dark corridor.

'I thought I heard a knock,' she said. At first Mansfield imagined that they had to transact their business on the doorstep, but the girl stepped back and into the front room shouting, 'Tom, it's your dad.'

The son was wiping his dinner plate with a half-slice of bread, at a small table by the wall. An armchair, a television set, three smaller chairs, two packing cases and a tea-chest made up the rest of the furniture. Mansfield found himself distressed by the dirtiness of the windowpanes which were thickly grey behind lace curtains filthy as fog.

They were left to choose their own seats. Tom pushed his plate to one side while his wife took a defensive stance in front of an unlighted gas-fire. The air oozed cold.

'Are you all right, then?' Hapgood asked.

His son waved an arm, as if inviting them to judge his health from his circumstances. If one disregarded the sallow skin, he was not unhandsome, featuring his brothers, Mansfield thought, but with a look of stupidity, as if from adenoids or a heavy blow. He wore clay stained jeans and no shoes.

'And Enid?'

'Could be worse.' And she grinned. She looked years younger than her husband, in a belted yellow mini-skirt, but her face, untouched by makeup, shone half-finished, malformed, with a nose like a boxer's. Her neck stretched long under the small head, the insignificant eyes, but her limbs were magnificent, large, shapely, smoothly tapering to delicate wrists and ankles.

'This is Mr. Mansfield, who's come with me.'

Tom poured himself another cup of tea, while Enid clasped her hands behind her back, thrusting her breasts forward and her frock higher.

'Did you get my letter, then?'

Man looked at wife. There was no collusion or question about the glance, no intelligence.

'Ah.' Tom crossed his outstretched legs.

'Then you know why I've come.'

'Clive.' Tom.

'We was going to write.' Enid. They spoke together. Both voices lacked resonance, squeaked ragged. Satisfied, Tom lit a cigarette, passed the battered packet to his wife who searched in a pot dog on the mantelpiece for a box of matches.

'Well then?' Hapgood sat straighter. His daughter-in-law dropped into the arm-chair, crossing her legs.

No one spoke. Two blew cigarette smoke about the room in silence. The younger people were composed, not unhappy, waiting. 'Your mother can't go on much longer,' Hapgood said in the end. His voice burst out, almost unreasonably against the settled quiet of the others. He received no answer to that so that he stared uncomprehendingly at Mansfield, who'd seen that expression on the face of a Tommy shouting at a French peasant.

'He's your child,' Hapgood said.

'We know he is.'

'You don't act like it.'

'What are we to do?' Tom got up, lazily awkward, and searched for an ash-tray into which he flicked the match he'd been holding. It was utterly uncharacteristic, as if he'd invited them to pray with him. 'We ain't properly settled 'ere. We've just got the two rooms, and we're payin' too much for them. We want to move. We don't know where we are.'

'So you leave it to us?'

'Me mam said she'd 'ave him.'

Hapgood suddenly bared his false teeth.

'That isn't good enough, Tom, and you know it. Clive's your responsibility. Your mother's getting no younger. And while we've had him you've written once. Not a word of inquiry, not a penny piece towards his upkeep. What sort of people are you?'

'He ought to be in an 'ome,' Tom muttered.

'If we have him,' Enid began, voice snuffling with catarrh, 'he's such an 'andful that I shouldn't be able to go to work, and then where should we be? We 'ave all on to make ends meet now.'

'So Tom's mother has to ... ?'

'He should be in an 'ome.'

'He should, Tom. Yours. He's your child, your responsibility.'

'It isn't as if 'e was all right in 'is head.'

All the son's remarks were delivered unclearly at the floor, his cigarette bobbing in his lips.

'It would 'a been better if he'd died.' Enid.

'He didn't. Somebody's got ...'

Hapgood broke off, hopeless. The conversation staggered. Nobody wanted an idiot.

'Well, what are you going to do, then?' Hapgood sounded truculent.

'I didn't know you wanted anything for his keep.'

'That's not what I asked you.'

Enid wiped her hands roughly on her belly, dragging skirt ends above the darker tops of her tights then, twisting, nearly slung her cigarette end into the fire-place. Sitting up, she jerked her frock decent.

'Now, come on, Tom. What are you going to do?'

'I don't know.'

'You've got to make your mind up, one way or the other.'

The pair were equally desponding, speaking non-existent minds, crossed, unaffected. Mansfield could not decide if Tom had assumed firmly that his parents would not put the child on the streets, or whether he was incapable of thinking anything beyond his instant comfort. On the other hand, Hapgood now seemed only to be reciting formulae, mantras to heathenish unknowns.

'Since that accident,' Enid said, breaking off.

Four of them in the family saloon, making good time for the beach, straight at an oncoming lorry, swerving at the last minute so that the parents in the back seat were killed, while the young couple tottered up, cut, shocked, alive. One heave at the wheel; two die, rumpled with the luggage.

'We're thinking of coming back,' Enid started again.

'Have you got a job in mind?'

'I can get one easy.' Tom spat a shred of tobacco from his mouth.

'When?'

'Depends. Don't it?'

Hapgood, in disgust, faced Enid.

'What about Clive?'

'Me mam would have took him. It needs two on us at work.'

'How's that?'

'Tom's nerves's bad. Can't always do a full week. An' who'd want to sit here every night?' Mansfield noticed wallpaper under the window, discoloured, buckling from the plaster. 'Sometimes, I'm at me wits' end. He just don't move out of his chair, like a statue. I don't know what to do or to say.' Her husband lit another cigarette, coughing on the smoke. 'It's awful. I don't know what t'think.'

'Your mother can't look after him. It's making her ill.'

'He should be looked after,' Tom said. 'We can't.'

'Your mother.'

'I've been badly. Enid's to'd you. Couldn't shift out o' me chair. And pain.'

Blocked, Hapgood turned to his companion, who

crouched in his chair, choked by the cigarette-smoke, the purposeless talk. Not much above a week ago, he was sitting in his son's polished rooms, exchanging words with the nobility, coddled, pampered among elegant furniture while now in this bare place, damp as a cellar, he was asked to judge. The other three waited, almost, he imagined, politely.

'I should set a time-limit,' he said.

'How do you mean?' Hapgood in hope.

'Name a certain short period.' Officialese, trouble-shooting. 'Say a fortnight. During that time, your son can change his job, his lodgings if he wishes, and on an agreed date you return his son.'

'How's that, now?' The father, reviving.

'A fortni't? That don't gi'e us long.'

'You've got to make your mind up,' Hapgood argued.

'We shouldn't leave here till the end of the week,' Enid said. 'We're paid up. Then we've got to move, get settled, find work.'

'It in't on.'

'You agree on the period?' Mansfield said.

'We agree,' Enid answered. 'But at the end of the time nothing's done. We're still 'ere. It's likely. You don't know 'im. I do.' She jerked a thumb towards her husband. 'I'm not blamin' 'im. He's badly. Nob'dy knows it better than I do. But nothing gets done, and then where are you?'

'It needs good will.'

'It needs summat. I'm bloody well fed up, I can tell you. Work all day, then home to cookin' and his grousin'. He don't do a hand's bloody turn all day. Sittin' there like a bloody ghost, waitin' for me t'come home and put the bloody food into his mouth. What sort of life's that? In this dump?'

The three men dropped heads at the outburst; it might have been a prayer meeting.

'If you can make a clean start,' Hapgood began.

'It's him,' Enid shouted, shriller. 'Him. Nowt'll change

him. Sit's there, too bloody idle to wipe his arse. And you talk about Clive. If I didn't go to work, d'you know what'd happen? We sh'd starve.'

'That isn't true, Enid.' Her father-in-law.

'What d'you know about it? If he runs out of fags in the day, he's too damned lazy to walk to the shop. Waits for me to come home. That's what it's like.'

'What do you suggest?' Mansfield spoke in an official voice. Contempt twisted her shiny face to rawer ugliness. Her mouth gawped, her broken nose in pallor.

'I suggest I bloody well leave him to it. That's what I suggest.'

'But the child.'

'Don't you think I'd 'ave the poor little sod if I could? He'd drive me daft, but he's my responsibility. Don't think you can come slummin' round here tellin' me what's right and what's wrong.'

'We want to help,' Mansfield said.

'You've not done much yet, 'ave yer?'

Silence again as she scratched at her belly. The room was clouded with smoke. Chairs clicked and creaked as each moved. Enid pushed to her feet, clattered the pots together, stacked them, banged them out to the kitchen. Returning she dragged the cloth from the table. A big tear hung by her mouth, dropped away.

'We'll fix a date, then,' Hapgood said.

'Do as you like.'

She stood, however, waiting to hear. A fortnight next Saturday was named. Enid nodded, folded her tablecloth.

'Is that all right for you?' Hapgood asked his son.

'It'll 'ev to be, wain't it?' Again a bout of coughing, as if the sentence had irritated his lungs.

'You'll write, now, and let us know?'

Tom's bloodshot eyes widened, as he wiped the back of his hand across his mouth, stood up, left the room. The visitors waited; from the kitchen they could hear Enid at work.

37

'What say, then?' Hapgood.

'Let's get straight back home. Tonight. Not stay here.'

'Won't upset you?'

'Bed all day tomorrow if it does.'

They scarfed up, buttoned the coats they'd not removed. In the greasy kitchen Enid turned from the sink to grunt them goodbye, arms glistening, hair in streaks down her face.

S arah Mansfield visited her grandfather.

Apparently, she and her friend had stayed in a hotel before returning to school late enough the next day 'to frighten the bodies concerned'. There was no regret in the account she gave her grandfather.

'Look,' she considered her nails, bitten short, 'our fathers are paying a lot of money for our education.'

'And you're not getting value for it?'

'That's what I say. They claim otherwise. Daisy, that's my friend, likes mathematics, but she doesn't get any satisfaction from Miss Stansforth who takes us. She just irritates me, but she doesn't understand what Daisy's getting at.'

'And it's no use complaining?'

'Who to? The headmistress? She's too busy considering the good of the school to bother about us. So we packed our bags by way of our little protest.'

Mansfield enjoyed hearing the girl talk; she spoke with the ease of a middle-aged woman, and the maturity of voice. Yet, as soon as she became bored, she rolled about, mooched, let her bottom lip droop. Sometimes she wrote or read, but more often she sat listening to pop music on a transistor set. With enthusiasm she set out for the shops, but by the time she came back, she was as glum as if she'd been crossed in love.

'Aren't you fed up here?' he asked.

'No.'

'Never?' He loved to think he was pulling her leg.

'Less than anywhere else.'

To his old-fashioned mind, she should smoke a cigarette in a long holder, a gypsy scarf wrapped round her head. In her mini-skirt, eyes lined and darkened, she seemed to be instructing him, dragging him into the present. That she was alert enough, her father's daughter, sparked in her sentences.

'I don't mind school for at least part of the term. Daddy was lucky. When he was there he had you. You thought well of learning, were impressed at every exam success. He isn't. If I get a good mark, he makes out he's pleased but what he thinks is that it's the judgement of some spinster who wouldn't last five minutes in one of his firms.'

'Is he right?'

'Oh, yes. But it doesn't encourage me to break my neck, does it?'

'It's a disgrace.'

'I knew you'd say that, grandpa. You like first-class honours degrees, and knowledge. You should hear daddy talk about science. His scientists are like old dears looking for bull's eyes in a sweetshop when the gas's blown out. That's what he says. And when you put 'em in teams they're like Sunday-school kids out for a nature-ramble.'

'Your father takes his metaphors from his childhood rather than yours.'

She laughed, quite out of character.

'You've never been to a Sunday-school, my lass, have you?'

'No.'

'I used to run one.'

'And daddy attended it?'

39

'Yes. And I know what you're going to say. That he's no great advertisement for the end-product.'

'He's not too bad.'

'When he's not too busy.'

On the second day, he learnt why she had come. After her escapade, she wanted to quit school for good, but the headmistress, preserving discipline, had suspended her for a fortnight. Daisy's father, a professor of English, very strict, had been furious and had spent two hours in the place, speaking his mind. 'You are squashing this child, in her "O" Level year, because you have not been doing your job properly.' Both girls were delighted at the uproar, regarded the enforced absence as a holiday, and now Daisy was to join her friend here for the final three days.

'Was your father angry?' Mansfield asked his grand-child.

'In a way. They'd rung Mummy, you see, and it worried her. He shouts a bit. "Before you do any more of your bloody-fool tricks, just remember that your mother's got plenty on her mind, as it is," ' she imitated, with charm. One noticed the irony, but no malice.

'What did he mean by that?' Probing.

'The rest of the family. Entertainment.'

When Daisy arrived, the two worked at their books, did some cooking, thumped the radio. The friend was small, a dark girl, with black inquiring eyes and a sly look, as if she fathomed deceit and found it mildly entertaining. Her name was Angélique, but who'd want that? She made free use of Mansfield's library, and passed information on at meals, and even asked advice where she thought him capable. The old man was pleased, fancied his own wits sharpened by her brightness, did his best, but in the end found he did not like her. If he'd been asked to say why, he could only have answered that her appearance was against her. She was polite, respectful, quick, full of ideas, but she looked like a knowing, scuttling black-beetle, as against Sarah's fair placidity.

They went out once in his car and pronounced the place ugly.

'Why don't you live in the country, grandpa?'

'It's foolish to move away from people you know.'

'Meet the new. I think we're going to move again.'

'Perhaps you don't make friends so easily when you're old.' Daisy.

'You don't get the chance.'

'D'you know,' Daisy said, 'I've never seen a colliery before. Not at close quarters.' Mansfield had parked, at her demand for information.

'There are some in Kent.'

'Like this?'

'Presumably so. I've never been there.'

'What's it like down a coal mine, then?'

'Horrible.'

'It isn't now, is it? Not so much so?'

'I think it is.' He laughed, sardonically. 'Even with modern machines. Very unpleasant, let's say, compared with young ladies' boarding schools.'

'Somebody's getting at somebody,' Sarah said.

'Isn't the logic slightly askew?' Daisy minced. 'I infer that you think we should not run away because our life's easier than a coal-miner's. Whereas I believe we should do our bit to improve our place if we can. It's not as if we make improvements at the expense of these people. Or only indirectly, and I'm not arguing that.'

'Nor that running away is a good method?'

'The only way to improve schools is to let people outside see what's going on in them. Our head doesn't like to appear ridiculous.'

'When I was a schoolmaster,' Mansfield said, and the children sighed 'Ha, ha,' but put on solemn faces, 'I found that the folks outside were more conservative than I was. They wanted whackings and punishments and discipline . . .'

'For their own children?' Sarah asked.

'Yes. Their children lived at home. Their fathers hoped somebody was doing something for the youngsters that they couldn't or wouldn't do.'

'Complicated.' Sarah.

'Our old Queen will look more auspiciously on us,' Daisy said. 'Believe you me. My dad's got a nasty tongue and Sarey's papa has bank-vaults full of money. They got a new chem. lab. already out of his firm.'

'We should have blown it up.'

'The Lord giveth and the Lord taketh away. Blessed be the name of Lord Charnborough and his son-in-law unto the ends of the earth.

They were giggling children again, and Mansfield, without permission, bought them ice-cream from a newsagent's. He confessed himself afraid, because these girls spoke so sharply, and yet trivially. Both were obviously clever, and yet to judge from their talk they might have been bottom-stream yobbos from a secondary modern longing for the day when school authorities let them finally out.

'You think,' Daisy said, 'that if you acquire a lot of knowledge, you'll have a happier, fuller life.' She spoke authoritatively; loved pronouncements. 'I don't see this. Suppose I learn all this stuff about the digestive system,' she tapped a beautiful drawing in her biology note-book, 'peristaltic action, enzymes, duodenum, villi, then what use is this if I decide I want to run for Parliament or play the organ for a living?'

'It gives you an inkling, helps you to decide which way your talents lie.'

'I don't need to learn Latin for four years to know it's useless.'

'Angélique Quinn,' Sarah said. 'You are super at Latin, and you like it, and you wouldn't give it up even if you could.'

'I know. It's easy for me. And it's one subject that's really well taught at our establishment.'

James Mansfield admired them; they were lost, but not

unintelligently so. They had turned his world upside down, but out of intellectual high-jinks. He tried to argue.

'I'm an old man,' he'd begin, and they'd roll about laughing until he had to join them. 'What's the joke?' he'd ask, recovering.

'Catch phrase. Everybody tries it on us. "Now, even you, Angélique, have to admit that I have been on this earth longer than you. Perhaps I have not employed my time quite so usefully, but . . ." '

'Miss Sneddon,' Sarah shrieked.

'Even my dad tries that one,' Daisy said. 'And linguistics is one of his things. Mark you, he's too clever. He picks things up too easily. My mother's always saying that.'

'Isn't she so gifted?' he asked.

'She's a journalist. I'd say she was quicker, really.'

On the last afternoon he walked down with them into the town, where they stood on a stone bridge over the river, built in the eighteen-thirties, a beautiful soft-gold span amongst the industrial sprawl.

'Why is this beautiful?' he asked.

Both girls were silent, sitting large-legged on the parapet staring down into the rusty-grey shine of the water.

'I know why you think it's more beautiful, let's say, than that one.' Sarah pointed downstream to a metal latticed bridge leading to the asphalted play-park.

'Go on.'

'You think what this was like when it was put here. It was a village with trees. Just across the road, there was a new Georgian mansion,' she pointed at a theatre, converted into a Woolworths, now being reshaped again. 'You could see the other few eighteenth century houses, the cottages with apple-trees; you could hear the mill-wheel. The river was clear; there weren't any factories. Only fields, and woods and little homesteads.'

'And birds singing,' said Daisy, 'as they soared into the empyrean, their feathered throats a-warble in the glitter of the sun.'

43

Sarah gave her a back-hander that almost toppled her into the stream. Daisy stood up, laughing, feet firmly down, laughing.

'I think of the agricultural labourers,' she said.

'Weren't they better off than . . . ?' Mansfield waved his hands at a group of women shoppers bunching for a bus.

'They were not.'

He argued, but found the girls ganged against him, warmly adamant, though as they walked back, he despondent at their materialism, Daisy took his arm and drew him to her. His eyes filled with tears; he blew his nose heavily.

Professor Quinn arrived at tea-time.

A dapper man, with longish hair and well-drilled side-burns, he was affable, but slightly hearty. It was as if, Mansfield guessed, he was talking to somebody deaf or dull. He expected nothing in the answers so framed his remarks as small social, sociable jokes.

'They haven't got on your nerves, then?'

'Should they?'

'They seem to offend against pedagogic susceptibilities.'

'Your daughter is very intelligent.'

'Except that she won't apply her brains to any accepted field nor for any length of time.'

'She's also got a heart.'

Quinn looked baffled, thrusting his lips negroid, making a gargoyle of his face until he wagged a finger at his daughter.

'Been deploying our little wiles again?'

'Daddy, you'll annoy Mr. Mansfield if you go on like that.'

'Shall I, sir?' Another comical monkey-face. 'Is that right?'

'Yes.'

The professor applauded with his large hands, but held his face wary.

'You find your way about, then, with these young people?'

44

They stood together at the picture window, looking over the valley, while the girls were elsewhere at their packing. Quinn had interpreted the landscape like a map, dating the housing estates, asking for, finding factories, miraculously apt with his questions. There wasn't any doubt about his intelligence, but Mansfield felt unjustly that once he'd charted the place in an hour of his valuable time he'd pack his traps and start elsewhere. Thus he'd know much, understand little, love nothing. Mansfield wallowed in his prejudice.

'I've enjoyed their company. They've put up with me.'

'That's something.' Quinn scratched his head. 'They're the revolutionary type. Good, affluent, middle-class background. They don't want to fight for academic success, or money. Their fathers have done that for them.'

'Isn't reaction against . . . ?'

'Oh, yes.' Quinn's hands bulged big in his trousers pockets. 'I can't stomach this objection to excellence. Some of my best students, the really thoughtful, quick, energetic, explosive, make sure they're in the second-class. I'm damned sure it must be harder to put themselves, keep themselves there, than to get the results they deserve.'

'If you know a man . . .'

'No. We don't know this. That's just about half of the trouble. We like to boast, as I've been doing, about our judgements, but . . . no, some awkward devil, on account of his obstinacy, might come up in the end with something important. We've only one criterion for excellence: a person must stick it out, put some time in. Matters are so complicated nowadays that, by and large, the amateur won't get anywhere.'

'You and your colleagues won't allow him to.'

'Granted.' He grinned, big teeth, Japanese man of business. 'But I think my point holds. Unless you persevere, you'll get nowhere. And this is what these young devils will not do.'

'Why?'

45

'Well, it's no answer to say they're unacademic. That means they won't do well at our courses. We could change our curriculum, I suppose. Or the exam system or the teaching methods or the content.' He sighed. 'We've a wider range, and they're more grown up. I thought my teachers were mistaken sometimes, but played it along with them. That would seem dishonest, now.'

'Isn't it?'

'Honesty has never seemed to me a prerequisite of academic, or any, success for that matter.'

'Disinterested search for truth?'

'One of the by-products.' Quinn laughed silently all over his face.

'No wonder the poor devils don't know where they are, if they have people like you gnawing their brains away for them.'

'No, sir.' Quinn spread hands. 'I talk about language to them. The words they learnt at their mothers' knees. It has its advantages. They think they ought to know all about it, but obviously they don't. It seems a fiddle, but they can't see how I get the rabbit from the hat, and they're not going to spend three years finding out.'

'Is it?'

'No, it is not. It's not final truth, either. Even if I do something outstanding, it'll be superseded.'

'Unlike a poem?'

'They say so. I doubt that, though. I wish sometimes I belonged to a fundamentalist, evangelical church.'

'You'd be a pastor?'

'Of course. Admirably suited. Hard worker, and very literal-minded. And quarrelsome enough to retain my place.'

'Do you know any such groups?'

'I was brought up in one.'

'So you don't mean it when you say . . . ?'

'I guess most people are moderately satisfied with what they have. That's the only way to keep sane in our sort

46

of society, isn't it? No, I wouldn't go back.' Quinn smiled again very broadly, as if he'd remembered a good story, and this Mansfield found disconcerting. 'I quarrelled with my father. But he expected it. He was also jealous. And polemics is part of their day's work; that's why they're a breakaway sect.'

'So you were the rebellious, heretical student?'

'To him, though, you must remember that the most conventional middle-class unthinking Anglican was held equally damnable.'

'These children want to set the world right?'

'Don't we all?'

'No. I don't. I can't.' Quinn looked up in surprise, subsided, nodded. 'But I still tell you it was a privilege to me to have these children. I felt honoured.'

'Good.' The professor transferred his thoughts elsewhere; perhaps in his childhood bethels it was invariably designated 'a privilege' to hear some plumber or porkbutcher blether through the scriptures.

The rooms stood silently empty after the visitors had gone, and Mansfield prowled restlesssly, finding a glove, a box of rubber bands, a pair of shoes. Dissatisfied he rang Hapgood, who invited him down.

'If I believed in answers to prayer,' Hapgood said, 'your phone call would be it. If my wife's not in the asylum inside a month, then . . .'

They settled before the fire; outside the sky spread moon-blue.

'She's gone down to the doctor's. I made the appointment, myself. She's as stubborn.'

'Where's she now? It's gone eight.'

'I expect she's called on Mrs. Radford.' Hapgood puffed breath out. 'By God, it's murder here. Like living in slavery. I can't satisfy her. She snaps and growls and bursts into tears at the slightest thing. You don't know what'll set her off next. If I bang a door, or knock something over in the shop, I'm likely to find her having

47

hysterics, screeching and howling and holding her head as if it's going to roll off.'

'What's your doctor like?'

'Pentland. Decent young man. But she'll tell him none of this. Just say she's run down, needs a tonic. By God, it's getting me. You don't know what's coming next. If I move a paper on the sideboard, you'd think I'd killed somebody. I daren't sip my tea too loud.'

'Has she been like this before?'

'She's nervy, always has been. But she's off her head. I keep asking what I can do, but she always answers the same, "nothing", but the implication is I ought to be doing something, not standing there asking. I take the lad off her hands when we aren't busy, but selling somebody a hasp and two or three screws is beyond her. It's a rum 'un.'

'Can't you get any help?'

'We have Mrs. Bradley to give a hand with the housework. Has done for years. It isn't that Clara's got too much to do. She can't cope with Clive, and that's the top and bottom of it. She's fagged out. She'll go up to bed at nine, and then lie awake half the night, wittling, crying.'

They heard the back door bang.

'She can't close a door quietly,' Hapgood muttered. 'Slam's 'em so I think the walls'll come down. But if I as much as drop a pin . . .'

They waited in dread, two old men.

Mrs. Hapgood sniffed, continued to do so, answered Mansfield that she wasn't too bad.

'Would you like a cup of tea, love?'

'I had one at Radfords'.' The tone, metallic, dismissed a stupidity. Nobody in his right mind would put such a query. She sat in her chair, slightly askew, like a naughty child. Mansfield began to ask about the garden.

'When do I have time to go out there?'

'You might get an hour in the evening now it's lighter.'

48

'Not as I feel.'

'What did the doctor say, then?' her husband asked.

'The usual. What else could he?'

'Did you mention Clive?'

'He asked me about him.'

'Did you say anything about getting him into a home of some sort?' Hapgood's exasperation was now as great as hers.

'The only home he should go into is his mother's.'

'That's ridiculous, Clara.'

'Ridiculous or not, it's what should happen. He's not so backward as all that. That's what that specialist said. He might have to attend a special school, but he should live with his parents. He's a human being, the same as you. That's what he told Enid. He needs love, as you do. Perhaps more so.'

'A fat lot she bothers.'

'She should be made to, then.' Mrs. Hapgood turned her face at Mansfield, pale as putty, dirty with hate. 'The pair of you went traipsing off to see her. Nice day's outing for you. Talking all the way. Very nice. Old folks' treat. But when you come back what do I get bar a cock-and-bull story. They might be moving. We'll take the boy up to them in a fortnight.'

'We will, Clara.'

'We will,' she mocked. 'You might just as well go stuff his head down a street-drain.'

'It's breaking up this home.'

'Then it'll have to. I am not allowing . . .'

'You can't go on like this.'

'Can't, can't, can't. I s'll have to.'

Her body writhed, jerked uncontrollably. It reminded Mansfield of the balsa and paper aeroplanes he and David used to make; they twirled the propeller to wind the elastic, but more often than not would find they'd neglected some other necessity and so have to let it untwist. The wild, short jolt thrashed the fragile structure so that

49

it seemed for seconds struggling to break in their fingers. So this thin soul.

'I think it would be worth a try,' he intervened.

'What would?'

'To take Clive back to his mother and father.'

Again the woman sniffed, vulgarly.

'God knows Enid's not much,' she said. 'But she's the one who goes out to work. Clive'd be left with our Tom. He wouldn't do nothing. Wouldn't change him. He can't control himself yet. All he'd get is a leathering. If not worse. And then you'd see a police-case.'

'You can't go on, Mrs. Hapgood.'

'Who says?'

'I do. It's too much for you. At your age. You can't be expected to . . .'

'Well, I am.'

She now stared into the fire, hands clapsed between her knees, her stockings wrinkled down to the ankles. This was the woman who'd fed, clothed, warmed her clever sons while they'd fulfilled her husband's ambitions. Dull herself, she'd darned and saved while she was young, vital to the developing scheme. Even with the younger boy, she'd sent him off scrubbed and decent, mothered him until he was unfit except to sit fraying his trousers' behind waiting for somebody to help him out. Now, down on energy, she'd taken this task beyond her strength, but was too stupid to admit her defeat.

'That boy stops with us,' she asserted, 'until the day his mother fetches him. Even if it kills me.'

'That's what it will do.' Hapgood.

'Then it will, then.'

There was nothing aggressive about the obstinacy; the sound grumbled with despair.

'Did you not mention Clive to the doctor, Mrs. Hapgood?'

'I've told you once. He asked.'

'I meant about taking him off your hands, in an

institution. If only for the time being.' Shipwrecked, he signalled his phrases into the storm.

'Waste of time. He'd do nothing.'

'Then you'd have to go . . .'

'Go. Go. When have I time for going? That child stops here till I can look after him no longer. After that, I can't answer.'

'But your health.'

'It'll break. And there it is.'

'There's your husband, Mrs. Hapgood. You've an obligation to him.'

'When you look at him, and then at the child, you know where obligation lies, and that's all there is to it.'

Her hands flew, winged crudely, then returned to a fierce wringing as if she'd wash rough skin from bones. She sniffed, turned her head from the men. The three sat in awkward silence; Mansfield wanted to comfort his friends, but had nothing, not a word. The clock ticked, hacked through ten minutes when suddenly Mrs. Hapgood clapped her hand to her mouth, hiccoughed a sob, high as croup, and staggered up from her chair out to the kitchen. As she passed between the two men she held her face tightly as if she'd vomit.

Hapgood stood, ineffectually, arms moving in vague loops, and sat down.

'Nothing's right,' he said.

'I'm sorry.'

'I don't know what we s'll do. I don't that.'

Mansfield shook his head, remembered the toffees in his pocket.

'Have a minto.'

The two unwrapped the sweets, noisily. The visitor shaped his paper round a finger to make a chalice, with a thin stem, and a base to rest on the flat of his hand, as when he was a child. He held it up for inspection, then rested it on his chair arm.

'My dad's favourites, these,' he said.

51

Hapgood nodded, as of he understood the purpose of these antics, but they were wasted, like conjuring-tricks on a dying man. The middle door creaked open; the wife pushed in, shut it, leaned on the sideboard with her back to them as if she were about to fall, turned, almost spoke, and made for the stairs. Shoulders drooping, she seemed to wrestle with the knob.

They heard her footsteps surprisingly steady.

'Has she gone to bed?'

Hapgood nodded, face doltish with pain.

'I'd better go before it gets too dark.'

As they went together to the shop-door, Mansfield put his arm round his friend's shoulder, but there was no response, neither word nor movement.

'Stick it.'

Hapgood's head dropped chin-heavy to his chest.

'We'll take that child back if it's the last thing I do.'

He might have been speaking to himself. The door was opened, held, finally closed by a dumb man whose eyes were gummed with tears. Now the world cracked, but in a leaden silence. Outside, in the street, a gang of children ran and shouted, haphazardly, out of excess of energy, powerful as God's kingdom. Inside the bar-light of the shop was switched off. Mansfield, shivering, dragged the mackintosh from his throat, hauling on his tie, in a darkish street of brick and blackening glass.

5

David Mansfield called on his father.

The old man found it difficult to account for the visit. He himself had been down in the mouth for some days. On the morning after his return from the Hapgoods, he had a phone call to tell him that a colleague was dead. This was Edwin Stacey, ten years his junior, still teaching at the school, who had collapsed while out in his garden, and died on the ground.

Mansfield had always looked on Edwin as a young man. He remembered him from thirty-two years before, with a bush of fair hair, a college scarf, a rugby player's strut, and later, on leave, in his officer's uniform. They'd walked out in the lunch hour, taken school parties together, and now, nothing, or a cupful of ash chucked down, blown away at the crematorium. He remembered the hearty voice; only last week they'd enjoyed a long argument on the phone about letters in the *Guardian* on intelligence-testing.

People died; Mansfield almost blamed himself. There seemed a casual connection between his interest in Stacey, their conversation and the almost immediate death. This might be ridiculous, and dismissed as such, but his gloom thickened. The congregation sat in the heavy-beamed church at lunch-time in Spring and sang 'For all the saints', the present staff, the row of shining prefects, long-haired some of them and side-whiskered, all unknown to him; the old headmaster, bent and nondescript, back for the service from Bournemouth, his successor, a nobody, the few well-heeled old boys who nodded, in black ties, the great words of scripture ringing hollowly past a jar of forsythia, the organ hauling through a Bach chorale. Poor Mrs. Stacey, face set, walked behind the mutes with one of her sons-in-law; neither daughter wore mourning. And above him on the wall, the brass roll of honour, Arthur William Tide, Thomas Eddington Varley, Arthur Wales, M.M., glinted, names of men dead before he came to the place, made himself a small instutution in the town.

As they recited the twenty-third psalm he had wept. 'Thy rod and thy staff they comfort me.' Only the prefects were perfectly solemn, as they learnt about death, at near hand. The old headmaster stood hatless by the west door, braving the sunshine, congratulating himself on his survival. Mansfield, walking away by himself to the street where he had parked his car, wished he could turn into the pub, stand swilling. He did not try; alcohol meant little. He wished it did, could alleviate that thirst in the heart. His head down on his chest he sat, in sun-drenched warmth, at the wheel of his car, hopeless, not wanting, numbed, incapable of self-analysis, sad, racked, a lost soul.

That afternoon as he napped, the phone jerked him to his feet. In a drowsy haze he heard a precise young woman telling him that Dr. Mansfield would call on him tomorrow, at eleven-thirty, and could he be ready to go out for lunch. He mumbled. Where was she speaking from? London. Dr. David Mansfield's office. Where was the doctor now? London. In conference. Was that all right now? Perfectly clear? His stupidity revealed itself over a hundred and thirty miles of telephone wire. Pulling himself together, he spoke too loudly so that his voice trembled.

He hated the disturbance.

David drove up in his Silver Shadow, smiling, with yellow scarf and gloves. He looked young from the garden's end, but wore spectacles which he crammed into a pocket.

'On the way north,' he said, stroking his face, inspecting the house. His father expected him to name a price, fully furnished. He sat down, sprang up again to look out of the window.

'Sit down, man,' his father said, bringing in coffee. 'You're worse than a dog in a fair.'

'I've been sitting all the way up.'

'All right.' He served his son. 'Now what's on the agenda?'

'Call to make. In Hull. Two days there, announced three months back. They work like blacks to straighten up for the big chief.'

Mansfield had no idea whether to believe these stories

which seemed simplifications for his lay ears.

'I like to drop in on you.'

'Straighten me up.'

'Not a bad idea. Like to see you're not overdoing it. I think quite highly of you, you know.'

'But rarely.'

'Of course.'

They could keep up this pseudo-talk easily enough, but like men chattering a foreign language they knew well. Now and then David would frown, drift off, tap his teeth with a fingernail and the old man would know he knew nothing about his son and his preoccupations. He ought to be sporting gold teeth to match his cuff-links. So they sat, making words, enjoying the company, knowing that it wouldn't last long. David followed his father into the kitchen to wipe the coffee-cups; that was touching.

'How did you get on with Sarah?'

'Oh. Well.' Splash of taps, reaching for detergent.

'In her right mind?'

'Very much so.'

'I'm glad. I very much value your opinion.' He hung the towel away. 'Her mother is worried. They've sent one or two special reports from school. That's what they do when a pupil's unsatisfactory. You found her all right?'

'Good company. But I didn't make any demands on her.'

'I see. And Daisy Quinn?'

'Clever. Affectionate.'

'Neurotic?'

'No.'

'She attacked one of the mistresses. She steals. She lies.'

'Why?'

David shrugged.

'I wouldn't have chosen her as bosom-friend for Sarah, I can tell you. How did you take to father Quinn?'

'Interesting. Not my cup of tea.'

'Yes. Clever arse-creeper. Apparently Daisy and Sarah got on to him to ask if they could spend the Whit holiday here. Did they say anything to you? They've nearly a fort-night, and then "O" levels begin.' David shrugged up. He stood magnificently, gigantic in his executive's casuals. 'They didn't ask me. Got Quinn to broach the subject.'

'Why not?'

'Just a moment. You didn't make the suggestion in the first place?'

'No.'

Silence while David scratched his head.

'Sarah's little time for me. That's how it appears. Since Eleanor and I don't hit it off so well.'

'How are things? I wasn't going to mention it . . .'

'As before.'

'Why didn't you tell me, David?'

The son took to an arm-chair, lumbering, like an old man, hands in pockets, face grave in board-room histrionics.

'I wanted to be fair to her, and you. You'd hear her side first, but also she'd put it better than I; spare you, you know.'

'Is that true?'

'As anything I say these days.' Back to the game. 'I go about spreading confidence.'

'As your grandfather went muck-spreading.'

'Muck. Luck.' He stretched his powerful neck. 'What about these girls coming here?'

'I'd be pleased.'

'The ticker? Won't be too much?'

'No. If they want to come, let them.'

They talked about business; David outlined the sort of problems he had, and possible solutions. His grasp and ingenuity frightened his father.

'Sometimes, my lad, I suspect you're clever.'

'Not at all. Make your mind up, then stick to it, hell and high water. Don't budge; that's the secret. You're as likely to be right as the other man if you've done your work properly, and from then on it's obstinacy.'

As they walked towards David's car, the father said,

'I like Eleanor, David.'

'Yes, I expect you do.'

'Very much.'

'I realise that.' He turned at the gate; behind him over stretches of blue, rain-cloud blackened. To his left in the distance a squally shower shifted like a thick grey pillar. 'The thing is, we just don't hit it. Now, everthing she does gets on my nerves. Vice versa.'

'That isn't true.'

'That's all you know. An hour in the house with her and I start to throw things.' He sounded amused.

'Then you're unreasonable.'

'I'm not saying it's not my fault, dad. I'm not blaming anyone else. But it's a fact.'

'I expect you know, David, but if you don't, I'll tell you, your mother and I were often at loggerheads. We tried to be civil when you were about. Did you know?'

'Yes, I did.'

'But there was never any talk of divorce or separation. We never considered it. I owed a lot to your mother. I don't want to preach.'

'I enjoy sermons. Economically, the split wasn't on for you. Therefore you kept the quarrels within bounds. I could do the same if I wanted to. Is that it?'

'Exactly. Or half-way. I put your mother first.'

'Even when you were rowing with her?'

'Basically, yes. I'm not saying I was a saint. But even when I was furious, it never entered my head to turn her out, or go away myself.'

David smiled, patronisingly. The shower approached.

'Get in, dad, before we get wet.' They sat in the front of the Rolls, in cushioned comfort, and, for the moment, sunshine. 'We can afford to part. We should have done so, if it hadn't been for the family. When they're a bit older, if we're of the same mind, which is a certainty, then I pack my traps.'

'Is there another woman?'

'Not in particular.' The answer dashed the old man. Money overrode morality.

'What's the effect on the children going to be?'

'I don't know. They seem sane enough. The situation's not unique.'

'David, I can't say that I'm very struck with the cold-blooded way you talk about it.' The father tried authority, to sound impressive, but even in his own ears his voice whined.

'I don't see, dad, why I should take it out on you. It's not your fault. I try to tell you as calmly as I can what the situation is. But if you think because I'm not ranting, I'm not serious, then you'd better think again. I know you like Eleanor. I know this goes against everything you've ever stood for, but there it is. Eleanor and I are quite different from the young people we were when we were married. And it didn't come easy to me, I can tell you, to realise that what I felt was not just temporary irritation, but that the way she breathed and walked about got on my nerves. We've tried to make it up. Bobby's the last attempt. No go.'

'I don't like it.'

'There's nothing you can do about it, dad.'

'I feel I'm to blame, somewhere.'

The rain pelted down, slapping, blurring the windows. David shrugged, drove off. He knew that before lunch was over, his father would speak to him again, attempt to extract some promise from him, and as they swished along the shining road he glanced at his passenger, at the fine nose, proud head, the schoolboy cut of the grey hair, the strong chin, the veined ugly hands. No, he felt no obligation to this man; if he had another heart-attack and died, his son would remember with tenderness the many good times they'd shared, but in day-to-day life, there was now nothing much between them.

Then sun shone through long windows as they ate lunch and feigned conversation. Neither drank. The whole exercise was a game, which both played inexpertly because each suspected the other. The son feared an intervention from his father, while the old man knew that this son kept something from him. They could eat lunch expensively, high in this skyscraper, the city's newest hotel, with nothing happening to either.

When Mansfield described, carefully, elaborating, the Hapgoods' struggle, David nodded, but barely listened. When, in return, he explained how a simple suggestion written illiterately and stuffed into the box by a factory floor hand had been put to use and saved thousands, his father raised no interest. What did concern him that somebody earning twenty-thirty-forty-fifty thousand a year had refined a notion from a twenty-pound-a-week labourer. That was expected.

'I'll drive you back home.'

'No, you won't. I shall shop here.'

'No. Let me . . .'

'Let you nothing.'

They said no more. Both were tired of the exchange. At the entrance to the car park, Mansfield said, 'Do you mind if I go to see Eleanor?'

'Why should I? Write to her first. I should if I were you.' The son donned his alpine hat, pulled on his rich gloves, just less than fiercely. 'You please yourself, dad. You've got your time to fill in, I suppose. But I can tell you this for free; where we've got to doesn't ask advice, moral, religious, even kindly. It needs a compliant judge to split us. Thanks about Sarah at Whit. Goodbye.'

The voice spread full, easily, controlled, but David walked angrily. He waved from his car as it left the forecourt, but somebody would pay that afternoon for his father's presumption.

When Mansfield wrote immediately to Eleanor, stating plainly what had happened, his daughter-in-law replied that he'd better come down, that she'd be glad of his company. She met him at Alton station.

'Tired?' She did not look well.

'No. No children?'

'The nanny has them.'

They stopped at a chemist's while he looked at the reddenned country faces. Eleanor bundled her purchases into the back seat, said:

'Right, now. You can begin.'

'Begin what?'

'The lecture you came here to deliver.'

He was taken aback at her rudeness. She yawned, not covering her mouth.

'If you believed that, why did you invite me down?'

'You'd think I was hiding something.'

'I don't understand you, Eleanor; either of you.'

'I don't suppose you do.'

'What does your father say?'

'He's sorry, because he likes, admires David. They'll continue to work together. No embarrassment. He considers we're grown up, know our own minds.'

'And I don't?'

'It appears not.'

They drove in silence the rest of the way, Mansfield stunned at his daughter-in-law's attack. He was shown into the small parlour, provided with a pot of tea and deserted for almost an hour. Eleanor apologised, explained why she had to phone, see the gardener, call on General Black. She sat in an arm-chair, almost exhausted, pale, a smoking cigarette in her fingers. From a distance, her elegance retained its grace, but her eyes were puffed, her arm movements jerky. She sat preoccupied.

'I've bitten off more than I can chew,' Mansfield said.

'Sorry?'

She had not heard him. Determined to get unpleasantness over, he repeated the inanity. In return she smiled, slowly, warmly, to disarm him.

'I didn't realise that it was as bad as this between you and David.'

'What did he tell you?'

60

'That you got on one another's nerves.'

'And you thought that we should grow up, stop molly-coddling ourselves.' No rancour there. Smiling, at her old phrase, she blew a cloud of smoke ceiling-wards. He thought, awkwardly, of something to say, to fill in the hiatus, to make her respect him, to ease her pain. Such remarks did not exist, so he drew a handkerchief from his pocket and unfolded it. She did not bother to watch. When he had smoked a pipe, his pockets were lined with specks of tobacco; now the handkerchief lay unmarked on his knee. After a pause, a fidgeting hesitation, he screwed the linen, pushed it back.

'I thought you were going to do a conjuring trick,' she said.

'I wish I could.'

She smiled again, widely, uncrossed her legs and stubbed the cigarette.

'I remember when you were married,' he said.

'Yes.' No encouragement.

'It was the perfect wedding. The crowds outside Mal-stead Church. I thought to myself, "I've no right to be here." And I said to myself, "You're as good as they are, Jim Mansfield, any day of the week." But I don't know. I'd produced a son who was a prodigy. But I stood there in the sunshine, and looked at you, and David, and the hired top-hat in my hand and I thought that it meant something.'

Tears swilled his eyes.

'It did, I suppose,' she conceded. 'Four children.' Her voice twanged cold. 'I think back with pleasure, some-times. But I can make nothing of it now, any more than I could go and sit at my school desk.'

'Are you bored?'

'Not really. The children, our social obligations keep me at it. I'm waiting for the next phase.'

'The divorce?'

'Probably.'

'What's your father say?'

61

She thought that over, brushing hair from her forehead.
'Nothing. Honestly. I've told you. He doesn't.'

'You call me "father", now. When you've parted, you won't any more. It's odd that a judge can deprive me like that.'

'That's because the word's inaccurate, isn't it? I should say, "father-in-law" and then it would be proper for a court to lop it off.'

'I thought you meant . . .' What? Parent until death do us part? He thrashed among words to hide his despair. This beautiful woman had been one of his possessions and now she snatched herself off, coldly, with a precise hauteur. What use would it be to talk about the garden, or Sarah, the state of the economy? She no longer, in any sense, belonged to him. He hung his head like a scolded child.

'Your generation puts too much emphasis on words.' Eleanor spoke again, rather impatiently, but not looking at him, in guilt. 'You think talk can solve everything.'

'I don't.' He denied in a daze, without conviction.

'You give that impression.'

That sounded feeble. Why were her ideas crumbling?

'I talk because there's nothing else I can do.'

'You could stay away, leave me alone.'

'Is that what you want?'

'I didn't say so. I'm listing alternatives. You could even buy a revolver and shoot me. Or something. Or kill yourself.'

She spoke mumbling now, might have acted a crone in a children's pantomime.

'That's cruel,' he said. 'I don't think I ever heard anyone speak so cruelly before.'

'You won't think.'

'I'm talking, though. And when I hear somebody speak as you've just spoken to me, I ask myself what's wrong with her.'

'I've told you. You're interfering. It won't improve

matters, and it makes me uncomfortable, embarrassed, angry.'

'You should see your doctor.'

'He's probably in the same quandary.'

'That's not even clever.' He braced himself. 'I accept that everything's gone wrong between you and David. And I'm sorry. But why do you turn on me in this rude way? I'm on your side. I want to help.'

'It appears,' she said, slowly, 'as if you can speak as frankly as you like to me, but as soon as I claim the privilege, I'm cruel, rude.'

'You weren't helping. You made brutal, silly, suggestions to hurt me, or get your own back on David, or the world, or yourself.'

'I'm sorry, then.'

'You're not, Eleanor. When I came into this place, I wanted to put my arms round you, hold you. It mightn't mean anything. I don't suppose you'd take any pleasure hugging a sentimental old man. But it would have demonstrated affection. I thought I loved you. Even if you divorced David, I'd have been your friend. But now, now ... I don't know. You seem to be ill.'

'I've said I'm sorry.'

'I am. Perhaps it's my fault. I oughtn't to have said anything. I don't think you can know, Eleanor, how much I feel this. Your marriage was one of my certainties. Like the walls of my house. I don't know where to go, now.'

He wept, openly, not moving, outraged to his soul, while she ignored the trouble. At that moment, he was in no way himself; his body had boiled into tears which he hated. Once more he fished for the handkerchief, covered, dabbed his face. From behind it he noticed that she glanced up at him, in distaste, face sober and wry.

'I'm glad Sarah can stay with you.' Olive leaf?

'I enjoyed her.' He answered steadily, face wiped clear.

'She's very like David. Wants her own way.'

'We all do.'

After dinner that night Eleanor's father, Lord Charnborough, called in from a neighbouring village. Drinks were served, and the old men were ordered into the small parlour.

'You talk to Mr. Mansfield, daddy. He's depressed.'

'What about me?'

'Make the most of your chance to talk behind my back?'

A fire burned in the grate, and they were glad of it in this chilly room, with its three dark varnished oil-paintings of Italian landscapes, keg-handed school of Canaletto, and its enormous curtains, grey and ugly as canvas.

'I'm staying with the Adamses,' Robert Mattison said. 'Eleanor pretty well ordered me over to talk to you.'

'About what?'

'I thought you'd know about that.'

Charnborough played with his whisky, stroked his belly. His barrel legs barely reached the ground from his high, embroidered chair, so that his feet were pen-pointed in their shining shoes. Mansfield never made much of the man; he was not obviously clever, like David, or powerful. He reminded one of those pre-1914 managers in furniture shops, dignified, solemn, well-dressed men who could wear eyeglasses without shame. Sure of himself, he made no fuss. Brought up in wealth, he appeared to know nothing else.

'It's not about David and Eleanor, is it?' Mansfield said.

'Could be, could be.'

'You know about them, I take it?'

'Of course.'

They moved to more comfortable positions, punching cushions, slightly shifting their chairs, white-haired, redfaced men.

'What do you think, then?' Mansfield blurted out, still tugging.

'I'm not surprised. Now you come to ask me. Are you?'

'Yes, I am.' Too loud. Accusatory. 'What more do they want?'

'Eleanor is not likely to be . . . Put it like this. David neglects her.'

'Why?'

'Business. Work. It interests him more. I'm not saying that's wrong. He's made high-flyers of us, I'll tell you. But Eleanor'll be second to nobody, to nothing.'

'It's his fault?'

'I wouldn't say that. David concerns himself with work. She does not. Won't talk about it. Insists on living in the country. He's not at home as often as he would if they lived in London. She feels neglected. He finds other pleasures.'

'Other women, you mean.'

'Other women.'

'Does Eleanor know?'

'Yes. And it does nothing to improve matters.'

'You take this calmly enough,' Mansfield said.

'My dear man, my dear man.'

Charnborough dusted his paunch again with fingertips.

'They must be unhappy.' Mansfield spoke sharply.

'I'd admit that. But aren't most of us at some time?'

'We get over it.'

'I think, if anything, I'm with you in this. But look at it from their point of view. We were a big, prosperous, family firm until David and Jack Stein got hold of us. Now we're millionaires, monopolists, monolith capitalists. There's all the money anybody can want. I'm not saying quite we could buy Blenheim Palace for fun, but we aren't far off. And there's power. Big. When David speaks, governments will listen.'

Mansfield almost enjoyed the exposition, the wheezing voice, the cigar, but he listened with caution as to a man not used to contradiction. Perhaps it was natural contra-suggestibility, but this flowed too easily, like a sermon. He remembered the pulpit-bashing parsons and their anecdotes: no modern saint dropped at his wits' end to his knees in prayer but a five-pound note floated through the front letter box. Lord Charnborough pursed his lips, as if to read the other's mind.

'Now, I'm not telling you that the effect on personal relationships is simple. I know one millionaire who's an un-complicated,' he gulped, 'secondary-modern type at home. Bit of gambling, but faithful to his wife. Homely. But, by God, he can be ruthless.' He tucked chins in. 'With these it's different. Both have changed, been changed. Both will do so. David will fondle his dollies; Eleanor will ransack the bank-account. Neither approves of the other's choice.'

'What sort of life is that?'

'You spent forty years, didn't you, educating the young? Useful, not unique, but by and large satisfying. Society hasn't rewarded you very well, but that doesn't matter, because your tastes are plain, and David won't see you starve. What sort of life is it though? Is it better than the Queen's, or a victorious commander's, or a machine-minder's or a navvy's?'

> " 'Could I be drunk for ever
> On liquor, love and fights",'

Mansfield quoted, in high irony.

'Something to be said for that.'

'I'm thinking of Eleanor, your daughter. She must be unhappy.'

'I've no idea,' Charnborough answered.

'Don't you ask? Don't you ever talk to her?'

'Of course. But she's been married sixteen years now. And I hardly made much of her when she was at school or at home. I don't think she'd any more come to me and say "Daddy, I'm in trouble" than I should employ the town-crier to shout my failings round the streets. It's not in us. Eleanor knows what she wants, and if she can't have that,

66

she'll make damn' sure she gets something more expensive still.'

'Spoilt.'

'Self-sufficient. Self-regarding.'

Charnborough blew smoke about, grinned, as if delighted with his analysis.

'I hate it,' Mansfield said, shouting his thought.

'It's only too common.' He slapped his jowls playfully. 'You'd like a John the Baptist figure, a Savonarola?'

'I want people to think, feel more deeply about each other.'

'In other words, to be like you, eh?'

No rudeness sounded, only a kind of sly intelligence so that Mansfield was taken aback.

'There's some truth,' he admitted.

'You schoolmasters are lucky,' Mattison said. 'You deal with human problems in ones.'

'That's the sensible way.'

Soon they reminisced together, two oldish, energetic men enjoying themselves. When Eleanor interrupted they looked at her in guilt.

'Sorted it out, then?' she said.

'Not that you'd notice.' Her father.

'Well if the two cultures can't do it.' She linked her arm in that of Mansfield so that he suspected she goaded her father. 'What are you going to do for me, mister?' She jostled the arm she held.

'I'm going home tomorrow.'

'Please, don't.'

'I think I will. If you don't mind.'

She withdrew her arm, said no more, mildly instructed her father that his man had come for him.

❧6❧

James Mansfield despaired.

Seated at home, he fought with himself. He had made no impression on Eleanor, had tortured himself needlessly. At breakfast on the day he had left she had carefully spelt it out again, that he could not help, that the children would be looked after.

'There's nothing can replace a loving mother and father,' he said. She opened her eyes.

'In many parts of the world, people believe otherwise. If I wanted a child's appendix removing, I'd call a surgeon, not David. We have money to employ experts. That's the way I was reared. If we were poor we'd have to try to learn otherwise. I don't know whether or not this is easier than surgery.'

'Shall I say something?'

'Do.'

'You talk to me in this cold, bitter, frothy way, and it makes me sure you're hurt.'

'I wish I weren't married to David, certainly, if that's what you mean.'

'Didn't you love him?'

'Father, you'll only upset yourself. We shall both be all right; you can reassure yourself on that. The children won't be harmed. You must accept it. Honestly. It's not what you wanted, I know. I'm sorry. David is. But we can't always have our own way.'

She drove him to the station, taking the two younger children whom she managed easily.

'I might never see you again,' he said. The youngsters circled her, chasing, well-behaved, lively.

'Whatever happens, I shall come and see you.'

'Promise.'

They kissed, shook hands; the children presented lips, waved, bounced off either side of their attractive mother. He sat in the green electric train amongst houses, sunny fields, shivering.

At home, he dosed himself, spent a day in bed listening to the wireless. He could not comfort himself, and in the end he telephoned Alfred Hapgood who asked him round, greeted him, shaking, distracted from behind the counter of the shop.

'Come through,' he said. He called to his wife in unease. 'I'll put the kettle on.'

Mrs. Hapgood thumped downstairs. They could hear an uncertain descent so that when she appeared Mansfield showed no surprise at her badly swollen face. The woman stood, as if on inspection.

'Show him your arm, mam.'

She lifted a loose sleeve revealing reddened, blackened skin, patches of vivid bruise on flabby flesh.

'Fell downstairs,' Hapgood. 'With the child in her arms.'

Mansfield clucked like a grandmother.

She sat, gingerly, into a chair, told her story. Her husband interrupted, was not checked. She ought not to have been carrying him at all, but he liked it. Suddenly, slippery as a fish, he'd leapt from her arms, as if he'd seen something on the ceiling and jumped for it. She thought for a minute he'd gone, flying downstairs, crashing to death, but as she'd reeled, staggered, he was by a miracle tight in her embrace again and she'd smashed arm, then arm again, then with a spark-bright jolt her face on the wall. Wonder both weren't killed. She'd kept her feet somehow, as her body bounced on the wall, her shoes twisting off as the last step had tippled her upright. She'd found herself sitting on the blanket-box, Clive screaming, and she muttering, 'God, God.' No pain, then; a paralysis of fright, of breath gone, a realisation of the slow nature of the fall, of its legacy of soreness, of limping agony. She'd let him run out as Alf came in, hair straight up, like a porcupine, mouth widening. Her face twisted into a shy grin at the description. Well, there she was, frock up over her bloomers, calling out to God. He'd fetched the doctor and no messing. Ambulance, then hospital, hours waiting, X-rays.

'And the boy?'

'I had to go to bed.'

'And the doctor, to give him credit, moved for once in his life.'

Again information flooded the double channel. No, there's no damage to him. Tough as old boots. Took him in to see after him, give me a rest. And to make a start on investigations. Well, he was old enough now. Tests. Psychology. See what he was capable of. No, they hadn't done anything yet. Only three days. Children's Hospital, no. Impossible. Full, perhaps, or not got the staff. He was in an annexe of the Queen Elizabeth. Little ward with another two children. Visit afternoons. Dad'd been.

Mansfield promised to drive Mrs. Hapgood as soon as she was fit. She opted for that afternoon. Argument began; she won.

The Haddon annexe was the oldest part of the hospital, a former isolation sanatorium, now on the edge of the campus, blacker than the new concrete blocks, less glassy-bright than the prefabricated wards, a three-storey factory surrounded by army-style huts and lime-trees.

The climb to the second floor dragged slow, painful. At least twice, he thought she'd given in, and once as she hung, face livid as the painted brickwork, to the banister he noticed her face wet with tears of frustration. At the end of the ward, she collapsed into a chair, croaked the word, 'Ask', jabbing a crooked finger.

A girl in uniform, aged thirteen, he'd guess, mumbled him the way.

The pair set off. A young man in a white coat joined them, had perhaps heard the inquiry, ingratiatingly smiled, sheepish but certain, like a shop-assistant. At the end of a long ward, where old men crouched in arm-chairs by their beds, dressed in shoddy, shapeless suits, he held open the door of a smaller room.

'This is it,' he said.

The room was surprisingly a-dazzle with sunshine and on the walls hung two sheets of wrapping paper attractive with silhouettes of rows of lions and elephants. On a carpet, under a radiator, Clive was squatting, a rag-doll, a teddy-bear, two matchbox lorries with him. He sat, one finger prodding the ground rhythmically, his right thumb fist-deep into his mouth.

But up and down the room, shouting a fanfare, another child marched. Much bigger than Clive, in jersey and sagging shorts, he pushed up and down the place howling his trumpet noise, his round head pale, cream-faced, sly.

'Soldiers,' the young man said.

The big boy paid no attention, but continued, his shrill racket having the edge, the edge of weariness.

'That's Paul,' the young man explained. 'Hello, Paul.' The boy turned, took the attendant's hand, as both went over to the small boy.

'Hello, Clive,' the man called. 'Are you a soldier with Paul?' The child looked up, not displeased. 'See who's come to see you, grandma and grandpa.'

Mansfield, who all this time held Mrs. Hapgood's arm, stepped across to fetch her a chair.

'On gran's knee?' The man swung him up, where he sat, quite still, except now his sucking became audible. Mrs. Hapgood moved him, wincing, muttering endearments, easing him, stroking his face.

'Has he settled?'

The young man, a male nurse, gave a short account of the child. He held Paul by the hand, talking brightly, vaguely, smiling at them. Clive slept well, ate marvellously, seemed to be amused in the company of the other boys. It appeared he'd no idea how to play with the model cars until he'd watched the others, who were now out, at physiotherapy.

'Has he had any of his tests yet?' Mansfield asked.

'Tests?'

'He was supposed to be examined.'

'He'd have the routine medical . . .'

'This boy is sub-normal mentally,' Mansfield said firmly. 'We understood that he was to be tested to find the extent of his subnormalities, to what extent he is capable of being taught.'

'I didn't know,' the young man admitted, still cheerful. 'I thought he was here because his parents, grandparents, couldn't look after him.'

'He wouldn't be put in a hospital for that?'

'Not for that, no.' He patted Paul's back, and the boy walked stiff-legged over to stand by Mrs. Hapgood's chair. 'They'd presumably do the examination elsewhere, at the Children's or St. Anne's. They'll have the facilities there, y'know. There's close co-operation, even if we take a day or so to get going.' More confident smiling.

'What sort of ward are you, then, by and large?'

'Geriatric.'

'That's what I thought. What's he doing here?'

'You'll have to ask the medical authorities.' The man swung to look at Mrs. Hapgood, hair in silver sunshine, black-eyed, trenched with wrinkles, who now held the hands of both children. 'This small ward's empty, and there are these four, two surgical, and these, all E.S.N., in need of constant supervision.'

'They set the place up to suit the need?'

'That's exactly right.'

Again the bright smile as if some important conclusion had been reached. The two rings on his right hand flashed.

'Excuse me. I'll leave them with you a minute.'

'Would you like a toffee?' Mansfield briskly pulled mintoes from his pocket.

'Just look. Toffees. Look what Mr. Mansfield's brought you.'

He proffered the bag to Clive, but it was the grand-mother who took, unwrapped the sweet.

'Paul.'

The boy turned away, the movement sharp as a cry.

'Wouldn't you like one?' The old man moved round, knelt down near the child, rustled the paper. Paul snuffled at the floor, and as Mansfield held the unwrapped sweet in front of his mouth, turned his head.

'Try it.' Touched the lips. 'Go on.' A hand flicked up, pushed the sweet in. 'That's it, Paul. That's a good boy.'

Mrs. Hapgood talked on at Clive who leaned back, head to her breast. His face looked squashed, triangularly ir-regular, while a bubble formed, burst at the lips. The squint seemed exaggerated, as if assumed, deepening the idiocy, the incomprehension on the unhealthy face. Yet he did not seem frightened, merely exhausted, lolling, barely living, the only movement expected a spewing, a wetting.

'He's worn out, poor little lamb,' Mrs. Hapgood crooned. 'It's a shame den. Does he want his beddy?' The child hadn't the energy to suck the sweet. 'Which is Clivey's bed, then?' she called across at Paul.

Surprisingly he pointed.

'Would he like his beddies, den?' She was loth to put him down, rocking him. Then she prised the sweet from his mouth.

He whimpered, but slowly.

Mansfield watched. The woman showed no sign of pain, concentrated herself powerfully, in love, on the flaccid body. Her bruised face, the veined arthritic hands, all demonstrated her care, and he found it indecent, un-healthy. Why should she lay herself open like this? Love expended on imbeciles was love wasted. He did not know that. If Mrs. Hapgood had been a young, attractive woman then this might have been bearable, but to see a crone, who'd sighed, pushed, grunted every step here, slavering over the cretinous grandson revolted him. He turned to Paul.

'Have you got a train, then?'

The boy put out his toe to touch his toy.

'Would you like another minto?'

He hung his head, ignoring the sweet held out on Mansfield's palm. The nurse returned.

'Worn himself out, has he?' he said, pleasantly, to Mrs. Hapgood.

'And he's wet.'

'Soon remedy that.' He laid the child flat, whipped down the plastic pants, and, humming to himself, changed the nappy. Clive, blowing like an old man, did not once open his eyes.

'Paul doesn't say much for himself, does he?' Mansfield asked.

'Can't. Hardly knows a word.'

'How old is he?'

'Six. Nearly.' He slipped Clive into a crib, fastening up the side. 'That's him until tea-time.' He dusted his hands, picked up the wet napkin. 'Coming with me, then, Paul? Let's go and look at the old gentlemen, shall we?' The child made no move, but dirty cloth in his left hand, the young man swooped across, grasped him with the right. 'Change for him, and the old chaps like it.'

'Is it suitable?' Mansfield asked. The pleasant expression on the nurse's face did not alter.

'Won't harm him. It's exercise. It's hard to know what the poor little beggar takes in.' He stopped smiling to wrinkle his forehead at Mrs. Hapgood who leaned over the end of Clive's crib, rocking herself. 'You don't notice much, do you, squire?' He swung the child's hand up and down, up and down. 'Except a tickle.' His arm circled the waist, a big finger explored the ribs. The boy's face lit into laughter, and he collapsed to his knees in wild giggling. The human sound shocked Mansfield; this tongueless, brainless body could laugh, behave with normality in this one insignificant area of humanity. 'It's coming again.' The man wagged, crooked his finger so that the child shrieked, but mildly, in delight. 'You like that, you little rascal, don't you? Bit o' tickley-wickley.' He touched the grey shirt, then scooped the lad by his hand. 'Come on, my friend. We've no time to be messing about here. Them old boys'll be shooting and murdering each other in no time, if we don't look slippy.'

They followed the two out into the main wards where old men crouched like toads. Paul stood like a skew statue.

Every afternoon, Mansfield drove Mrs. Hapgood to the hospital. He hated the task, her grumbling, obvious pain, the slow climbing, her self-pity. When she lavished love on the child, he turned away, staring out of the window at the normal world of straight trees, the bright borders of flowers.

Hapgood struggled to get sense out of his daughter-in-law.

He wrote, enclosing stamped envelopes, paid a second visit, contacted welfare workers here and in Hull. Nothing happened. Enid did not reply, avoided him and officials. She was never at home to responsibility, and no one could coax a word out of her. The grandfather spoke to the almoner, made it clear that he was not prepared to take the child back, but the hospital authorities failed to nail the parents.

Mansfield had to hear the bickering.

'He'll be put into a home,' Hapgood told his wife.

'He will not.'

'You can't look after him. Anyway, they've got the professionals, trained people.'

'If Enid and Tom don't take him, he's coming back here.'

'That's lunacy, Clara.'

'Blood's thicker than water.'

It seemed as if Hapgoods deliberately forced him to witness their altercations, perhaps in case of development to speak for the rightness of one side or the other, or, more likely, to keep the row within bounds. The old woman did not recover quickly from her fall; her face was dabbed mottled yellow, and she dragged herself about the house. Mansfield wondered what bound these together. Economic ties? Certainly it was not self-interest. And as far as love was concerned, they never showed, or spoke, one iota of affection. They were like two tramps who, even at mealtimes, seemed to be robbing each other. When they heard from their successful sons, they vied with each other in sour criticism.

Once, while Mansfield waited, the shop-bell clanged. Hapgood was upstairs at the lavatory, so that his wife struggled, not quietly, wrestled with her chair, to go serve the customer.

'Don't bother; I'll see to it.' Mansfield went to the front, chatted until Hapgood appeared, flustered, tugging at his cardigan. When he reappeared in the living room, he turned on his wife.

'What do you send Mr. Mansfield in there for?'

'I didn't.'

'You'd be in no hurry to get up.'

'Neither would you if you'd got the leg I'd got.'

'Any excuse. Any excuse.'

Children, nagging street-brats.

Yet there was no overt misery, rather a present energy of struggle. If they relapsed into apathy, then hope disappeared. He remembered this creaking woman letting down the crib's side to kiss Clive, and Paul all eyes before some rag-bag of an old man. These fragments. One couldn't help concluding that the rich organised matters better. Eleanor and David avoided each other, paid servants to arrange it. These two, married forty-odd years, grew towards hate, but dared not admit the fault, hypocrisy yoked to dislike. Both seethed.

He watched flies spiralling in a couple of square feet by his window that evening. There buzzed his picture of life. He thought back to Annie who brayed and banged her displeasure about the house, whom he'd neglected for his son and his school. His wife, tall in her youth, gold-ginger hair in a heavy plait across her head, with long shapely legs, and dynamic arms flung at, round him. She'd soured on him, but when the doctor told him that she'd not recover, he'd stood mutilated. Guilt burnt; he'd not done his duty and now she was dying. If he'd have, she would . . . In a cold misery he'd trembled before a cold hearth, back from the hospital, had written carefully to his son, who was taking finals in a month or two. What he said on this sheet of paper, out of his bowels' fright, his remorse, his ingrained selfishness might affect the lad's career. He need not have worried. David did right, came down at the weekend, visited his mother, looked pale, never raised his voice and went back to score his brilliant first. Mansfield had reported the success to his wife before she died. She smiled with a thin irony. She'd never shown much enthusiasm for examination results; she had been pleased, of course, but did not understand either their importance or their hierarchies. Now she seemed to grasp, nodded, showed the ends of her teeth. Her son had satisfied, astounded the examiners of London University; hers was a harsher tribunal. When Mansfield took the returning hero to the ward next day, she was unconscious, barely rallied. But the hour after her husband had left the previous visit, she'd asked for paper, hutched herself up in bed and had written, untidily, in struggling pencil: 'Please give dear David his grandmother's little gold watch with my love.' Now, vaguely alive, she breathed brutish, eyes shut, as bad as dead, but with this note, this congratulation, courageous on its Woolworth pad. Yet she recovered, if shortly.

Today when Mansfield thought of her it was as a young woman, with wide mouth, hair gleaming, and he'd stare at the brown photograph on the sideboard, E. P. Short, Market Street. It stood there when she was alive, ramming round the house, scorching him with her tongue, blasting his vanity, and he hated the thing. Now, gently, he picked it up, put it down, did not try to be fair, even to assess

77

the beauty of his smooth face, but turned his attention to the
dodging gnats, chasing and dipping in a whirr of grey-dun
wings against the blackness of rhododendrons and laurel.

Hapgood failed to get sense out of his daughter-in-law.

When the authorities had concluded tests on Clive, they
sent for his grandparents. From Hapgood's account, Mansfield caught a live impression of the interview, the jargon,
the friendliness concealed by patronage.

'You see, with an IQ of 0 to 19, we categorise as "idiot",
20 to 49 "imbecile", 50 to 70 "feeble-minded". But
Clive's none of these. It is even possible that he is not
educationally sub-normal, and with an interested home
could work his way through primary, secondary schools,
find himself work.'

The picture glowed.

But grandfather spoke obstinately; his wife couldn't take
the child back; it was more than she was capable of. Couldn't
the parents be forced . . . ?

Addresses were taken, inquiries would be instituted, but
really they couldn't keep the child much longer. They
weren't furnished for such work; under-staffing made it
worse; it wasn't good for the boy.

'What will happen,' Hapgood persisted, 'if his parents
won't have him?'

'He'll be committed to the care of the local authority.'

'I don't want that.' Mrs. Hapgood shouted, her discoloured face drawn. Once again, kind words were ex-
changed, carefully chosen, camouflaging. As soon as they
were home, the grandparents put the alternatives into plain
language and quarrelled.

'He'll have to come back here.'

'He will not, Clara. Whatever happens, he will not do
that.'

'I shall do as I say.'

'You will not have him here.'

'It's no use your shouting, Alfred. We've got to take
him. They won't. Nobody will. He's our grandchild.'

'You're the one I'm thinking about.'

'You'll have to think about somebody else, then.'

'As soon as he comes, you'll be back where you started. It was your squealing and howling that you couldn't go on, that it'd kill you. Not me. It was you. And I'm considering you, now. I don't care what you say, or anybody else, he's not crossing that door-step.'

'He'll have to.'

'Have? Have hell. I'm not having you as you were. Couldn't boil an egg without scalding your fingers and bawling and screeching all over the neighbourhood. We're getting on, Clara. I can't stand no more of it.'

'That's more like it.'

'That's God's truth. That's God's truth.'

They wrangled; in the end, both wept and rolled angrily sleepless. Touchingly both rang Mansfield who talked, fluently helpless, like the hospital official. After the second call, he sat down in his chair and tried to work a solution out. He'd no idea what would happen. He walked his garden, willing himself to think, in the sunshine until the east wind drove him in. He could reach nowhere, arrive at nothing in no future.

He recalled, a tenth, a fifteenth time how Eleanor had taken him to the National Theatre to see *Twelfth Night*, the play he'd done at school, and as the actors spoke he'd known the text again, word by word:

> 'It gives a very echo to the seat
> Where love is thron'd'

savoured it until the box-tree scene when Sir Toby, he'd auditioned for Toby at university but they'd made him Orsino, had called 'Would'st thou not be glad to have the niggardly rascally sheep-biter come by some notable shame?', and like a cold cloud, the magic blackened, he'd known: 'This is the last time I shall ever see this.' The play he'd learnt so well fifty-odd years back, so that it was part and parcel of his life, a jewel, would be prised out of his consciousness by death, would mean as little to him as it did to Shakespeare, rotted in the damps of Stratford Church. He thought he was about to start another heart-attack, there, in the theatre, chest split, jugular vein throbbing to bursting, so that he sat, chilled, weazened, a thin tremble of flesh among these scented well-to-do people, and when that fear died, the original dread savaged him again. Those marvellous words he was hearing for the last time. He might be sitting at his own funeral service, shrouded and chill, a ghost-body, a wisp, air, buffeted by the golden, flying syllables.

Another phone call from the Hapgoods.

They seemed incapable of acting without his knowledge or permission. It was not, he thought, that they expected any help from him, but they were so much at loggerheads they needed an umpire. Tom had come down to see them; they had quarrelled.

Mrs. Hapgood's account struggled. In spite of emotional upheaval, she'd determined to enjoy the full drama of her tale.

'He turned up at dinner-time. We asked him if he'd come for the boy. He said no, he hadn't, and he just humped there in front of the fire smoking. He'd never start telling you anything. But he ate a good dinner. I don't know how a man so thin and pale-looking, as if he'd been reared on chips, could eat so hearty. In the end, his dad had to ask him outright, and then you never heard such mumbling. Dad spoke quite sharp to him, as if he were a child again, before he'd say anything properly.'

Then apparently he blurted out that Enid had left him.

The last weekend, she'd walked in as he lay on Saturday morning to tell him that she was going off with Frank Bruce, a young man who lodged next door. She'd shoved a kid's white purse into his hands; it had three pound notes inside. He'd got up, tried to detain her, failed, and she'd locked him in the bedroom. By the time he'd dressed, clambered out of the window, she'd carried her cases in next door. He'd created a scene; neighbours jumbled a crowd in the front garden. Without any fuss the lovers absconded over the back fence and into the next street while he hammered on the door and frantically shouted his grievances.

Nobody helped.

A busybody sent for the police; two well-wishers led him to the pub. On Monday and Tuesday he'd been to the factory, but by Wednesday he caught an early bus for his parents' home.

'You should be at work,' his mother said.

'You made not a move, nor a sign of one, to fetch Clive, nor even to see him. Now you come down here.'

'What can we do, you silly boy?'

'You've had enough work for the week. That's what it is. So you take a few days off, at our expense. Well, I'll tell you one thing. You'll get no money either out of me, or your mother. You've made your bed; you can lie in it.'

Tom had looked from one to the other. There was no aggression about him, but a kind of bemused helplessness etched in the blank grin of his face.

'I didn't treat her bad,' he said.

'How often have you done a full week's work since Christmas?' his father asked.

'I've been badly.'

One might have tried to reason with a cat or a monkey. Mother and father raved, but he sat, penitent, humbly contrite, to judge by his shoulders, but mindlessly unaware of his responsibility or their words.

'What are you going to do, then?'

'I can't do nowt.'

They'd no idea at the end of two hours whether he loved his wife, or even if his pride were hurt. He lived at some low reptile level, coldbloodedly. At four o'clock, exhausted, they'd given him a good tea, showed him the door. He'd taken the shabby raincoat on his arm, and gone into the back-yard where his father had told him to get back, work for once in his life. He'd listened, listless as ever, and then said, 'Can you give us a quid or two? As a sub, dad?'

'No, we cannot,' Mrs. Hapgood flared.

'Just to tide me over, like.'

'Earn yourself something.'

He'd turned, shambled down the narrow yard until he reached the fern growing in a wide wooden tub. Half-hesitating, he shoved a boot underneath, prising out a house-brick, leaving the plant toppling. With a growl, he'd grabbed the brick, taken a short run and heaved it, a feminine awkward throw, at the back window which cracked with explosive force. Glass splashed. A great black star of a hole disfigured the glass. 'Bastards,' Tom yelped. 'You bastards,' and then ran off, full tilt, studs scraping the entry.

The old people gaped.

Mrs. Hapgood wept, but admitted that it hadn't taken dad long to cut a new pane and putty it in. Inside an hour, they were normal again.

'But we can't send Clive back,' she said.

'No.' Mansfield hated the word.

'He'd neglect him. Leave him to run wild in the streets.'

Sarah arrived for her Whitsuntide holiday.

David, who had brought her, delighted his father. Somehow they had begun to talk about the stock-market, and the son tried to explain dealings there. He spoke modestly, as an amateur, but quoted his own transactions, and those of close friends, and flashed his knowledge of the morning's quoted prices. James Mansfield found himself caught up by the exposition, in this new world, this language. He'd visited the stock exchange, seen their film, knew of bulls and bears, but 'contango', the word baffled, attracted, was explained. They walked round the garden between the lines of primulas, as David explained how much such a man earned, how much he had made, how long he worked.

'It doesn't seen like work at all,' Mansfield had said, elated.

'You can lose money. It's as if at the end of a bad teaching period, you found some of your salary docked.'

'But is it necessary?'

'I'm not saying it is, ideally. But our society's traditional.'

He was off again, easily explaining, listing alternatives, suggesting what happened in Russia, all fluent, charming, interspersed with compliments for the early pansies or aubretia, camellias, guelder-roses. A huge, efficient, shining machine he moved in perfection. It was no wonder he could win confidence.

'What are you like when you're crossed, David?'

'A bastard, a four-edged, double-dyed bastard.'

'You'd have made a marvellous teacher.'

'I know.' Confidence. 'But only in short bursts. I want to do something. Not talk.'

'I taught boys all those years. We looked at economic history, I suppose. But I hadn't the remotest notion what it was like to start a factory. It's ridiculous, really. I thought it was a case of saving or borrowing or having money, and then paying a bricklayer or an engineer to do a bit of work for you. You know, as I might employ old Jack Jordan to knock a pantry wall out or put me a new door in.'

'That's what it is like.'

'Nonsense. I'm not talking about small concerns.'

'Nor am I. What I do is basically the same as if you built a shed at the bottom of this garden, bought half a dozen sewing machines and hired some of the biddies down here to make frocks.'

'I should be ruined because the mass-producers . . .'

'Of course. Unless there was something special about your product.' He went on expansively; they'd just acquired a well-established firm in Leicester. The directors were retained on salary, no redundancy threatened the workers, but new plant and sales direction would steeply increase profits. 'And yet, it's not much different, from your going down to Hapgood's shop, buying yourself a can of oil and going round the old biddies' machines.'

'And wearing the frocks myself.'

He could not be sure of this man, feared irony in all the suavity of talk. That his son came down to mock he would not believe, but his delight cooled so that after an hour he wanted to sit indoors, on his own. When his son asked a name he was suspicious.

'What's that, dad?'

'Ornithogalum.'

'Don't believe it.'

'Ornithogalum umbellatum. Star of Bethlehem to you. Closes up when the sun goes off it.'

Mansfield felt himself shrivel, in shadow. The name sounded ridiculous. And David, enormous in a rich suit, with heavy cuff-links, legs astride staring down at the flower-clump, put him in his place, his backyard, out of the real world.

'How's Eleanor?'

'You needn't start any of that, my man.' David shook a waggish finger. 'Exactly as before. No miracles. Nothing silly.'

'No love, either.'

'I know how it must appear to you. I'm not insensitive. But there's nothing you can do about it. Except pray.'

'I deduce from your last remark . . .'

'Correctly. It's a bloody nuisance to me. I wish it hadn't happened. She said to me one night, when we'd been

84

badgering each other, "David, I don't love you. I don't think I do." D'you know, I admired her for saying it. It was true. And for me.'

'You told her? There and then?'

'No. I didn't. I apologised for nattering at her. She looked at me as if to tell me diplomatic chat wouldn't edge me out of this one. And I thought, "You chilly bitch." '

Mansfield looked over his primulas, a row proud upright, yellow, deep red, velvet purple, which would in two days stand with shrivelling specks of colour on their stalks. Sarah walked out into the garden, very ladylike.

He had fitted a long desk in the girls' bedroom, so that when Daisy arrived they could revise together. Vaguely he hoped they'd apply to him for help, but guessed they'd grass him with ridiculous questions about the total mileage of Telford's roads in the Highlands of Scotland.

When David had gone, without more conversation, Sarah settled down. She outlined her plans coolly enough, explaining how she'd modify these in days of bright or bad weather. On this Saturday night she sat with her chemistry note-books on her knees as she watched television, sometimes making a note or telling her grandfather with an air of surprise that she'd completely forgotten some fact.

'Do you like chemistry?' he asked.

'I do not. They teach it badly, I think. Just make us learn reams of notes.' She flicked the pages of her books. 'Wouldn't be so bad if I saw any sense in it.'

'Your father used to be very good at chem.'

'He'd be good at most things. He'd want to learn.'

'Don't you?'

'Not really. If I read something interesting, I can't help remembering it. I'm like Daddy in that I'm a competitive type, I don't like being beaten. So I shall mug all this up, and then forget it.'

He grew surprised at her cheerful cynicism. Her teachers were foolish, she thought, but since she had to keep their company she'd play to their rules within reason. He

85

imagined that if he claimed, as to himself, that education was a privilege, an apostolic succession, she'd show total incomprehension. In another school she might have shaped better, but fundamentally she saw no difference in quality between the selected facts of chemistry or the Industrial Revolution or the principal parts of Latin verbs and the names of the hounds in the kennels near her home or the stitches required for some garment or the date of a friend's birthday. All these were knowledge, and utility for examinations conferred no lustre, no rank to one fact over another. Perhaps she was right.

Mansfield remembered his own father's awe.

Translate into Latin: Balbus built a wall. And the old man stroked his moustache with pride as his clever son wrote down the foreign words. These are the lively oracles. And he'd ask the boy how to pronounce the classical phrases from the back of the dictionary, and try his own tongue round them. They'd laugh, dad, Jim and mother watching the menfolk, because the old man often aped stupidity, but these words 'ab imo pectore', 'facilis descensus Averni', 'pallida Mors', these were learning, scholarship, above the pence of the workbench, the shop-counter, the kitchen-sink. Perhaps. Basically their sorcery was economic. He who could translate Balbus's wall into, or Caesar's Wars from, Latin, earned a stiff-collar, a soft-handed job. 'Hard-headed men who have never laboured in their minds till now.' The snobbery of court officialdom. Learning late deceased in beggary. Not here where the 'beggary' of court circles would be counted as wildest affluence.

Sarah smiled, not down-hearted.

He looked at her, on the settee, composed as her mother, almost grown-up. That sounded askew. She appeared to him, at least as old as some of the young mothers with two or three children he'd seen squatting alongside pushchairs outside the supermarkets. His years or lack of interest left him incapable of judging a young woman's age.

86

Sarah always smiled at him. While she poked fun at her teachers or described the boredom of lessons she took care to be polite, speaking formally, not making him an accomplice. She seemed to understand that he'd prefer matters otherwise, and therefore assumed an air of apologetic truth. Even Daisy, whom she admired, received a lashing now and then.

'She's all right, up to a point. Very clever. Gets A-marks all the time without trying. But she's boy-mad.'

'You disapprove.'

'It's crazy that somebody who can do maths, and music, and hockey all so well should be mooning over some dripping wet-head you wouldn't look at twice.'

'She may see something deep in the man.'

'Something that's not there, then. Besides she sees it in a different one every week.' Her eyes lacking malice, glinted.

'You don't suffer from this, these drawbacks?'

'Not so often.' She suddenly straightened, hauled her skirt-ends. 'I've been struck once or twice, I can tell you.'

'It seems serious, doesn't it?'

'At the time. Yes.'

They looked each other over, warmly, making contact. Mansfield did not remember any such confidences from the adolescent David. He'd talked to, escorted girls but said nothing to his father, who'd never asked. Now this young woman spoke with detachment, without embarrassment, treating him for once as a colleague.

'Daddy never lived up here, did he? In this place?'

'No. It's only been built five years. We lived on Kirby Road, down in the town. I'll show you the house.'

'Who's there now?'

'I don't know. I think it's flats.'

'He'd have a lot of girl friends. At eighteen he'd look marvellous.'

'I suppose so. I never really knew. Sometimes I saw him with them. With one. She went to the university. But he never said much, and as long as he got on with his work . . . I ought to know more, but I don't.'

'Weren't you interested?' she asked, and her face, in repose, seemed both beautiful and sly, mocking now, cordially critical.

'Yes. But we didn't say . . . My wife and I. He was young. And he could mind his own business. We were friendly, but I think he knew, even at that time, that by his standards I was a failure.'

'That's horrible. I didn't like to hear you say that.' Her voice sounded clearer, younger, while the past tense made its one point disinterestedly, without recourse to abstraction. 'Do you think you are, grandpa?'

Now he smiled, wondering how near the truth he'd venture today.

'I've done one or two things I wanted. And David has done about fifty times better than I could ever have managed.'

'Is that good? Or are you jealous?'

'I hardly know. Honestly.'

He did not think he'd failed her then, and she groped after a success that appeared only momentarily, a flash of fool's gold, a grail glimpsed.

On Sunday afternoon, Daisy Quinn arrived, in flowered trousers and pink shirt, accompanied by her mother, a dry, brown woman with glasses, who smoked heartily and croaked advice. Mansfield could not make out the relationship between mother and daughter; they seemed not unfriendly, not quarrelsome, but slightly bored, or exasperated. Mrs. Quinn would be glad when Angélique could drive herself; she was capable now. This led her to a short expository paragraph on the compromises of law, a kind of footnote on foolishness. Her host found this odd, not entertaining, like garlic, endured once a year and bragged about. The woman was obviously clever, with a wide range of learning; she did not boast, treated listeners as equals, one aside on transformations in language floored him in no time, but she was not, obviously, fond of her daughter, or of demonstrating love. The girl treated her mother equally casually as a piece of furniture, a telephone, useful now and again, but otherwise ignored. The brown triangular face of Mrs. Quinn presided over the table; she did most, all of the talking but she reminded Mansfield of a sparrow he'd once seen, reared by a family and let free, which fluttered in at mealtimes from its hedge, perched on the potato dish to peck. When there were visitors, the children squealed, perked up; on their own they greeted the bird, fed him, ignored him.

Mrs. Quinn disappeared after tea to belt the M1, shaking hands sharply, thanking him with her don's squawk, her quick eye-dropping. The girls disappeared to a bedroom and he was left happily to wash dishes.

On the bank holiday Monday he cleaned his car, took the guests breakfast in bed and offered to drive them out if they weren't working.

'We did some last night,' Sarah said. 'Half-way through three revision sheets.'

'So you'd like to go?'

'Where to, grandpa?'

'How about the Tramway Museum in Crich?'

Their look of incomprehension before they composed themselves to habitual boredom made him laugh outright. Daisy laid down the rules; they'd do the sandwiches. He demurred. While he prepared food, they must do an hour's work. Agreed, agreed. A maths paper, Daisy thought, that'd be fun. Sarah pulled a face.

'Then you'll need to give her another hour to put her glory on.'

Inside five minutes they were at it, head to head on the hearth-rug, chins propped, toes drumming, pencils quickfire; they competed, hating each other's skill, but never stopping, mentioning methods, occasionally criticising, neither in difficulty. It pleased him to see the two, straight hair cascading so that a slit of face showed, hard at it, never

uneasy, even stopping once to say something about a class-
mate, Elizabeth Large, who had shouted out in lessons that
maths was only fit for milkmen. They laughed uproariously
but not for long, returned to straight faces. As soon as he
gave the word, they packed up their papers, put on a pale,
ridiculous make-up, mini-skirts and coloured tights. They
appeared different, as if masked, faces daubed stiffly inex-
pressive, but they chatted to him, read his map, ate ice-
cream cornets like solemn children.

They parked in the white dust of the quarry floor under
Crich Stand, swung down to the tramcars, took leather
seats on a closed-in Glasgow tram. The conductor, in his
speech of welcome, addressed himself entirely to the girls,
ignoring the mums and children, putting on a show and a
half. The two sat like queens so that Mansfield thought it
should be double fare to be allowed to sit with them. A
young man with a paintbox explained what he was
about, took the three along a loop-line to show them a spare
the enthusiasts had been trying to beg, borrow or steal for
three years. There it lay, rather rusty, by the track side,
uninteresting but a treasure, to be shown only to these long-
legged, posh-voiced misses.

They took lunch on the moors, drove over to Haddon
Hall in the clouded half-brightness of the afternoon. Now
the girls walked with decorum, added lustre to the stately
length of the long chamber where branches of late cherry
flowered on a table in the alcove. They peered from the
gardens down to the river and Dorothy Vernon's bridge,
but they did not giggle, and Daisy, suddenly catching
Mansfield's eye, said fiercely:

'Do you know what my father would call this?'

'No?' Amused, fascinated.

'A jewel.' She drew herself up. 'He's never been here.
If he had, he would have said so.'

'Will he visit it now? Is he interested enough in this
sort ... ?'

'One never knows.' The use of 'one', its tone, seemed

aristocratic, feudal, suiting the panels, the subdued airy light. 'Not with adults.'

That spoke for the child. Enough is enough.

The afternoon of the Hapgoods' visit, the girls went for an hour's tennis. On their return they took Clive out on the lawn, and played with him. The three old people stood at the window to watch the swooping young ladies in their brief skirts circling round the child, who tottered, staggered but mainly sat down. If they held on too long to the ball, he howled after them, a wild squawl.

'Not much wrong with his lungs,' Mrs. Hapgood said, resigned.

'Young man,' they heard Daisy address the boy as she returned the ball, 'you make far too much noise for one of your size.'

'And so I must appeal to you,' Sarah mocked, 'to conduct yourself more equitably.'

Clive gaped up at them, snotty-nosed, and held out the ball again, for more frustration, or the pomp of language.

'Marvellous, the way those clever girls deal with him. He seems to know,' Hapgood said. 'School'll perhaps be the making of him.'

'We've got to get him there, first.'

They began to talk again. Only yesterday the child had been sent from the hospital, and he'd seemed much improved, less grizzly, almost as if he was grateful to be back. His grandfather, however, expecting the worst had written to Enid, care of a married sister, and had set it down plainly, once more, both claimed, that whatever she thought of Tom, whatever her present fly-by-night plans might be, she'd brought this child into the world, and she should assume responsibility.

'I put it straight and simply,' Hapgood said.

'For all the good your putting did, you could have banged it straight in the dustbin. Her sister's as bad as she is. They wouldn't send it on; they wouldn't know how to cross one address out and write another on even if she bothered to tell them she'd flitted.'

'I wrote to the welfare people.'

Mrs. Hapgood's sour smile smeared her face. This naive belief of her husband that if you got it down on paper something would happen clashed with her methodistical upbringing. It spoke the same feckless behaviour that put its trust in football pools.

Outside the girls were swinging Clive, one, two, three and aw-a-a-y. His screams of delighted fear ripped round the windows, and all three rushed in breathless and flushed.

'Blow your nose, Clive.' Mrs. Hapgood advanced with a handkerchief. He allowed the indignity, but turned immediately to the girls, who bibbed him, fed, fussed him at the tea-table.

'He'll sleep tonight,' his grandmother said.

Peer's granddaughter entertains idiot. The headline presented itself to Mansfield, who wished he'd thought otherwise of the visiting pathetic trio. After tea, the sleepy child grizzled on the hearthrug when his playmates went upstairs to study.

'He's really enjoyed himself. He won't forget this.' Mrs. Hapgood.

'It's done us all good.'

'Come again, then. Give those girls something to think about.'

Mansfield considered these dully-delivered sentences. They had the resigned stolidity of remarks offered after the early-warning siren had sounded. Some would writhe and pray, but others, and God bless them, would add that the weather was fine for it, or order some slatternly kid to tie his shoelaces properly. It might never come to that. But for thousands, millions, it had happened; the sentence of death, the waiting, the final five minutes before the hangman's noose tightened, the stark-naked walk of Jews to the gas-chamber, the mass grave. They were no less sensitive to shame, to fear, then he, and they had been publicly summoned to die. What had they mouthed? Shema Yisrael. A frightened gentleman pointed upwards to an aeroplane to distract his infant son from the executioners' rifles. But perhaps they muttered, stuttered, something banal, and of good report.

Why did he torture himself in this way?

Torture? Smock-ravel, rather.

He knew how to die; the depression, the sense of sick heaviness when indigestion would not yield, and his blood thumped and banged him silly. As sweat and tears mingled he thought that he'd met his end. Did he speak? Frightened through every pore, he'd waited, clung, in a limbo, a tearing death for the tablets and the unhurried men in white coats in the disinfected stink of the ward. He'd not said a word, good or flat, but as the ambulance men had carried him out he'd noticed, pain near-bearable now rescue'd begun, the number on the garden gate, a metal two, plain on blue wood, shadowed, in relief. Relief.

From upstairs faintly he could hear the pocket tape-recorder.

Pop dribbled quietly as the girls worked.

'We shall have to be going soon, mother.'

'Yes, but it's that nice here, and he's so well behaved. That's if you're not busy or anything, Mr. Mansfield.'

The phone shrilled in the hall, and Eleanor inquired after her daughter. Carefully, and when he'd chaffed her for not waiting for the six-thirty cheap rate, he explained what he was about.

'You're not overdoing it, father, are you?'

'I expect so.'

Both had come up when he'd been ill. He could see their faces now, stiff with concern, as a youngish consultant, curls thinning, explained drily why there was no need to move the patient to the pay-bed block, that he'd been as well cared for . . .

'Of course, if you insist, I shall do as you say.' The voice snapped sharply, nasally, as if the physician's métier

93

consisted of protecting invalids from relatives.

'Then you're very silly, father. Filling your house will all these people and their troubles.'

'In my father's house are many stanchions.'

'But you will take it easy, won't you? I feel bad enough wishing Sarey and Angélique on to you.' She disregarded, or misheard, his word-play.

'They'd make marvellous nurses, Eleanor.'

'They'd make marvellous anythings, that pair. Don't get putting lunatic ideas into their heads, will you, darling?'

'I don't think they listen to a single damned thing I say.'

'That's very naughty of them, then.'

'No, they're like you. Too many concerns.'

'I'm quite idle, now. Nobody about. Nobody wanting anything. If things stagnate any more, I'll be round the village with a bell.'

Oddly, to him, she did not want to speak to Sarah, inquired after her work, made one or two comments about Angélique Quinn. Eleanor disliked the professor who was a snob and his wife who regretted that she sacrificed an academic career to bring up a family.

'If he can get on telly, and she can write a book, they'll be made.'

'Is it likely?'

'Anything's possible with the mass media. If she produces a book, it'll be one of these diligent biographies, Life of Herbert Spencer or Thomas Love Peacock or somebody. And some equally industrious don'll find three mistakes in seven hundred and forty pages and spoil it all.'

'They're lost, then,'

'With the rest of us.'

They talked past pips so that when he returned to the Hapgoods he hummed, light-hearted.

'We'll have a glass of sherry first,' he said, when they made a move. The three drank, in his wine-glasses, present from David, as Clive snuffled himself to sleep on his grandmother's lap.

'Quite the high life.' Hapgood. 'We're thinking of selling the shop.'

'Where will you live?'

'We did think of up here,' the woman answered. 'If it's not beyond us.'

Mansfield meandered on about mortgages and good-will, the need for a car, the distance of the shops. Wine cheered; this talk committed nobody but suggested a grasp of affairs. Overdrafts, money tax and value had no connection with tantrums and bed-wetting. All boasted, as if about football or sex.

Soon after eight the girls came down to see a comedy programme on the box.

'Work well?' he asked.

'Moderate,' Daisy said. 'We can't raise much enthusiasm.' They watched, never laughed once, commented adversely, and during the news-bulletin Sarah suddenly said of an item gloomily galloped-through on the failure of a travel-firm, 'If he'd read that like that in the Frank Derby Show it would have been killing.' She was correct, he thought.

He produced cocoa, and they talked about school. Now they seemed younger, less intelligent, trotting out the feeble eccentricities of the staff, the headmistress's sniff, the geography mistress who ate biscuits in the lesson, the chemistry master who frightened himself to death by saying 'Bloody hell' when Felicity Worth spilt acid all over a bench-top. Mansfield expected chatter of this sort, was even pleased to find it, but became apprehensive when they shredded the chemistry syllabus as educationally useless. That was too adult. For Daisy could pout, 'It's time old Leadbelly learnt that there is no intrinsic value in a fact of chemistry acquired by memory and reproduced with a formula and a diagram which is an exact copy of his which is itself a reproduction and of no artistic merit.'

'What a sentence,' he said.

Sarah grimaced, shook her seat.

'A double,' she said. 'This child is not merely offering a valuable comment, or at least one fruitful of discovery, she is also parodying her father who does not consider that he has spoken a complete English sentence until he has said something rude and included the word "value".' Both laughed now.

'And what about your father, Sarah? Or should I ask Daisy first?'

'We admire him,' Daisy said, 'in his way. But that's because we've no ideals. He makes a lot of money.'

'I don't suppose,' Sarah added, 'that he's any more distinguished in his line than Daisy's papa in his. But everybody in this country admires wealth.'

'Are you fond of your fathers?'

'I don't know,' Daisy answered, first, with hesitation. 'I sometimes wonder what I'd feel if he died. That's morbid.'

'I like Daddy,' Sarah said. 'But I don't see much of him. Even when I'm on holiday he's not about. And now he and Mummy are . . . well, disagree, it's worse.'

'My mother often contradicts my father to show him she's as clever as he is. She's probably right, but he's a tremendous worker. He really does drive himself.'

'The whole thing's cockeyed, though,' Sarah followed, lips pursed. 'What's he get out of it in the end?'

'He impresses my mother. That's what his life consists of. Sad, isn't it?'

'He could do a sight worse.' Mansfield sounded dogged.

'But it's adolescent. Mature people should know their thing, and either like doing it, or know its value . . .'

'Bull's eye,' Sarah shouted, but neither laughed, looking at Mansfield for his reaction. Now they sat scared, babes in black wood.

'Do you talk to your parents as you're doing to me?'

96

'Do you know,' Daisy whooped, like a north-country comic, 'he never listens to me? He says a few congratulatory words when I've done well at school, and, give him credit, he opens his wallet. But he never listens.'

'So you want to impress him?'

'I suppose so.' Suitably chastened.

'And you, Sarah?'

'I don't know what I want. I think I'd like to please them. If I knew how.'

'Doing well at school?'

'Yes. I know that. I once did something for daddy. He mentioned something about the Lake District. I think some minor advertising campaign. And I went to the library, the man there's very good, and copied information down; I was really interested after a bit and spent three days working it over. And when I showed my file to daddy, I could see he was impressed. I'm not boasting. It turned out it wasn't important, or even anything to do with him, but he was pleased. But mummy was furious. "So that's where you've been hiding yourself," she said. She's often angry, but not with me, if you know what I mean, with herself, or facts, or circumstances.' She laughed at her own fumbling. 'But this time, she was jealous. Jealous of me. I ask you. I didn't think it was possible to know, but I did. Just because daddy had praised me.'

'What did you do?'

'What could I? Pretend I didn't notice.'

'It would have made me feel important,' Daisy said. 'As if they asked one's opinion, and meant to listen to it.'

'I wouldn't have touched it,' Sarah said. 'I just started, and became interested.'

Mansfield shivered, put his feet together, wished he could take a drink or light a pipe to smother his uncertainty. These poor, clever children, batting above their league, with only their intelligence, their glib words to help them out. Not until they'd hardened themselves, soiled, spoilt themselves would they be able to cope, and then they'd be handing punishment out to the defenceless un-deserving in their turn.

'I'm an old soldier,' he said. Was it aloud? Both stared at him, in mock alarm, but looked away.

He should not have spoken.

It was his shibboleth. Whenever he was in trouble he thought these five words, remembering he'd been in the trenches, frightened to die, but with a crust, an exo-skeleton, of rigid unfeeling, of hard support so that he could look at the spilt entrails of a friend, or his teeth in death's stiff grin. He'd been wounded. He always said now it wasn't too bad, like a punch. Dying was perhaps no worse, a mere schoolyard scrap. The words comforted him, had stiffened his civilian back, but now today he'd said them first time, out loud, breaking that piddling spell.

'My password,' he said.

They nodded in incomprehension so that he went to the cupboard and took down the silver biscuit tin where he kept his fruit drops.

'Who wants a toffee?'

The three unwrapped their sweets, and he collected the litter.

'Toffee or tuffeh,' he said. 'Sounds better.'

He had enjoyed the girls' company, and was now pressed by Eleanor to stay again in Hampshire. One day when she'd rung up, he'd mentioned his fears at the performance of *Twelfth Night*. He could almost hear her brain; given a suggestion she was at work at once.

'I know exactly how you felt,' she said. She reminded

him of a breezy woman doctor they had once. None of your nonsense, now. Open your bowels for you. 'We can do something about it.'

'You can?'

'There's an admirable amateur performance in Winchester next week.'

'That's tempting providence.'

'No. Or not for long. If it were weeks ahead I might agree, but it's next week.'

'Hubris.'

'No, father. Will you come?'

'Yes.'

'That's settled that.'

She loved these decisions, and yet she acquiesced in his irrational fear that fate would intervene before he managed another performance. He travelled by train; she feigned anger as he stepped from a second class carriage, and enjoyed the fuss with grandchildren and servants. They drove in style to the play, which was excellently presented; Eleanor did not keep him hanging about drinking with the dozens of people who wished to talk to her. He spent the next day in bed, and they saw the performance once more on its third night.

'That's showed the immortal gods,' he said.

'It's shown you,' she said.

David did not appear, and the father said nothing. This woman had delighted him, exerted herself to exorcise his fear, and he was grateful beyond words. To see the beloved play twice inside a week seemed a gift beyond generosity. She had settled his fear, but largely, handsomely, with élan.

'Now, I know what "ineffable" means,' he said.

'More than I do.'

' "Not to be expressed in words." You've done a marvellous thing for me, Eleanor. If I could . . .'

'Don't exaggerate, father.'

By the prim pronunciation he knew she recognised his

joy, and he left it at that. If he flung his arms about her, it would be anti-climax; if he spoke he might not control the one violence left to him, his emotions. So he sat, between the two performances re-reading the play in the Arden edition, relishing the notes, the appurtenances of scholarship, but best, head singing through those golden words, remembering school, college, dallying with the innocence of love.

When he returned home, he took himself steady for forty-eight hours. He had enjoyed the break to the full, but knew his limits. A long journey by train, however clement the weather, however pleasant the company or scenery, had these days to be paid for in fatigue, and he, because he had found delight, sat about, rang nobody, did nothing in the garden until he had made terms with his demanding age.

He was hoeing his rosebed, basking in the sunshine tempered thus high with a flutter of wind, when he noticed his neighbour, a Mrs. Fisher, watching him. She had retired here from the valley where her late husband had owned three prosperous shoe shops. A decent woman, her voice recalled the front-door step of the terraced cottages by the hosiery-factories rather than the spruce bungalow she owned, and the mathematically tidy garden she employed professionals to manage.

'Mr. Mansfield.' She called very unusually. Grudgingly he went over. 'Y'know that Mrs. Hapgood, Clara Osborne as was, keeps the hardware on Newmarket Street?'

'Yes.'

'Y'haven't heard, then?'

'No.'

She tried not to beam, twisted her face in suitable sorrow. 'She put her head in the gas-oven.'

He paused, the whole world greyly unnoticed. For these seconds he was not concerned even with himself. He registered nothing but the initial impact.

'Is she dead?' His voice?

'They rushed her to hospital.' She determined to

lengthen the recital, postured, decided on a stance, continued. 'She's very ill. On the danger list.'

'When did this happen?' Now his legs trembled, eyes misted, hands ached. He must sit.

'Yesterday. Her mester found her.' Again the shift. 'I only seen her last week. In the shop. She didn't look very well, then. 'Ighly strung, if you know what I mean.'

He stared rudely at her.

Now, he muttered thanks, brusquely left her standing. In his arm-chair, he seemed to fade, to disintegrate before a long spasm of weary, painful violence. Without will to combat the weakness, he sat captive, shaking, inhuman, vague. Finally, he struggled to the kitchen and the brandy bottle.

After almost an hour, and vacillation, he dialled the Hapgoods' number. Doubt harried him as soon as the ringing-tone chirped. He hoped for reprieve, a respite, but Hapgood answered. Mansfield muttered he had just heard. The other coughed, weakly. How was she?

'Out of danger, I'm thankful to say.'

'I can't tell you how sorry I am.'

'Everybody's been very good.'

'Is there anything I can do?'

'I don't think so, thank you.'

Both breathed audibly. Mansfield wanted details, a good sign which he hated. Two men stood at either end of a telephone connection, unspeaking, aching for contact, one afraid to offer, the other to ask help. So they licked lips, noticed the inadequacies of their bodies, stared listlessly at clocks and calendars, tugged spectacles off and said nothing. There must be some word, some expression of sympathy, some key to the situation, but Mansfield, groping, did not know it. He made the attempt, cleared his throat, blurted out:

'I'm very sorry. Alfred. Is there anything I can do?'

He had used the Christian name for the first time. Halting or not, it supplied the solution. Alfred.

Hapgood began to talk.

Clive had been off-colour, had tired his grandmother. He had been put to bed, crying, just before Hapgood had gone to call on a joiner about a new set of racks for the shop. His wife sat in her chair in front of the fire, white-faced and exhausted, but there was nothing to do, and the child slept quiet.

'She was whacked, but I'd made her a cup of coffee and put the wireless on for her, quiet so could hear him if he woke. She was all right, and I told her I wouldn't be long, but she said there wasn't any hurry, she'd just sit there. I never thought twice about it, because the lad had been ever so good for a week or more now till then, and I wanted to get Jed Holmes going on with this job. I thought it'd please her, modernise if we're to sell, and, anyway, you know what these little men are, like snails.'

The large voice rumbled on, diminished by the phone, but impressive, slow, dignified, a local preacher.

'I wasn't away more than an hour and a half. I'd walked, and I came in the back way, down the yard. The door was locked, so I slipped my key out, it's a Yale, and rattled, couldn't open the thing. Bolted. But nothing struck me, even then. I knocked on the living room window, rapped, you know. Not that I could see anybody inside though it wasn't very dark. And then I saw the curtains in the scullery window. They were drawn. By God, it hit me. But you know, you can't believe it. It don't happen to me, to people . . .' His voice crumbled away, and Mansfield heard him clear his throat. 'I stood there. I'd look such a fool if I smashed a window for nothing, especially after our Tom had gone breaking one. I stood there like stuffed pork. I don't know how long, but I wasn't weighing it up or anything like that. I just stood, and then I bent down and picked a big round duckey up and belted it at the window near the catch. I wasn't frightened, not in the slightest. I thought, "Another bloody job putting this pane back", and then I knocked the fastener aside and upped the bottom and when I pulled the curtain, the gas, by God, the gas it leapt out as if it was solid. You wouldn't think standing in the air in the yard you'd hardly get a whiff, but I'm telling you, it fairly leapt out as if it was alive and heavy. I don't remember climbing through that window.'

Pain seeped in the silence. Outside Mansfield heard an aeroplane pass, thumping the ground with its roar.

Hapgood breathed, unaware of his listener, in his ache of slow memory.

'She was lying there, stretched across the floor, her head sideways on a little stool-cushion we've got. I pulled her out of the stove and her head fairly banged the ground. Then I put the tap off. I think I did. You know, I don't remember this properly. It'd be sensible to turn the gas off first, wouldn't it? but I couldn't swear I did that. Then I jumped up for the door. I was that dizzy and choking with it, I hardly knew I . . . what I . . . I couldn't . . . My fingers were all thumbs as I bent down for the bolt and I fell over and gave my head such a whang, but I didn't notice. And I jerked at the latch and the door squeaked on the kitchen tiles, it sticks with heat or damp, but I got it open, wide open, and I pulled Clara out in the yard. And I thought when I dumped her there, "Not near that damned door. That's where it's coming from", so I drags her up the yard a bit, though that all felt drowning with the stuff. Perhaps I'd got it in my lungs. She was alive. I didn't know what to do, first-aid nor nothing like that. I didn't know whether to give her artificial respiration or what. She looked a bad colour, and she's none so young. I ran in and dialled emergency. What they asked me or what I told them I don't know to this day. It smelt gas all over the house. I thought I couldn't have turned it off properly, and I looked at all the taps, fiddled a minute, and got out in the yard again. She was lying spread-eagled there, by a little rose we've got in a wooden tub. She seemed to have moved, but I don't suppose she had. "You can't leave her there. You can't leave her there, like that." I just stood gawking at her, gawping.'

Again the narrative trickled dry.

Mansfield cleared his throat, not daring.

At the other end of the line, Hapgood seemed to puff little bubbles at the phone's diaphragm, like a short-winded smoker.

'I went in the house.' His voice regained its large normality so that the sentence rang with breadth, a power in simplicity. 'I got a cushion off one of the chairs and an old coat of mine. I made her comfortable, and put the coat round, and then I seemed to go myself. I hung over the wall, and I heaved and heaved as if I'd sick my heart up. Gas and shock. I could hear myself dragging my inside out, and fighting against it but making this groaning noise; it scraped my chest near raw. It's the biggest wonder Bellamy next door didn't come out at the racket, but I suppose they've got their sitting room upstairs and they'd be watching the television. And when I knew I'd finished I thought of her. I knelt down. She didn't look too bad, but she was unconscious and I sort of pulled her up a bit, sitting, and got my arm round her. Her head lolled, and I thought by God I was going to start again. My head swum and there we were. And d'you know, it started to rain. I'd been wanting it for the garden, but I never thought I'd get it like that. It fairly flung it down and her hair was all streaked over her face. She'd looked a sight, I can tell you. But I thought to myself, "She's outside, in the air, breathing fresh air", so I didn't take her indoors. I covered her head as best I could and there we were when the ambulance men came, me squatting and her lying in the pouring rain.'

'They took her?' Mansfield's foolish question relieved both.

'They didn't waste much time. Asked me a few questions and one of 'em said, "You get yersen inside, dad, and in a hot bath, and have a hot drink. We'll see to her." '

'That's what you did.'

'In time. And then I drove down to the hospital and asked at the lodge how she was. They rang up somewhere and said she was as well as could be expected.'

'They didn't let you see her?'

'No. They told me to go home and ring in the morning. Red-faced chap on. Was very nice. Phoned one or two places. Did his best for me, though it didn't mean anything to him.'

Now he paused, for exhaustion, fetched himself a chair for the rest. He described with poignant artlessness, as if he'd decided to spread the rich voice on the flattest words, broken-backed sentences, the morning's first call, the police constable, the visit that afternoon.

'And how did you find her?'

'Last night? Not too bad. Weak, if you know what I mean. As if she'd got nothing about her, no strength, no gyp.'

'And the boy?'

'A neighbour has him. Mrs. Dunn. Young woman with a family.' He stopped again. These pauses did not disconcert Mansfield who held the phone in a slow chaos, a maelstrom of inaction. 'I thought she'd be guilty, feel it, y' know. But she's never said a word. She'll talk, but not about that, why she did it: anything else. And I daren't ask her.'

'No.'

'I keep worrying myself what it must be like, t'have made your mind up to do it, and then wake up in a hospital.'

'She probably feels physically ill. Exhausted.'

'But to have to explain it, Mr. Mansfield. She knows she'll have to do that. Our Clara faces up to it in the end. She realises what she's done. But I daren't . . . To think what must be in her mind. I didn't think she was capable of that, Mr. Mansfield.'

Mansfield, on a tentative invitation, visited the hospital that evening with her husband. He made up a bunch of roses.

'Those yellow buds are beautiful,' Mrs. Hapgood said.

'Ducat.'

'Beautiful.'

She seemed normal, shy, taciturn. The men chatted easily about neighbours, a new road being built, Mansfield's garden, while she, reserved, eyed them, ate an apple, drank lemonade. They left, rather relieved that no confessions had been made, the elder proud of himself, of his good works. Hapgood thanked him, harassed, on the pavement, a puzzled man in dark suit and cloth cap.

At the weekend he received a phone-call from Enid Hapgood asking if she could call.

The Saturday morning scorched the garden where he sat, waiting. She arrived about eleven with a young man in a multi-striped shirt and long-bobbed hair.

'This is Eric,' she said.

As they sipped boiling coffee in the fierce sunshine, Mansfield looked at her. Her face was brown, freckled, but raw, half-finished, unattended. Her features were complete but botched; the eyes small, slyish above the large nose; her mouth slack, unshaped. And yet her body under its neat orange frock, no larger than a bathing-dress, moved superbly, and her legs, bare, golden, stretched magnificent.

'Our Wendy wrote up about Mrs. Hapgood,' she said. 'I'd heard from him, from mester. I didn't do anything about it, though. Didn't see my way clear.' Aggressive, self-reproachful, she stirred her coffee, explained how she'd told Eric they'd have to come. The young man poked a hand down into his trousers top.

'I didn't want to go round there. Our Wendy says she's improving, but you don't . . . I looked you up in the phone book. Well, you came to our house.'

'Yes?' He disliked his assumed superiority.

'I'm not going back to Tom. I'll tell you that straight. We've done, once and for all. I've left him, and that's that.'

'You're living with Eric?' He'd no idea why he asked the impertinent question.

'Yes.' Jaw jutting, she stared her dislike. 'But I, we, want to take Clive. We'll have him.'

'I thought you had a job?'

'I have. But I've got it all fixed up. He'll be looked after.'

'Why have you come to see me?'

She raised a fist to her mouth, bit her knuckles at his stupidity.

'You know the Hapgoods, if she's getting better. You can put it to him about Clive.'

'Why can't you?'

'Because I know what he is. I've left his Tom. I'm living with another man. I'm not fit.'

'I don't think so.' She looked up at his assertion. Her face shone in the heat. If she'd taken ten minutes' trouble over make-up she'd be presentable, not disgracing the trunk, the perfect limbs. 'It drove Mrs. Hapgood to suicide.'

She considered that in the shimmering air. At this time in the morning it was already so hot that the white houses on the other side of the valley shivered, and sunshine pressed through one's clothes. Massed to his right roses burned above dried soil, Masquerade, Ena Harkness, Peace, the Doctor, Dagmar Spatte, Albertine on a trellis, Nevada like a great tree of creamy saucers. Magnificent. Nothing out of the ordinary, but fiery in the clear light, and to the left, their scent heavy over the grass, beds of pinks.

'I should go and see him, then?'

'Yes.' He considered. 'You haven't asked me where he is. Or how.'

'I know. Ethel Dunn's got him.'

Intelligence rattled in the fresh voice. She wasn't without sense in that she'd made enquiries, rooted about for his address, made her way here to put her case. Suddenly in the heat, in flaming June, his eyes strained, seemed weak. It was not that he did not see properly, but about him settled an imminence of feebleness; his body, which functioned respectably now, could easily give way, and no amount of will-power or grit on his part would by one jot alter that failure. His hand lay weak on the arm of the garden chair, discoloured, fat-veined, brown-spotted. He had reached old age, and he'd better accept it. The realisation spurred, did not discourage. He set his coffee-cup on the ground with something of a flourish, smiled, said:

'My best line is to ring Mr. Hapgood now. Tell him what you say.'

'It might be a shock. If you blurt it out.'

'There are such things as pleasant shocks.'

Nodding, she dabbed her face with her handkerchief rolled into a pad. While Mansfield was indoors, she spoke once to Eric saying how nice it was up here, in this big garden. Then they sat drowsily until the host returned, sat gently down.

'That's all right, then.'

'What did he say?'

'He thinks you should take Clive. He'll tell Mrs. Hapgood this afternoon.'

'When do, can we collect him?'

'Tomorrow morning. If that suits.'

She turned to look at his roses, thighs exposed, without self-consciousness.

'Did you mention Eric?'

'I did. There's something to be said for speaking the truth.'

'There wouldn't have been if he'd turned awkward.'

'Well, he didn't. If you can go round after eight this evening he'll have Clive's clothes ready for you, and you can pick him up at Mrs. Dunn's after breakfast.'

'All cut and dried?' she said. She did not exactly mock him, but her voice withheld praise, cut into complacency. It came amiss. He watched the pair walk down the road, over the hedge-tops, a nondescript couple. With the full stretch of his imagination, he wished himself into her mind as she walked between new sandy gardens, the Little Dorrit, the fresh-laid lawns turning brown, the white paint, brass coach lamps or cart-wheels. She couldn't want the uncouth child; he'd be under her feet and Eric's with his illness and mardy squealings, but she'd seen it as her duty to fetch him, perhaps superstitiously to allay God's anger at her adultery. Where had she learnt these notions? How deep were they ingrained? She had come here, at her own expense, to do something he himself would have shrunk from. Standing in his kitchen, swilling the coffee cups, he admired her, but, uncertain of her motives, could not claim his admiration reasonable. Now the couple would be on a bus, on the way to her parents' crowded terrace-house, the fish-and-chip dinner. The complexity of human behaviour left him empty, without resource. He'd no business meddling here.

A day or two later, the Hapgoods invited him for tea.

Mrs. Hapgood was up and about, and though the husband fussed over her, at least verbally, she bustled round. If he expected overt remorse, shame, he saw none. She appeared vigorous, and grateful.

'People were very good to me,' she said, cutting a slice of fruit cake, still warm from the stove where she'd tried to kill herself. 'You don't know until the time.' She walked badly, waddling to the sideboard for spoons.

The meal was pleasant, but after they had cleared away, washed up, Mrs. Hapgood went out to a meeting.

'She goes with a Mrs. Sheldon,' Hapgood said wryly. 'Lame woman, lives over the street. Came to the hospital. Said she felt a call.'

'What sort of meeting is it?'

'Religious. Evangelical. Tin-tabernacle sort of place.'

'What do you think?'

'We shall have to see about that.'

He said no more.

Mansfield read a post-card from Sarah.

The picture was of Stonehenge and at one of four gum-marks at the corner she had written, 'Ripped from history book'. The message stood clear. ' "O" Levels not too bad. Can we, Daisy and I, come up when we finish on Tuesday week? Love.' He answered at once that they could.

To his discomfort, the weather remained hot, without rain, and evening by evening he carted his watering-can round the garden. Exertion soon wearied him, and he sat idly in a deck-chair during the day's heat, promising that he'd begin to cook meals for himself as soon as it turned cooler. He had no time for life, listening listlessly to music on his radio or passing his leisure drinking tea he did not enjoy or sitting of an afternoon dabbing himself with a sponge in a warm bath.

Young people shouted, running near-naked at the weekends, complaining but brash with energy. Some old-age pensioners played bowls or set off on day-trips to the seaside, but they seemed to him foolishly aping their grandchildren without youth's excuse. Yet he resented his inactivity, waited desperately for the postman to bring the letter that would set him to work, or the phone call, the summons on the door-bell. Nobody needed him so he could not occupy himself.

When the girls arrived he brightened. The weather had broken and he stood on his porch relishing the rich sweetness of wet earth, the thunder-grey of the clouds.

'Look at it,' Sarah said. 'Tropical while we're in exams.' Daisy wore a stiff straw hat, with a coloured ribbon, untidily attractive on the back of her head. Their luggage seemed excessive, great round-cornered portmanteaux.

'I have to tell you something first,' Sarah said.

'Won't it wait?'

'We should be at school. For another fortnight.'

'They don't know you've come here?'

He needed no answer to that, but felt only sympathy for them. Why should they be cooped up, obeying petty regulations, loathing institutional cooking, when they could be up and away? With a pang he realised he would never have taken the risk.

'I shall have to ring your headmistress.'

'Yes, grandpa.'

The two watched him, standing by their enormous cases, noses shiny but testing him, putting him to the judgement. 'O that I knew where I might find him, that I might come before his presence.' A voice swooped in his memory. Mendelssohn, Elijah and Obadiah, the polished chapel-pews of his young manhood. The rain dripped brightly, sedately from the rose-leaves.

'I'll tell her some cock-and-bull story. The examinations have turned your head.'

They smiled politely, as if in their world there was no call for excuses, delivered from goodness of the heart or not.

'We'd planned it,' Daisy said.

'I know,' he answered. 'Sarah sent me a card.'

Equal now, he and the children.

'I'll ring Miss Esher, straight off, before she worries your parents.'

'That's a good idea. And we'll write to them.'

Though he disliked long-distance calls with the waiting, the difficulty of hearing, he enjoyed his few minutes with the school bursar, who told him that the headmistress was away. He felt incisive, giving name, address, first, asking her to take a note. Then he announced the defection of the two girls; the authorities had not yet noticed, it appeared. Next he proposed to get in touch with the parents and hoped that this met with the bursar's approval. She, to judge from her voice, fluttered, aware of charges of ignorance or inefficiency, unwilling to take any line without the sanction of higher authorities. Mansfield spoke loftily, in Ercles' vein, half-ashamed of himself. All was well. They were tired after their examinations. Perhaps she'd agree it was a little upsetting. He would see they were cared for. Not to worry. They seemed basically sensible children. So on, so on; he pranced with his voice, imagining the dim woman rushing off to institute searches and inquiries in tremulous excitement.

The girls each took a bath, and came down in mini-skirts with faces made-up.

He had already spoken to Eleanor who answered crossly. Sarah had no right to inflict herself. He hadn't been well, and could not be expected to wait hand and foot on these two.

'I think I should tell you, Eleanor,' he said firmly, 'that I take their side.'

'Then I don't.'

'This examination's a big strain, and if they need a change . . .'

'Both will be going away on expensive holidays at the end of the term. That should be soon enough.'

'I don't presume to give you advice, Eleanor, but . . .'

'You're as silly as they are.'

Her rudeness cut him short, jabbed him breathless. Shivering, he waited and then very slowly like old Mrs. Moody laying a slice of bacon from machine on to greased paper replaced the phone into its cradle. He slumped in his armchair, cold in spite of his electric fire. Rain splashed and dulled his windows. In the bedrooms he heard the excited voices of the girls.

After five minutes' physical debility at her words melted, and he tried to think reasonably about Eleanor. Deserted by her husband, satisfying the family's demands, presenting a smooth public face it was no wonder she could not control herself. She looked for a weakling to bully, from her own distress and incapacity. He ought to ring back, apologise, but his own temper glared; he was as sulky, as touchy as an adolescent.

'Your mother's furious with me.'

'She's no right. If she has to be angry with anyone, it should be with me.'

Hoity-toity, Sarah flounced, bridled so that he had to take care to hide his smile. Oh, for that energy which forced her to strut and toss her hair. All he had was nostalgia; a short burst of passion for some old scene, tune, face, which dissipated itself, ash-cold, in minutes, leaving him to wonder at his foolishness, or his sham.

'I don't know whether I dare ring yours,' he said.

'I'll do it.' Daisy went straight out, but left the door ajar so that he could hear all she said. She explained in a high, clipped voice where she was, why she'd come and even asked if they hadn't lost Mr. Mansfield's telephone number. She next inquired if the school had been bothering them and after listening said, 'That's quite reasonable', and then, 'Two things. Don't forget to tell daddy, and, secondly, I could do with some money, actually.'

When she returned, he expected her to be complacently dusting her hands.

'I don't know whether I made her understand that we're still supposed to be at school.' She laughed.

'She's not as mad as all that, Dais.'

'You never know with her. It might be affectation. On the other hand, when my brother Francis broke his leg she took him to hospital, sat with him ages there until they'd X-rayed and plastered him, brought him home, put him to bed, and then, after all this upset and patatras, she asked me, not an hour later, to go and see where he was because he was so unusually quiet.' They laughed.

'You think I'm disloyal, or,' breath, 'unnatural, don't you, talking about my mother like this?'

Mansfield started. The thought had not crossed his mind; he'd been putting an age on this clear, prim voice; had decided thirty-six.

'Well . . .' He hesitated.

'Did you feel affection for your mother at my age?'

'That girl,' Sarah said, 'has to be seen to be believed.'

'Fifteen, sixteen?' he mused. Ragged with anger, he'd sat his school certificate while his mother nagged. Was he doing enough? He ought not to go watching a cricket match. Harold Sharp was down to it all hours of the day and night. Decent, harassed woman with her coarse apron and her flowered apron, with hands purple-red as the tasselled tablecloth. Well-to-do relatives had stayed, unusually, with them just at that time. He'd hated everybody.

'I'd nothing much to say in her favour,' he said.

'She loved you, though?' Sarah's eyes danced.

'I've always assumed so.'

The girls played tennis in the afternoon, gadded about in the evening. By the third morning they had two young men in attendance at the garden's end.

'Good morning,' Mansfield greeted them ironically polite with an inclination of the head. 'Can I help you?'

'Good morning,' one answered, completely assured. 'We hoped Sarah and Daisy would be here.'

'Perhaps you'd like to come and wait for them.'

'If you don't mind.'

'It's if they don't mind that counts.'

He offered cigarettes which they both refused. They talked nineteen to the dozen; the one with dark side-whiskers seemed personally insulted by the placing of the shops in the estate. The other, curly hair and spectacles, argued that all owner-occupiers here had cars and that his friend began with antiquated ideas about time and distance. They argued, fluently, with point, as if he were telerecording their performance. It reminded him of colleagues' anecdotes about two-minute lectures in pre-O.C.T.U. courses. When the girls appeared, eyes lined, lids blued, the young men stood and all decided to sit in deck-chairs where they told inconsequential stories of school, dances, parties; they now seemed absurd, young, shy, trying it on. Mansfield carrying mugs of coffee listened, delighted, a man with treasure.

He went indoors where he reread a stiff letter from the headmistress who recorded herself as waiting for instructions from the parents of the children. David had phoned to say he'd arrive on Sunday, that Eleanor was furious and he demanded civilly enough, what his father was up to.

'They've finished exams. They dislike school. They're welcome here.'

'I don't think you'd have taken that attitude with me when I was a boy.'

'Very likely not.'

David laughed, without humour.

'Eleanor's playing up. If we allow Sarah to do as she likes, there'll be no holding her in a year or two.'

'Sarah represents you, a vulnerable you.'

'You've probably got something there.'

'The child shouldn't suffer on account of your quarrels. That's a high priority.'

'None of your tragedy, now.'

Over lunch he enjoyed their discussion of the young men, both of whom had finished 'A' levels, but were returning in September to their public day-school for open scholarships. The girls showed real delight when he intervened, asked questions; it was as if they had suddenly noticed that an adult could pay attention to an idea instigated by them.

'Have you paired off, then?' he asked.

'Well, no. We both like the same one.'

'Who's that? Let me guess. Side-whiskers?'

'How did you know?'

'His name's Basil,' Daisy said. 'Basil on the razzle. The dazzling Basil.'

'And what's his line of learning?'

'Classics. But he wants to change to Chinese.'

'Why?'

'He just got interested. Learnt some from the radio.'

'And what about Curly, then?'

'He's going to be a doctor.'

'He'll be superb,' Daisy said, 'masterly. He's got it all weighed up. He reminds me of dad, in a humorous sort of way. He'd kill you and cut your cadaver up without turning a hair.'

'That's horrid,' Sarah said.

'It's right. I've known one or two like that gentleman.'

'And that's why you prefer Fu-Manchu?'

They rolled around at his nickname; it seemed odd that intelligent girls should be so taken with the feeble witticism. He decided that if they were paraded for a Sunday-school bus ride to the Zoo and issued with a sticky stale bun they'd achieve a summit of attainable bliss. Touching.

'But how will the eternal triangle be resolved?' he asked.

'We shall be off these in a day or two.'

'Or button up grief,' Sarah said.

'You don't think we can feel grief, do you?' Daisy astonishingly serious, whispering.

'You don't know what I think,' Mansfield answered. 'I took some boys of your age on a holiday party to Devon. We had a girls' school staying in the place, but they went back the night before we did. And when I did my rounds there was one lad, I remember, flat on his bed sobbing his heart out.'

'Because his girl had gone?'

'What did you say, grandpa?'

'Nothing. I couldn't. I pretended I didn't notice. I thought something like "God bless you". If I'd been asked to talk, I'd have said something stupid about Elizabethan behaviour.'

He asked about drug-taking. Yes, they both knew people who claimed to smoke, claimed, Daisy emphasised. Nobody at school. Where'd they find it at that dead-and-alive midden? Once at a party, Daisy had taken a drag at a reefer they were passing round.

'What was it like, Dais?' Eager Sarah.

'I was frightened to death. Sweet. But I hardly dare take it in, because ordinary tobacco chokes me. Besides, I didn't like the idea of some wet-lips passing it on to me.'

'So?'

'I haven't finished up on the "Dilly".'

'What would your father say?' Mansfield.

'I think he's conventional. Sideboards and levis don't make one any younger.'

'So he shouldn't dress like that?'

'Nobody minds. He's clear-headed enough to know it makes no difference. He's not bad. And he can say "No".'

'My daddy will play hell when he comes up on Sunday.'

When David arrived he made no attempt to cover his displeasure.

'Have a cup of coffee, will you?'

'No, thanks, dad. I'll have a word with this pretty pair first.'

'A cup of coffee won't delay . . .'

'I had one on the motorway.'

'Perhaps we could have one, Mr. Mansfield,' Daisy said. 'We might need it.'

David frowned, looked in his petulance ready to kick the furniture. His father took his time over the milk-saucepan, could hear the voices, moderately calm, from the sitting room.

When he finally knocked at the door with his tray, the girls were seated together on the settee, while the father handled a handsome pipe in a fireside chair.

'Guilty or not guilty?' Mansfield asked facetiously.

Neither girl spoke. He handed them cups, for which they briefly thanked him, in whispers, and then he made for the door.

'Don't go, dad.' David's big warning finger. 'I can't see any reason why they shouldn't catch the train back to school tomorrow. Can you?'

Catch the train. The phrase came from David's youth, when his father hadn't a car. He felt sympathy for the resplendent man.

'I see.' As he spoke the two eyed him, together, in disappointment. 'Will the headmistress take any steps to punish you?'

'We shan't be allowed out of the school grounds.' Sarah.

'Are you usually?'

'There are trips. Museums. An archeological site. At the end of term.'

'That wouldn't worry you, presumably.'

'We shall survive.' Daisy, who seemed the perkier, spoke shrugging. Sarah sat drained white. 'They won't let us play games, and I expect she'll set us tasks. "Go to the library, Sarah, and find out all you can about baroque architecture. I don't want you to regard this as a punishment, but as a small piece of research. And when you've written it up, I shall be pleased to discuss it with you."' The imitation seemed not unlikely.

'You don't want to do that?' Mansfield asked.

'I don't.' Daisy, emphatic.

'Sarah?'

She looked up, sighed shortly, let her head drop, then shook it. She appeared no more than twelve now, with a pinched face. Her father had frightened her.

'I see. That's what you wish, is it, David?'

'This pair,' the son spoke without speed, 'have taken the law into their hands. They may have shown initiative or even acted sensibly. But they have put some people to some trouble. The headmistress. Their mothers. Me.'

'You think they should be punished?'

'Provided it's civilised, as it will be at the school.' He smiled, massaged a kneecap. 'So I'd be glad if you could get them to the Midland Station for 10.15 tomorrow morning.'

Daisy spread her hands in mock despair.

'Doesn't that seem reasonable?' Mansfield asked her.

'In your eyes, yes. Annoy adults, interfere with their comfort and they'll punish you. We came away from Beanhurst because we were sick of the place. Now we're sent back.'

'Sarah?'

'What does it matter?' she spoke dully.

'Your father thinks that if he doesn't make some sort of a stand now, you'll go on doing,' Mansfield grinned proleptically, 'more and more inappropriate actions, finally murdering the headmistress in her bed or . . .'

'I'm more likely to slay her if I'm sent back,' Daisy said.

'Except there'll be sanctions.'

'Deter, deter. To the Lord High Executioner.'

In time, the girls took coffee cups out. David yawned widely.

'Why is Sarah so frightened of you?' Mansfield asked.

'Is she?'

'David. Come on, now. Look at the way the poor little miss sat there.'

'She's a sympathetic child. She realises somebody's been worrying about her. That she's loaded you with a burden you could well do without. So she's not pleased with herself. That other shining example there puts a bold face on it, chirps up, cheeks her way out of trouble. But Sarah knows she's done wrong.'

'Why didn't she know at the time?'

'Spur of the moment. Led into it by the other idle little bitch. She's young for her age. Don't you think so?'

'I'll tell you what I do think. You're unfeeling about this.'

'Don't exaggerate. I've done exactly what they expected me to do, played the medium-weight father. They know where they stand. That's what children of their age need. Standards.'

'Love.'

'What makes you think I don't love her?'

'There's not much evidence, David.'

'No, dad. Not either way. I've come up here. I could have phoned my orders. But I preferred to see for myself if there was anything really wrong. I love Sarah. I think highly of her.'

'Have you told her so?'

'She knows.'

'Have you told her so?'

'No, because she'd find it embarrassing in front of Daisy and, two, I'm not pleased with her.'

'That's the time to tell her.'

'I never noticed that you prefaced your punishments to me with an announcement that you loved me. And if you had I'd have taken you for a hypocrite.'

'I wasn't much good.'

'I'm not grumbling.' David grinned, cleanly.

'When they put Charles Dickens in a blacking-factory it made a novelist of him. But it's hopeless for run-of-the mill people. That child's frightened of you, David, and I don't like it.'

'Dad, you're exaggerating. But I'll be frank with you; if you go on like this it'll end with my saying something we'll both regret.'

'That I'm an interfering old fool, for instance.'

'I'm not specifying, at the present. But you're getting on, and if I blurted something out in temper, it might have more effect than on somebody younger, not so vulnerable. So, I'd be pleased, dad, if you'd let it drop. I love that child.'

'You'll tell her so?'

'At the appropriate moment.'

'Why don't you admit you're wrong, David? You've come here because Eleanor badgered you, and you feel guilty enough towards her to have to comply. She's taking it out of that youngster, and using you as the instrument. You desert her. She makes you punish Sarah.'

'Very unlikely.' David shifted, crossing his legs. 'You don't know Eleanor. This thing between us is mutual. Your notion of a helpless woman betrayed and deserted,' he snorted at the phrase, 'is so much fantasy. She's capable of caring for herself, I can tell you. But we've one or two things in common still. Concern for our children.'

Mansfield's weakness shut his mouth. The girls returned, to sit side by side. David nodded at them, as at a pert dog, sparrows.

'Mummy said I was to pay the train-fare,' he began.

Sarah did not answer.

'I don't suppose she'd mind if I added a bit to it.' He waved the large right hand. The children looked pleased, almost to order. Mansfield wondered if a pound note or two changing hands made all the difference.

When David left, he seemed short with his father.

'It's no trouble to you to get them to the station?'

'If I said it was?'

'Phone for a taxi.'

'You're not pleased with me, David, are you?'

'I don't think you should have given them permission to come.'

The old man nodded, looked over the garden, at his son's shining car in the drive.

'And if I do it again?'

David laughed, affably enough, and bunching his fist playfully knuckled his father's biceps.

'We must love one another,' he answered, 'or die. Didn't you know?'

The girls spent the evening at the house of one of their boy friends. They reduced the chaos of their bedrooms to conspicuous tidiness again, and left without fuss. Both shook hands; Sarah kissed him awkwardly. As he sat in his car outside the station, he amazed himself at the fierce strength of his emotions. If the children had suddenly died, he could not . . . Rubbish. He was surprised; this was unintelligent; he'd be throwing public tantrums next. He watched two taxi-drivers spar with each other, grinning and grimacing. A small Sikh boy, top-knotted in yellow, solemnly, eyes wide, took it all in. The girls travelled back in the care of engine-drivers, signalmen, platelayers, into the care of teachers, the bursar, the headmistress. He brushed his distress from his cheeks.

≝ 10 ≝

Mansfield met Hapgood in the street, inquired about his wife.

'I don't know what to think.' The voice vibrated vaguely. 'Clara has taken to religion. I honestly don't know what to make of it.'

Hapgood shifted from foot to foot.

'Come on, man, come on, then.' Mansfield spoke jovially; the news cheered him from his own doubts.

'While she was in hospital, a Mrs. Sheldon from along the street visited her. We hardly knew the woman, but she was one of several neighbours who looked in. And she came up home, and invited Clara down to their meetings. Little Pentecostal place, tin tabernacle affair, built it themselves. She's been going ever since.'

'And now she's getting on at you to join?'

'Well, not nearly so much as I should have thought. She asks, but she'll take "no" for an answer.'

'You?'

'I wouldn't say I'd anything much against religion.' The deep, muted voice sang in the street. 'I was brought up to it. Sunday school, Band of Hope, whole bag o' mashin'. But I haven't been for years. I haven't thought about it. Hasn't crossed my mind. You know what they say. "When a man's frit, he'll run to God", but with all this bother and hullabaloo we've had the last month or two religion never entered my head. I didn't pray. Never occurred to me to.

Now I think back to it, it's a bit odd that I didn't, but that's the truth. God's nobody I know.'

'Well, then.'

'Since she's been going, I've turned it over in my mind, I'll admit. I've asked myself if I believed there was a God.'

He stopped, toeing the pavement, face comically screwed. Mansfield waited for him.

'The nearest I can say,' the voice purred, deeply, scarring the air like a furrow in clay-land, 'is that the question's meaningless. I've forgotten what the Bible says, pretty well. I can remember a few hymns and they're no help, but as to what and who and where God is, I might just as well be asking where yesterday's cricket match has got to or our wedding-day.'

'God's dead, in fact?'

'I wouldn't say that. He'd have been alive once on such an account. When I was a child at Sunday school, I believed in Him, I can tell you. As soon as I grew up, and could think for myself, I never thought about Him again.'

'But when your children . . . ?'

'They were christened. They got sent on Sunday afternoons. I went to the high days and holidays, anniversaries and the like. I didn't know the hymns and the parsons didn't come near my conscience. To tell the truth, the kids were as bored as I was with it. Chucked it up.'

'And your wife?'

'Same as the rest of us, I'd have said. But now here she sits with her little card, reading the Bible morning and night.'

'Is she comfortable?'

'I don't know. That's what beats me. She says there's hell for unbelievers.'

'Did you . . . ?'

Hapgood put out a large policeman's hand. Halt.

'I've learnt to keep my mouth shut in this last month or so. And talkin' about hell's preferable to livin' it.'

'I see that. You've not been to the services with her, then?'

'Once. I made it plain to her. I believe in saying what I mean. She was pressing me, every verse end. But I said, "Look, Clara, I'll go with you once or twice, company for you, but that's all." This Mrs. Sheldon was there at the time. I told her, "Don't expect to frighten me to death threatening me with hell, because there's no such place in my opinion, and if there was I'd have no truck with a God who either made it or used it." ' Hapgood's face creased, lively obstinate. 'And she said a funny thing, Mr. Mansfield. She's a nobody, hat on her head straight off a jumble-stall, but she surprised me. She said, "It's not the hell-to-come we bother about so much as the blessing here and now." Good for her, I thought.'

'So you went?'

'I did.'

'It still meant nothing?'

'Just like sixty years back. Hymns, choruses, Sankey's, sung damn' loud to a harmonium. Long prayers. Bible-bashing. My say-so, if you understand me. All about salvation. While we were yet sinners. I thought to myself, "I'm not much of a mucher, but I'm not such a wrong 'un as all that." I don't go round publishing my misdeeds, I can tell you. Friendly, though, plenty of hand-shaking, how are you? And they have a devil of a big collection. I will say that for them. But I'd have been better employed listening to the wireless or the telly. I like some argument, some reason. It's no use telling me Saint Paul said this, that and the other, and expecting me to believe it's true. I want it explained and discussed. Old Elias Harrison at the Adult School always used to call out, "None o' your dogmatism now." That's me.'

'Even geometry has axioms.'

'Ye', an' pigs have wings, if you believe some people.'

Mansfield stood aside, wondered what the pair of them looked like to a passer-by; shabby old men, himself with shopping bag, grinning false teeth and well-made National Health spectacles.

124

'I don't mind,' Hapgood said, 'as long as she's quiet in her mind. If she wants heaven and hell, she's entitled to it.'

'You don't wish you could believe, yourself?'

'No. I should be a different man.'

'And you don't want . . . ?'

'I've thought about that, an' all. We'd all be different if we could, but only in the sense that we'd be better. Like we are now, but not making so many errors, if you know what I mean.'

He hitched the sleeves up his arms, and pushed off. He had done his companion good.

Back at home, Mansfield reread the note of thanks from Eleanor. It said nothing; it did not apologise and her harsh words rankled still. More than anything he wanted to impress and please his daughter-in-law; yes, and comfort her, if that was on. But here was his dusty answer, precisely folded into three. David, too, had written, but he'd showed sense, warmed his father's heart. The old man knew his son was hypocritical with his talk of generosity, eccentric kindness, clear-headed whimsy, but at least the lad, the tycoon, had tried, had served his customer to liking.

The girls had both written, short notes, not unhappy. Sarah's, strangely enough, read more worldly than her friend's. 'They didn't punish us. Old Fanny gave us a long lecture. Actually it was fairly sensible. But she's overawed by daddy or thinks he'll write a cheque or two for the funds, so we're allowed to ramble out with the rest, looking for Roman roads. I quite like it.'

He smiled to himself at this. Children soon recovered.

The Hapgoods asked him down to witness signatures, because they'd managed a quick sale of their shop to a young couple who were bursting to be in and settled before winter. They themselves bought a small, Edwardian semi-detached off the main street and now looked forward to their strip of garden.

He grew excited with the couple, down at the solicitor's office, in the back-room of the shop.

'It's been cosy here,' Hapgood said.

'That's not to say it won't be so up Ragdale Road,' the wife said. She seemed heartier, redder of face, more fleshy. 'He's a proper wittler, Mr. Mansfield.'

They had not heard from Tom since he'd broken the window, and nobody had seen him. Mansfield felt unable to say how this affected them, whether they were pleased or conscience-stirred. As to Clive, they'd received one letter from Enid, a side of note-paper which they produced so that he'd credit their account of the girl's spelling.

'Beyond that, nothing,' Mrs. Hapgood said. 'But it's what I expect. You can write and write, but she'll none bother her head.'

'If you look,' the husband said, 'that letter's written in ink, with a steel-nibbed pen.' Mansfield had not noticed. 'How'd she get hold of that? Anybody in her right mind can buy a ball-point pen for a few pence.'

'It's probably been round the house for years.' Mrs. Hapgood. They'd obviously worked this out between them. 'Nobody there ever puts pen to paper.'

'A sociological curiosity,' the visitor said, and all were delighted with themselves.

On this visit, Mrs. Hapgood said nothing about religion, but a newish soft-backed Bible lay on the sideboard with a packet of pamphlets. Outside in the yard, Mansfield asked.

'She's not so bad. She talks about it. And she insisted on writing to the children about it.'

'Tom included?'

'Yes. Though she might just as well have posted that one down the first drain she came across. But it was the other two as interested me. Fred didn't say a word.' The doctor in Africa. 'And I'm not surprised. But our Billy,' principal of a teachers' training college in New Zealand, 'he laid it on thick. It was important. He was touched and delighted. Surest source of comfort. He himself had known the stirrings.' The deep voice mouthed these inanities with relish. 'You never read such stuff. I should have thought he'd have known when he wasn't talking to his students. And what I should say to it. Not him. He's forgotten. He's been out so long that we're strangers. If I met him in the street, I'd know him, to guess from his photographs, but his wife and children. No. They'd all be strangers to me, our Billy biggest of all. With his talk. He's got a voice like mine.' Mansfield remembered it, deeply rich from the thin throat of a spectacled lad with neatly greased hair in the sixth form. 'But it pleased his mother. She kept opening the envelope and looking at it. Read it out to me, and Mrs. Sheldon. Thought you might be treated to a stretch.'

Shirt-sleeved, Hapgood put a hand to the buttress of his narrow dividing wall, shook his head.

'It in't a bad thing either. If I could write to New Zealand with that effect, I'd do it, like a shot.'

'Even if you didn't mean it?'

'Mean? Mean? That lad seems to understand his mother's present frame of mind better than I do. That's all. Whatever it means.' Hapgood grinned, skew-whiff, wickedly. 'Our Billy's a great fat chap, now. All of fifteen stone. You remember him when he was so skinny the west wind'd blow him over? Now he's a man of substance.'

'And talks like it?'

'He might choke on every word, for all I know. I some-times think of him standing there on his platform, laying the law down, and I wonder what I've done.'

Mansfield drove to the east coast, spent a few days in a boarding house by the flat sands. The weather turned colder, whipping the sea white, piling and shedding the clouds. Other guests kept coats on, hung on to hats and complained that the summer was done before July was out, but Mansfield felt well, walked in the chill evenings, took half-pints in a saloon bar, wrote to nobody, needed a hot-water bottle in bed.

On his return he found a letter from Sarah in Brittany.

Her daddy wasn't there, and she spent most of her time quarrelling with her mother. 'We get on each other's nerves, I can tell you. When I put it down here it seems funny, but we'll end up scratching eyes out over the gender of a glass of wine. I hate it. I hate her. And yet, she's marvellous with the kids, better than Nanny or Susan. She's generous, and wonderful at straightening things out, but she's got it in for me. I daren't open my mouth, sometimes. I don't know what I'm going to do.'

He wrote back by return, telling her to grin and abide, inviting her again. By the end of a week, he'd received a reply, describing how she had found twin girls her own age with whom she knocked about, met boys, and how Eleanor's temper had sweetened beyond miracle. The child, at a loose end, must have loitered all day at her mother's heels, playing up, nagging. Immediately he wrote off to Eleanor, describing how Sarah complimented her on her organisation, building a fantasy of praise in which he compared her to a general in battle. It read ridiculously. Logistics. What might have been acceptable for two sentences sprawled over four pages, surprising its author. Hardening his heart, he sealed, posted the envelope.

Her reply fell magnificently.

He'd spent time at Skegness one blustery morning in an amusement arcade, where'd he'd won a jack-pot, a handful of coins. This letter arrived with the same silver heaviness, the clank of surprise, of unworthiness. She'd been sorry for what she'd said, could have bitten her tongue out, but now he'd written generously like this, fresh as the blue morning, and she had to tell him. It was, she said, like religious conversion, the lighted mind. For a moment he thought her answer scornful, a black parody of his imaginative vapourings, his own heady conceits, but as she went on to describe the children shouting in Anglo-French all day with kids on the beach, hilariously described, a local noble family, the night-clubs, the sea-trips, he realised that this was seriously intended, split generously into the winner's tray of his heart. He walked down his garden, a giant.

Down on the main street Saturday afternoon, he occupied a seat with two other old men. They treated him with suspicion, but informed him that a 'Procession of Witness' would shortly appear.

'What's that?' he asked, ironically.

'The churches and chapels wi' banners.'

The crowd thickened so that they had to stand. In the distance a drum thumped as Hapgood pulling Clive appeared.

'My missus is in it,' he said flatly.

The Salvation Army band blasted neatly at the head, their blue and red and yellow standard, Blood and Fire, high, first. Behind them were four parsons, the rector in his cassock, the Methodist, young with bushy sideboards and a light hacking jacket, one without a Roman collar, one with long grey hair. Then came a decorated lorry, A. French, Builder and Contractor, with children diffidently waving, being warned with finger and voice to sit down. Scouts, Boys' Brigade, bugles gleaming ready but leaving it to the band, their drummer keeping the step, Sunday schools with ornate banners pre-first world war and then raggedly marching grown-ups, ordinary people walking the street, half in formation, embarrassed in Sunday suits. A second policeman and a bunch of semi-officials, marshals, organisers brought up the rear.

'There's your gran,' Hapgood shouted to Clive.

The woman saw them, smiled, waved widely horizontally across her face at the boy, then set her mouth and marched on. She might have been on the way to a public execution. In her rank were two middle-aged women, a small man with staring eyes, a goitrous throat and then a youth with shoulder-length hair, like some Liszt or Cortot, his lips curved gently in a ruminative smile.

'Didn't think they did this this sort of thing these days,' he said to Hapgood.

They were on the seat again, Clive between his grandfather's knees.

'Coming back.'

'Nothing like the size before the fourteen war,' one old man said.

'Well, you should 'a joined 'em, then.' His companion.

'This is advertising the chapels, not the pubs.'

Pipes were lit; reminiscence spread.

'Where d' they go?' Mansfield asked.

'Round the new houses, bit of a service and back to the Wesleyans for a cup of tea.'

Mansfield smiled; the 'new houses', a council estate, had been built in the thirties. The old men were breathily recalling thick ears Sunday school superintendents had doled out in their prime, and recommending the treatment for modern youth.

'Isn't there too much violence already?' Mansfield asked.

Silence; sudden, blank silence. They looked away. No doubt they knew him, would rough him up verbally when he'd gone, that schulemester, one o' them new bung'lows, poking his bloody fool's nose in. They ignored him, biting on pipes, pulling waistcoats down. He'd no right to interfere with their enjoyment. They could argue if they wished, but he was allowed only to ask questions, to echo agreement, by their uncodified rules, so that when he transgressed, they broke off the conversation, glared across the street, banked the fire of their discontent until he'd gone when their comments would be slowly, boilingly, proffered, one to another.

'Thinks he knows it all.'

'He in't talkin' to a class o' schulekids now.'

'Who asked 'im 'is opinion?'

'Always bin the same. Ever since I've knowed him.'

' 'Ow's he come to learn so much, then?'

'Reads it off th'back o' match-boxes.'

'Please, teacher, may I leave the room?'

Mansfield, saddened, slouched away with Hapgood, Clive between them, holding their hands. Now followed the explanation of the boy's appearance, the unexpected letter from Enid asking them to look after the child while she and

Eric had a week in Blackpool.

'She can write ever so well when she's a mind.'

'And Tom? Have you heard of him?'

Clive was swung up between them, one, two, three and a-jump, the old men aping youth's energy, so that his grandfather couldn't speak until the game had ended in breathless delight.

'We have. Chap as used t'come in the shop. Didn't know him very well. Stopped me in the street, said that he'd seen Tom working on some new housing up in Retford. Don't know why he came out with it. Any other day he'd have nodded or passed without so much as a word.' He bent to wipe Clive's nose with his own handkerchief. 'I didn't let on as there was anything up. I just asked him what Tom had to say for himself, and then made inquiries, the whereabouts, y'know, as if I was interested.' He clearly admired his tact, ruffled Clive's hair in pleasure. 'I told Clara and straight off, no argy-barge,' she says, "We'll go and see him." Out with the van and there we are.'

He sighed, roughly, quickening his pace. In the distance the bugles of the Boys' Brigade mildly ripped the afternoon air.

'We found the place all right, and there he was, stripped to the waist and as brown as a berry, pushing a wheelbarrow. Clara, she calls out, and he comes across. He looks fit, with a knotted handkerchief on his head. My wife didn't mince words, she just calls out, "We've found you, then" and "Why haven't you written?" He shifts from foot to foot, standing there naked as a Red Indian, shrugging, more like this child here than a grown man. "We've written to you," I said. "You know how it is." That's all he can say. "You know how it is." '

Clive jerked away towards the road, but grandfather dropped a second hand.

'Whoa, hoss.' The boy's face reflected pride. 'He said he was all right, got good lodgings, but he hadn't heard from Enid, and didn't particular want to. "Are you going to answer your mam's letters?" I said. "Might." That's all we got out of him. Said his mate'd be wondering where he was, picks the handles up, and off. We stood there, it was a lovely afternoon, just looking at him, Clara on a plank. He never came up again, though he waved once. And that's all the change we got for our efforts.'

'What did his mother say?'

'What could she? While we were talking, she said, "Tom, I pray for you, morning and night," but he never noticed, or if he did, he never let on. She's never said anything like that to him before, except in her letters, but she might as well 'a said she was using Persil.'

'She'd be upset?'

'Not only her. I wonder to myself sometimes, Mr. Mansfield, what I've bred.' Now they stood outside a hairdressing saloon with rucked lace blinds bound with pink ribbons. An assistant in a mini-overall, blond hair screwed back from pasty face to a flapping pony tail, passed them, grinned at Clive, stroked his head, flounced leggily into a pastrycook's. Both men watched as the child sat on a low wall, drumming his heels. The girl returned, carrying a paper bag and smoking; she called Clive 'mah duck', ignored the old men. Hapgood put an arm across the boy's shoulder.

'One of these days,' he began, 'I'm going to die. Can't be long, now. And what shall I have done? Served tons of nails and screws and paraffin across my counter. That's useful. Y'know, when I'm out on my own in the evenings, I can't see properly. Whether it's my eyes, or the light or lack of it or both, but there I am peering at things, like a goldfish goggling out of water. And that's how I feel when I sum up. It's not the stuff in the paper that puzzles me, permissive society and unrest. I don't understand that, either. But it's my own three boys. They're all different and two of 'em done well. We lived our life through those lads. We sacrificed and planned and kept ourselves awake and where are we? For all I can make of 'em, we might just as well have spent our earnings in the Bull.'

'That isn't true.'

Hapgood pouted his lips as if he were willing to be convinced, caressed his grandson's shoulder.

'You gave them their chance.'

'Look at our Fred. Writes once every three months if we're lucky. Never comes to see us. Bachelor. Whisky and hospital, all he thinks of.'

'He's an expert on tropical diseases. You can't evaluate the good he's doing.'

'Why doesn't he do his mother a bit, then?'

'You've given him the opportunity to specialise in his branch of medicine. If you hadn't, thousands who are alive today might well not be.'

'All asking 'emselves, like me, what the hell they're here for.' Hapgood laughed, not convincing himself.

'Your case isn't logical. You, by your efforts, helped two of your sons to create careers for themselves far beyond the average of children of their class and status in this town. The fact that the personal relationship between you and them isn't satisfactory's unfortunate, but it deducts nothing from the first.'

Before he'd finished, he impersonally, or with the ears of those other old men, recognised the schoolmaster's tone of harangue, but he completed his sentence, as strongly. Hapgood rasped the bristles upward, time and again, hungrily on his long upper lip.

'Grandad. Grandad. Ice-cream.'

'So you shall. I promised you.'

When the two men returned from the shop, Hapgood said:

'You're lucky in your David.'

'He's as bad, or good, as the rest.'

'Ah, well,' Hapgood coughed. ' "What a friend we have in Jesus." '

✄ I I ✄

Mansfield spent the first part of August helping an old colleague to build a greenhouse.

This was a satisfying pastime, because George Collis, though five years younger, had been an old woman all his life. He had consulted catalogues for three months, talked his wife to distraction, and finally made three calls to Mansfield, who offered to take him round merchants' yards.

'I'm not starting from scratch,' Collis beamed. 'Prefabrication is the line now.'

He had no idea how big he wanted the greenhouse, nor where he was to place it in the garden, nor, as his wife pointed out, what he was going to do when he'd got it.'

'One obstacle at a time,' Collis said. 'I'm a bookish man. When I've got the structure, I'll then study the probable contents.'

'He's like a child,' the wife said. 'Once he's made his mind up he'll have it, but he's frightening himself nearly to death.'

They drove to see specimens, but the only one erected for inspection was the sort Collis had decided against. He spoke to the young man with hauteur.

'Pictures, I find,' he patted his lips, 'are often deceptive.' He tapped the catalogue. 'That, for instance, I like the look of, but I've no idea what the wood's like.'

'I can show you.'

'I'd be glad if you would.' Judicial calm.

'You'll have to walk across the yard.'

They inspected panels, brown cedar, rich as navvy's tea. Pressed by Mansfield, Collis approved, but waved his hands about.

'Now,' he said, 'there's the small question of size.'

Mansfield remembered how his friend always raised his

inanities in staff-meetings with this faintly unidiomatic expression.

'Depends what you want,' the young man said. 'You're not thinking of supplying the country with tomatoes, now, are yer?'

Collis's pride wilted; his face immediately puckered in hurt.

'You want, if I may say so, sir,' the young man had noticed, 'a place of retirement. Go in for little jobs first, as you said. If the bug bites, well you can always come back.'

'Ah,' Collis appeased, 'but two small would cost more than the one large.'

'Right. I can see I'm not going to catch you napping, sir.'

They ordered the smallest, while Collis blew eloquent with questions on the explicitness of the enclosed packet of instructions, of stories from friends about badly drilled screw-holes, mis-measured lengths, missing bolts.

'I'll personally check it myself, sir. It'll be all there, plastic bag o' putty an' all. We can put it up for you, but I'd have a go myself, sir. You'll enjoy it. You'll need a screwdriver, an' a little hammer for the tacks, and a scraper for the putty and that's that. You c'n borrow a spirit-level for the concrete base-blocks.'

'I've got one,' Mansfield said.

'My friend'll give me a hand.'

An hour of Collis boosted Mansfield. The man was uncertain, but talked all the time, boasted, prognosticated. Mansfield chose the site, levelled it, said he had put ashes under his.

'But we've got no fires at this time of the year, man.'

'Then we can't have ashes.'

'Does that mean . . . ?' Collis's face fell.

Once the materials arrived, Mansfield adopted a routine. He'd arrive at the Collises' house by ten-thirty, when they'd start work until lunch. Then all three would have an hour or so in the darkened lounge, after which the men would potter until four-thirty. The weather was good, and the pair took the job slowly. Though Collis talked, he acted merely as labourer, and his amazement that the structure actually coincided with the plan was touching. Mansfield, busy, erecting, issued orders, sat down often to rest, never heard a word of his companion's monologue. He made the work last, knowing he'd be sorry once it was done.

The last pane of glass went into place on the morning he'd received news from Sarah of her 'O' Level results. She had done outstandingly well, and clearly was in favour at home. He sent her a cheque before he appeared for his last chore.

'Thought you weren't coming.' Collis wore a paint-splattered raincoat for these operations.

'Thought you'd have a band here this morning.'

'Got something better. Bottle of white wine. St. Croix du Mont.' Collis flourished his French accent at Mansfield who had thought him a teetotaller.

Twenty minutes saw them through, and they ceremoniously collected the tools, and then sat in deck-chairs to eye their wine-glasses, and their handiwork.

'You're a craftsman.'

'Screwing a few pieces of wood together?'

'You know, Mansfield, I could no sooner have put that thing up than I could have taken wings to fly.'

It was true. Utterly conservative, he repeated over and over again the skills he'd acquired in youth. He pruned his roses, cut his grass, his fingers, polished his boots, marked his exercises as he'd done at twenty-five; he re-read his old books, went every year to the same district of Paris where he'd been a student. Now and then, his wife pushed him into innovation, but with difficulty. How many hours he'd lain awake over this greenhouse Mansfield could not guess. Yet he listened to the French radio every evening, read *Le Monde,* still acted as secretary for the Modern Languages Association. A narrow provincial

Englishman, he'd spent his life drilling foreign words into the pens and tongues of his pupils.

Unaccustomed wine went to their heads. The man next door, in pin-striped trousers and black jacket but collarless, wished them good morning. He ignored the glasses they raised to him, banged the dustbin lid, went indoors.

'He's got a mistress.' Collis whispered, face vinous with mischief. He nodded, blubbered his lips about, wrapped the paint-smeared coat-tails over his knees.

'Go on, then,' Mansfield said. 'Don't keep me in suspense.'

Comically Collis peered over his shoulder at the closed back-door in the next house, then as suspiciously at his own.

'Seventy-three years of age,' he began. 'Wife died, oh, fifteen years ago. Lived on his own, didn't say much, but meticulous about his housework. He's got one daughter, married, down in Exeter, but she never comes. Didn't even when the mother was alive.'

A back-door flew open. The neighbour reappeared, but this time wearing an apron, to throw potato peelings on his compost heap. He avoided their eyes as if he knew they'd been gossiping. Collis rolled with guilt.

'Well,' doors were green-shut, 'about a year ago he started going to the Oxford Arms with another old man down the road. Don't know how they became so thick.'

'He's got money?'

'Not a lot. He was some sort of clerk. They always say his wife bought the house with her money.' Collis picked the bottle from the shade. 'Drop more?'

'No, thanks. Not till I've heard what the demon drink did for . . .'

'King. His name's King. Gilbert Theodore King.' More peerings over the fence. Mansfield thought his companion would pull his coat-collar up to keep the story in. 'Down there, at the Oxford, he met this woman.'

'How old is she?'

'Forty at the outside. Married. Got a grown-up son, just the one, eighteen, twenty.'

'And she lives here?'

'Yes. Brought her here. When he does mention her, mumbles something about his housekeeper. He might just as well brazen it out. We all know where she comes from.'

'And her husband?'

'Said to have been round, threatening. Appeared in the Oxford, but we've seen nothing of him.'

At that moment Mrs. Collis arrived, round-cheeked, with a tray of crockery.

'Now, you two,' she said, 'put that stuff away before you're drunk, and have a decent English cup of tea.'

'Grown in your own garden?' Mansfield said.

'You know what I mean.'

He did. Collis, who'd spent his life introducing children to a foreign language and culture, had anchored himself to this Anglo-Saxon. Every year since their marriage she'd accompanied him to France, where she'd not disapproved, merely taken little notice. It was part of her husband's job to live a few weeks a year in that place, and just as she would have carried his dinner to the close site if he'd been a bricklayer, so she went to Paris, without grievance, cheerfully superior, and sat unmoved.

Now she poured the tea for them, smiling.

'What are you two so conspiratorial about?' she asked.

'Ah, ah.' Mansfield.

'King,' she said. 'The reprobate King.'

'Good subject?' Mansfield chaffed her.

'He's not had much of a life.' She did not lower her voice as she waited for her husband to drain the last drops of his wine when she commandeered the glass. 'It's ridiculous, but who are we to talk?' She challenged them, sturdy, commonsensical.

'You wouldn't invite them in for coffee,' her husband said.

'We've been neighbours for thirty-odd years, and we've

not been in the habit of running in and out for coffee or anything else. We never thought of such things when we were first married. Why should we start now he's keeping a fancy-woman? George Collis, I mistrust your motives.' She wagged an indulgent finger.

'He thinks the poor chap needs a cup of coffee now,' Mansfield said.

'He wants to see what she looks like, sounds like, how they behave.'

'Don't you?'

'Yes. But I'm no bursting hurry. It'll come out.' She picked up Mansfield's glass, went indoors, not flouncing, stopping once to lift a buddleia spray to her face.

'Hope for us still,' Mansfield said.

'Eh? Eh?' Collis thought elsewhere. 'Yes, oh, suppose so, yes.'

'Have you noticed any difference in the man?'

'Yes, I have. He's less tidy. In himself. In his personal appearance. He used to dress up to go in the garden to pull a weed. Now you'll see him in the street in shirt-sleeves and his carpet slippers.'

'Doing what?'

'Going to the shop. She's out at work. One of the big places in town.'

'Earning the beer money?'

They finished their tea, re-inspected the greenhouse, discussed brushing the woodwork with linseed oil.

'Raw or boiled?' Collis with his quibble.

'Don't know. Don't suppose it makes an atom of difference.'

Collis cocked his head, prepared for a longer catechism.

'We're all ignorant somewhere,' Mansfield said. 'You'll have to reconcile yourself to it.'

As he parked at his own front gate, he was hailed from the other side of the road. A large man, in his forties, waddled across, declared his name was Trenton and that Mansfield wouldn't remember him, but his boy had been at the school, in 'your house'. Mansfield recalled neither man nor son.

'And d'you know what he's doing now?'

'No.' Hypocritical expression.

'You wouldn't guess in a hundred years, Mr. Mansfield. Before he got his "A" Levels, he said, "Dad, it's too soon for me to go to university," and when he got accepted it was for a year ahead if you follow me. Fixed it all up himself.'

'And he's gone abroad.'

'No. I could have understood that. See the world. No. He got himself a job up in Scotland, looking after alcoholics, in Glasgow, meths-drinkers, God knows what.'

'Good for him.'

'The tales he tells. The muck and filth. Crawling with fleas and bugs. You wouldn't think it was this country. They die in the street, some of 'em. Did you know that? Makes you shudder.'

'And he likes it?' Mansfield asked.

'I wouldn't say that. There'd be something wrong in you yourself if you actually liked, enjoyed working in such conditions. But he said to me, "Dad, somebody's got to do it. You can't just rope 'em in and put 'em to sleep. They're men, not dogs." And I look at him and I think to myself, "Why's he doing it?" and I look at his hair, typical scruffy student he is, and his hippy's bangles and I think to myself, "Well, by the Christ he's doing something I'd never do." '

'Good.'

'I missed the war. I regretted it, though I did national service. But it would take a war to compel the likes of me to do what that boy's doing. But he's got no religion. And talk about permissive society. "If they want to drop out, dad, or women want to sleep around, it's their own lookout," he says. I could swipe him sometimes and his mother's that there upset. What am I to say to him, Mr. Mansfield?'

'Say what you think. Speak your mind.'

'I do. Don't fret yourself about that. But when I've calmed down a bit, it comes in my head as plain as daylight, "Jim Trenton, that lad's doing something you've never done, nor never will if you live to be a hundred." '

The man chuntered on, repeating himself, asking questions to which he wanted no answers. He tried to be proud of his son, who did well unacceptably. In the end, he retreated to his car, muttering,

'It's a rum 'un; it's a rum 'un.'

Collis's neighbour, Trenton's son, two in one morning, stepping outside propriety. Standing by his front door, he'd refused Mrs. Collis's offer of lunch, he stared over the town, smoky in summer even, vaguely examined himself. What had he done? Fought in a war so filthy that would make young Trenton's job clean as a super-market. To what end? He'd been shipped abroad, vilely swearing, bullied, frightened but never hopeless, to see men die. Now? At thirty he'd married Annie Frances Kettlewell, a woman he'd loved, but never fathomed. She'd always seemed one-up on him, better prepared, more occupied. However often he'd flashed his opinions at her, she'd lost nothing in her own estimation, chosen her own strong way. When David was born, a bare year after the wedding, she'd loved the child, but distantly, with discipline, as if she derived her action from a system of morality that covered, or invisibly supported, love. What that system was, if it existed, he'd no idea. She did not talk much, as if it ever came to argument, he'd bustle in and easily beat her, only to find her unmoved, or regrouped to defend the same objectives.

Now he asked himself how they'd come together, what she'd made of him, but failed to answer. Annie was not a cold woman, could fly off the handle, squeal in the frenzy of sex, but her notions were foreign. David, their only child, they'd lost two by miscarriages, had been a brilliant student, constantly winning prizes and competitions and commendations, had been everything his father had hoped, so much so that the older man feared that the boy's accomplishments were tinsel lures, flattering, masking some headlong final catastrophe. Yet the mother, at each marvellous stage, expressed mere conventional approval, as if she'd no grasp on the quality of her son's achievements. This could not have been true; she was capable of comparing his results with those of other clever boys she knew, had heard about from her husband. But, no, 'He's done very well' or 'You won't get a swelled head, will you, David?' were the extent of her enthusiasm. How far she felt differently he did not know, did not know how to find out.

When she became finally ill, she was frightened, but even this was diffident, hidden, and twice as he had found her, out of the way, in tears he'd not known what to say. He'd put his arms round her, and made comforting noises, muttered it would turn out right and she'd dried her cheeks, hugged him briefly, and gone downstairs to her housework. As she feared, she died at home after a spell in hospital, nursed by her husband and an elder sister. Her cancer had not been painful and in the end a heart-attack had killed her as she sat downstairs watching birds squabbling on the lawn in September sunshine.

Mansfield had just started back at school, keenly basking in David's finals result, his prizes, his prospects. It had been a pleasure to lord it in the class and not the sick-room, and now just as he began a new year, jerked lethargic brains into action, the secretary had sidled in, face blank, to ask him to see the headmaster immediately. He'd walked down the stairs mildly annoyed; this was the sort of interrupion one expected at the beginning of term, but surely it would wait until break or the lunch-hour.

The head asked him to sit down, and then had stood himself. 'I'm afraid, Mr. Mansfield, I've some bad news for you.'

David. Damned tremor. Catastrophe.

'You must prepare yourself for a shock.' They did not look at each other. "It concerns your wife. I'm afraid your wife has died.' He stopped, fingers splayed on polished wood. 'Your sister-in-law phoned. Apparently, it was a heart attack. I'll drive you home.'

He'd put his coat on, gone into the common-room for his attaché-case. A colleague had called, 'Had enough already, then.'

The headmaster waited outside. When he'd broken the news, his eyes had been large with tears. He was dead now, and his unsuitable wife, who'd shouted out in her county voice, in the common-room, 'This is the most untidy bloody place I've ever set my eyes on.' In the car, the old man had spoken a few conventional words of sorrow, had dropped Mansfield, and driven off, scared.

The bereavement was unexpected. Doctors had warned that his wife would hang on for twelve months, more, wearing him, bullying, enslaving her sister. Now he was released and, moreover, he'd paid a sop to the black powers who threatened David's progress. But for this moment, walking in, noticing that the blinds were as yet undrawn and that a knot of neighbouring women grouped to stare sympathetically, he wondered what Annie would look like. She stretched, in fact, almost unrecognisable; the day before her sister had permed her hair, at cost to both, and the unaccustomed curls above the pale slack face had altered that look of sly cursory attention, that quickness near the edge of affairs that, he now realised, had livened her face. He would have claimed that his wife's features were almost expressionless; once he saw them in set in the dull plaster of death, he knew the observation false.

They had been married twenty-two years, had listened to the radio, gardened, had discussed outings, holidays, schemed, taken insurance and mortgages together. Most of the time she'd done the talking so that now he wondered if he had been selfishly, mildly dominated. Her father had been an Anglican clergyman, but he'd no idea if she'd believed in an after-life. They'd lived, as it were, in parallel, but had produced this marvellous boy. That was to be their defence;

whatever their personal shortcomings they had reared the Feldhouse prizeman, the prodigy who'd turned Cambridge deliberately down against his father's wish, who'd topped the degree lists. Suddenly he grew sad, and for months had short periods of not-sorrow, something nearer loneliness for which he was not prepared. He recalled Annie's kindnesses, the comforts she'd put in his way. Then he not only missed her, he expected that, but felt guilty, wished there was some way he could make up. In these bouts of loneliness, or thin desolation, he'd act honest with himself, think what he'd say if by some miracle she returned from the grave. As tongue-tied? No, he'd talk, but with the wrong words, asking her if she were comfortable, how she felt. He could no more have said, 'Annie, I've loved you for twenty-odd years. You mightn't think so. It's the truth,' than he could have slit her dog's throat. Perhaps it was not so, was merely the result of nostalgia, of having to prepare his own tea, and if he were given the opportunity to spit it out, she'd glance at him, say, 'That's very nice, Jim,' and pick the kettle up or lay the tablecloth.

As he looked over the valley he tangled thus with his thoughts, allowed them vague recognition. If someone pressed him now whether he was sorry his wife had died, he could answer little and the rag-bag of memories offered were trivialities. Of course he could remember the day he 'passed the scholarship' but why should he remember passing a grocery shop on the walk home from school one Christmas holiday at the age of eleven? Why that year? That place? Or his parents standing in the back-garden talking in high summer to the next-door neighbours? Why had that struck sharply in his head for sixty years? To him, there seemed a mere ravel of meaningless events, one crowding out, clouding the next. His father on the weighing-machine at Mablethorpe, Annie waving one Saturday morning from a passing bus, his stepping over his mother's arm as she scrubbed their front-door step in Leicester, David convulsed with laughter at a terrier, racing flat-out in the park, the cold boat ferrying him to French trenches for the first time.

Yet, each was vague, tenuous, tantalising. Once one put words on the memories they became fixed, clearer, yet less real, no longer part of his substance. This fog, no, that metaphor misled; it was as if he'd been shown a bright picture to which he'd paid insufficient attention. He concentrated on the African lily by his door, simple enough in design, the bunch of broadish, spear-tipped leaves, all curving downwards, some sunlit, upper surfaces hollowed, lower faintly shadowed, then three stalks, two feet high, leaning sunwards and the clusters, fifteen perhaps, of flowers, whitey purple. He closed his eyes and the reality faded; he could enunciate the words he'd mustered to describe the plant, but the exact, beautiful reality his eyes revealed disappeared into crumbling light. He could hold one leaf, two perhaps, but nothing more complicated, and that for the shortest time.

Man of words.

Words only brought certainties. Poets complained of their imprecision, of the slippery, evasive nature, but they only offered a steady reward to him.

> 'Breaking the silence of the seas
> Among the farthest Hebrides.'

That held. Ideas, mind-pictures shifted but that stayed. Like his beloved *Twelfth Night*, 'and my desires like fell and cruel hounds e'er since pursue me'. Solid. Diamonds for ever.

He gave in, walked a step or two.

Painters, men of the eyes, might remember differently. He was an elderly pedagogue, who'd taught history and literature and Latin, who now had paid the penalty for his bias. But all paid. There were no free gifts, no windfalls from his own God. If one worked, one prospered. He laughed at his own puritanical fancies. Had he deserved

David? Had his history and snippets of poetry and principal parts combined to make a millionaire?

God help us all.

Had he been lucky? Or happy? One of his girl friends had compared love and infatuation fifty years back. Love lasts, she said; that's the difference. 'We shan't know till we're dead, then,' he'd argued, 'whether we were in love or not.' 'That's right.' He loved her more than she did him, and that's why she was prepared to leave it at that, with her complacency unpunctuated and his lust a dance of uncertain servility on her most fatuous wish. But she was right, right. That left pap where heart doth hop. Still, still.

He eyed his agapanthus again. Now it was manageable, monstrously difficult no longer.

Grinning as he stumped indoors he wished sanely to God that he'd accepted Mrs. Collis's offer of lunch.

≈ 12 ≈

David arrived for a two-day visit.

First came the telephone messages from his secretaries, business-like but kind, then the remainder by first-class post. Next, a lady made three separate inquiries over three days to see if there was anything he needed, anything they could send. Mansfield remonstrated with her, comically serious.

'While he's up here, it'll be plain living and high-thinking for him.'

'I'm sure it will, Mr. Mansfield.' What did she think? Shut up, you silly old billy-goat. Or did she speak as she typed, automatically? A pound to a penny this wasn't a typist at all; some neat-ankled graduate in Greats or sociology pouring a creamy voice over her master's contacts.

'You know, I think you're just reassuring yourself that you can actually reach this place by phone.'

'No, sir. Your son is just a little concerned that you, you might over-exert yourself.'

'So, he gets a beautiful young woman to ring me every day to cool my courage.'

'You haven't seen me, Mr. Mansfield.'

'I know my son.'

She concurred, syrupped him, then returned to her charge. He must not chase needlessly what she could organise so easily from her end. He enjoyed the exchange, doubted if she did.

David, arriving, was pleased with himself.

Yet the man looked tired, puffy, pale, with his hair as if it had died.

'Overdoing it again?'

'Yes, dad, and a half.'

His father thought that any minute David would take a bow. Soon the story was flowing. They'd broken into the American market, against odds, advice, trends, the will of God almost. Hadn't he heard it on the B.B.C.? Mansfield had, at least five times, with appropriate comment from our economics correspondent and our man in New York. He'd known that the named group was one with which his son had connections, but as there was no mention of David, he barely remembered the facts, refused to jig to the excitement of those fast-talking commentators with their wary eyes fixed on an off-screen script.

Apparently the deal had been on, 'in the pipeline', for nearly two years, but had been settled, bloodily, in the last three months. David had been in America, Mansfield knew, just recently. He described difficulties, lucidly, with a lurid energy, so that the telling mounted climax after climax, a celluloid epic. Mansfield admired the asides, caustic description, the way he was driven to understand the ordering of the affair which was as complicated as a hundred years' religious war. But it saddened him, for compared with the tale, the teller shrank, body comparing poorly with voice, movements sluggish against the blaze and drive of the outlining mind.

'And now the millions'll come rolling in?'

'We shall make money, certainly. But it's a prestige job, mainly. We've broken into their markets. We're super-efficient. Very good effect in Europe.

'You haven't drawn your lines of communication out too far, have you?'

'No. It doesn't work like that. You see . . .'

He was away again. This time he lost his father, but did not notice. The old man considered his son, idly catechising himself. Did this smooth, convincing talk cover David's uncertainty? Perhaps he'd undertaken negotiations which in twelve months would be found unprofitable, and then the go-getters, now guardedly praising David's initiative, would claim Mansfield had lost his touch, would criticise, grab, gang snidely up to shift him. A success is as demanding as, more enervating than, a failure, and now here the boy sat, having worked his heart out, waiting for his results, which themselves depended on incalculable contingencies. James Mansfield, hearing the strong voice and understanding nothing, eyed his son, and behind him the sideboard that had stood in the old house with its cut-glass fruit-bowl and its silver-rimmed oak biscuit barrel.

'You look whacked, David,' he said in a pause. The son frowned, affronted at the interruption or suspicious of his father's inattention.

'I've been going it. We had to tie this up sharp.'

'I thought you said it'd been two years. '

'Nobody believed in it. I didn't. Then six months ago there was a dog in hell's chance, but what with bureaucracy over there, and they can be a thousand times worse than we are, and cold feet this end, it really was like trying to strike a match at the bottom of a lake. The number of people who want reassuring, need their hand holding, beats me.'

'I thought that was the characteristic of my brigade.'

'No. People with five-figure salaries and they act as if they're running a corner-shop.'

'So this isn't so gilt-edged as you make out?'

'Risk's always there.' David bit his finger, scowled at his father, then laughed, now loud, deeply. 'I'll tell you now what you're thinking.' Immediately he began to describe the doubts that had troubled the old man, choosing the exact words his father had used, an impressive performance. In the end, he clapped his hands together with a frightening smack.

'How's that?' he smirked.

'Not bad.'

'Reassure you?'

'Not about your business acumen; it merely shows that you've got your old man weighed up.'

'And that's something.' Smiles that converted his father. 'Now, friend, some other good news for you. Eleanor and I have decided not to pack it in.'

'That's good.' Slowly, grudging, after a pause, the coarseness of expression.

'I thought there'd be more excitement than that.' David measured his father's reaction, and chaffed him.

'I want the full story first. You know me.'

'She's been a trojan while this lot's been blowing. Her dad's heart, Sarah's tantrums, Robert's scarlet fever and frantic phone calls when I wasn't there. Managed the lot. And I thought to myself, in the thick, "She's doing you proud." I was winning on this job: I ought to share out the spoils. Hardly that. That's wrong. Might I slip up and then need somebody to stroke my forehead? I thrashed it out, parallel with this other thing, in spurts, in the middle of conferences, and then I wrote her a note from Washington . . .'

'Outlining tentative conclusions?'

'Yes, sir. Very brisk. I told her not to reply, just to mull it over. I could not believe it. I told myself, "As soon as I see her, the house, the kids, back to status quo." Not so. Not so bloody ridiculous is it?'

'You don't like Damascus roads, then?'

'Don't like anything I can't reasonably fathom. I was convinced we were finished. Sick of the sight of her. Then . . .'

'Ah,' Mansfield baaed at his son. 'It's that scientific education of yours. Unfits you for life.' David considered, laughed, rubbed his knees.

'My experience at university was that if you really got stuck but had worked on a problem, it was quite likely the way-out would show up, be handed to you. Sometimes. Not always. I've known really clever people up the creek, but the other happened regularly enough to be counted as, well, not unusual.'

'So you used to wait for an answer. Talk about Damascus; this is more like the upper room and Pentecost.'

'Don't get me wrong. Usually you arrived by slog, trying this or that, using all the dodges, the techniques you knew. But now and again you'd be beaten, leave it and then the method would suddenly be there, on a plate, gratis. Might take a bit of working on still, but you knew you were home.'

'And what conclusion do we draw?'

'Doesn't seem suitable for human behaviour.'

'Why not?'

'There aren't any real solutions there, are there? Too many imponderables.'

They sat, the pair of them, chins on fists, elbows on knees, *penseurs*, for some time, immersed in the happiness of their own conversation. Mansfield was suspicious, didn't trust his son's conversation, guessed it might have been mocked-up as largesse, his own share, in the American triumph. The whole thing was too theatrical, too unlike the calculating strength which latterly distinguished David's personality.

He began, almost as if tipsy, to describe how he had been listening to the Radio Three as he worked in his kitchen, and suddenly came to as a woman sang Schubert's *Geheimes*.

'D'you know it? "The Secret"?'

'Don't think so.' Further negative head-shakings as his father whistled a bar or two.

'I heard the announcer outlining the story. Youngster in first love. The neighbours all guessing and gossip. But she doesn't let on, looks forward to the next meeting. They're in love. Nobody else knows. That's the secret.' He looked at his son, expecting mockery. 'Then they started. That stuttering, tripping accompaniment, like a young girl, uncertain but darting about, marvellously nimble. Perfect. It was perfect. Took my breath clean away. There I stood leaning on the sink, face dripping tears, utterly happy.'

'Yes.' David sat, carefully.

'That was my free gift.'

He soon stood, towered over his father, darkening the room for him

'Dad,' he said, 'you must be the chap they're always writing about in *The Times*, who won't have any lowering of standards.'

'You don't approve, do you?'

'For all the notice I take, they could broadcast silence all day and every day, and for telly a white kitten in a snowstorm. I don't take a thing in, even when it's on.'

'More's the pity.'

Both felt the warmth of the moment, loved, wished each other different. Mansfield cleared his throat.

'What's Eleanor say, then? About this change of heart?'

'She's pleased, I think.'

'But what are you doing up here? You ought to be with her.'

'Her suggestion. This isn't young love, you know. None of that sort of secret.' He dug his handsome chin into his hard, spotless collar. 'We're both a bit suspicious. But she said, "David, go and spend two days with father. You've made your fuss of the youngsters, and me. Now go on up there and talk about particle physics or demography or Mahler or whatever it is your old man's interested in today." '

'Any reason?'

'I didn't ask her. I think I know. She and the youngsters and the locals are all part of my business set-up. Not so here. I'm nobody.'

'And it's hard work.'

'It is, by God. I put my brains to specialist uses. But I hardly read, never hear anything serious, only go to the theatre when I can't avoid it. None of my people, friends, would say anything to me about Schubert.'

'None?'

'Not that I can think of. Let's be fair, they talk about matters I'm more interested in. Money. Advantage. But I expect she's right. *In statu pupillari* again. Like the old school. It was a good place. Of its sort.'

'You regret . . .'

'I do not. To be in the frame of mind where your *Geheimes* or a line of poetry is the most important thing in the world, even temporarily, needs training. And rejection of everything I think counts.' He sat again. 'Only in this room, father Mansfield, would I say that.'

'It is easier for a camel to go through the eye of a needle than for a rich man to enter into the kingdom of God.' He aped a parsonical delivery.

'It would be, if the kingdom existed.'

'Don't you wish it did?'

The two unbelievers shook their heads over nothing, delighted with the conceit. When Mansfield had recovered he found he was recalling a series of visits to a factory

152

site. David, almost insistent, had driven bis father over one Sunday morning.

The place looked bucolic enough now, with a row of railway cottages, some hawthorn hedged fields and beyond, not far from a small council estate, oblongs of neat allotments, with bean-poles, fruit-bushes, lovingly built huts of brick or wood, half-covered with rambler-roses. David outlined the advantages: near a main-line railway, with no chance of closure, fifteen minutes from the M1, sufficiently large population to man the factories.

'Why's nobody else taken it, then?'

'It's not the only site, by any manner of means. But you must have a lot of money and be prepared to push and kick government departments and local farmers.'

'And fight retired colonels?'

'Aren't any. The place is spoilt already. They've flitted.'

Next time they visited, bulldozers had smashed down hedges and trees, even shifted top-soil so that the ground was raw, thickly scarred with tractor-ruts, scoop-pits, puddles and small deal crosses like home-made children's swords, or cats' graves.

'We're off,' David had said. 'This is when I really think I'm doing something.'

Now came the reinforced concrete, the metal skeletons of the smaller buildings, the cranes on their lengths of track, the diminished crews in helmets, seemingly few and unbusy in the vast stretches of unfinished newness and sprawl.

'How long?'

'A year,' David said. 'If we manage to keep 'em at it.'

That spelt power, and Mansfield shared it, distantly. This did not rape the countryside; the railways had done that over a century back, and besides these acres of undistinguished farm land were nothing much, neither in profit nor beauty. If some sentimentalist had been born in one of the toppled cottages, then he must learn a new pride in glass, straight walls, machinery, gleaming end-product. This place spewed out the heavy plant to ram the motor-roads, pile the sky-scrapers, richen the wealthy.

They walked together round Mansfield's garden, and as David asked the names of flowers, his father remembered that they never strolled like this when the son was adolescent. Both parties gave heavily then, wanted to accept nothing.

'Peaceful here,' David said.

'Until the evening when the cars and motor-mowers start.'

David looked over the valley, the houses, the dark stretch of woods, a line of poplars, five chimneys on the extreme sky-line.

'Not much of a place, this,' he said.

'You don't feel any nostalgia?'

The slow, searching shake of the head.

'I doubt if I would even if it were beautiful.'

'It's nothing to do with beauty, in that sense.' Mansfield might have been at the history fifth, on a summer Friday, last period. 'Certain people, sights, move you when you're young and you remember them. But there's one overriding advantage. They don't change. The girl's beautiful as the day you first saw her; she's grown no older, lost neither teeth nor temper. Life is disappointing now so we hark back. God knows it was dreadful then, but we revise and prune. Isn't that it?'

'If you say so.'

'Are you listening?'

'I'm trying,' David said, 'to decide why you think life's disappointing. Mine isn't. At least, I don't think so.' Modestly.

'You're not chasing one achievement after another?'

'Of course. But that's how I'm made. That's what I do best.' He pointed below to a stretch of buildings, covering acres of land, widely, whitely. 'Little family firm. You'd say they were doing well. We nearly took 'em over last year, with a couple more concerns like them. Wasn't worth it, in the end. Not for us. Rampoles will get it, you'll see.'

'You used to play tennis, there. When you were at school.'

'So I did.'

'Had you forgotten?'

'No. I remember the groundsman. Officious pot-belly. Showed us up, to his satisfaction, in front of the girls. But I remember better that one of our subsidiaries, now, put the money up for their first phase of expansion. You pays your money, dad, there as anywhere else.' He pulled himself upward, stretching, broad, in the sunshine, a big man, and then screwed his eyes. 'Life's a disappointment to you, is it, then?'

'You might say so.'

Mansfield tried to speak coolly, not to think what he said.

'Why's that?'

'I'm near the end of my lick.' Still calmly. David flexed his muscles, took up an exaggerated statuesque pose.

'If,' he declaimed, 'you have any tears prepare to shed them nee-ow.'

'In my sort of job, it's difficult to assess how well you've done. Clever boys will score as high with somebody else. You can point to this factory, that road, these hundreds of machines. I can't. . . .'

'Nobody can. Except the simple one-man business. The craftsman, the novelist, poet. Scholar, perhaps. Old-type scientist. They're not well regarded. Hard times for the ego.'

'I've had one go at death, David.'

The son grimaced. His father pressed.

'I was certain I was going to die. One further slight mechanical failure in a bit of muscle or artery, and I was a goner. That would be it. Name on tombstone for a hundred years, in people's head for a bit less, then end of James J. Mansfield.'

'You never know,' David spoke pacifically.

'I do.'

'You don't. Some insignificant creature dies, sinks on to the mud. A hundred, two hundred, I don't know, million years later, he turns up at the seaside, perfectly preserved as a fossil for dad and the kids to enthuse over. How's that for immortality?'

'I haven't done anything, David.'

'That's wrong. In any case, why compare yourself with Alexander or Jesus or Beethoven? That's ridiculous. Just look round you. At other schoolmasters, fathers. Never mind your delusions of grandeur.'

'I'll conclude the whole human race is a failure?'

'May be. But it's not logical. Each individual may not do much, but the sum of progress is remarkable. I know it's not perfection. But we've got somewhere. And if you think that somewhere's hopeless, you try to change it, which knocks your case for universal individual failure on the head. T'other way about, you might just as well take the hippy view, and opt out, if you can.' David had adopted his father's manner to the life. 'If your character allows it.'

'Or cut your throat.'

'Yes. There is that. Do something for me, dad, will you?'

'Oh? What's that, then?'

'Will you have Sarah again for a bit? It's like this. She's creating about having to go back to school. We think it would be better if she did. She doesn't know what she wants to do, but objects to going back to the hockey and the prefectorial round. Says she should be going to a good, co-educational comprehensive.'

'Something in it, David.'

'Of course there's something in it. But Beanhurst gets admirable academic results, and isn't anything like as old-fogeyed as she makes out. She should do "A" Levels.'

'In what?'

'That's the snag. She doesn't know. Frankly it doesn't matter much. But you know about these things, and you can talk to her. She likes you, and, I don't like to say this, dad, you're one of the few people she's not sick of who think education's worth something.'

'Isn't it?'

'I've not thought about it. I should. I know, I know. I've an old-fashioned prejudice which suspects that as long as education is going on, one might just pick up something of value. Anyway, she needs "A" Levels for university. She'll enjoy that, socially. You don't think much of me, do you?' He pulled a rueful face.

'I don't make head or tail of you. That's for certain.'

'You'll have her?'

'Yes.'

David stared again over the valley, big as a viking, and his father, coldish in the sunshine, afraid, made nothing of him.

Sarah gave no trouble.

Her grandfather put it straight to her why she was there. Warmly she walked across, linked her arm through his, and said:

'I'm going back.'

'To study?'

'English, French, German. Then university, I hope.'

'But your father . . .'

'My father isn't used to rational argument. Not even for enjoyment.'

She gently made fun of David and Eleanor, summed the advantages of her school sanely, said why she'd chosen this course.

'I'm glad,' he said, 'that I haven't got to sort it out with you.'

'Why?'

'Young people are different. Their standards . . .' His voice tailed.

'They haven't changed much. You can't bluff us quite so easily, that's all.' Her mother's control spoke there, her father's energy.

Awed, puzzled by his victory, he pampered the child, uncertain whether he or his son was being fooled. Sarah demanded little, played pop on her machines in her room, knitted as she listened to the Third with him downstairs, and became suddenly, one evening, magnificently acute in her observations on a television programme where she noted the weakness of plot, the failure to exploit created situation, the shifty nature of the dialogue and the actors' inability to use material credibly inside the genre. He himself was quite crushed by the devastating skill she used in spotting weaknesses, as much as by her lack of savagery and her verbal flatness. She did not score by cutting phraseology, with gibes, but merely picking out deficiencies which were obvious once she pinpointed them. This was intelligence. At the same time, she apparently never noticed the effect of her criticisms on her listener. She spoke her piece, uncomfortably reminding him how fitful his own attention to the programme had been.

While she was out one afternoon, at a skating-rink, Alfred Hapgood telephoned. He spoke thickly, choking on his words.

'Clive's dead, Mr. Mansfield.'

'How's that?'

'We don't know, really. Details. Caught a cold somehow, on a seaside trip, I think. Turned worse. Chest or heart. Dead in no time.'

'How is your wife taking it?'

'That's it, Mr. Mansfield. She's so quiet. Struck to a stone, like. But she's blaming herself. Says if he hadn't gone, he'd still be alive.'

'That's rubbish.'

158

'You try to tell her. She ignores you. Turns her back.'

Unwillingly next day, while Sarah was out, he called on the Hapgoods. The wife opened the front door, said she was 'all right', and led the visitor straight through the house to the back door.

'He's working.'

Certainly she seemed laconic, but not unusually so. He might not have noticed, if he'd not expected trouble, any difference. Preoccupied, she showed him to the garden where he'd find her husband whom he'd come to see. Mansfield was in the yard, not having spoken to her about Clive.

Hapgood was building a greenhouse, but his, unlike Colis's, was no prefabricated affair. The foundation, the brickwork of the sides and the skeleton uprights had been completed. A furnace with hot water pipes was in place.

'Nice job,' Hapgood said, patting the rusty ironwork. 'Bought this cheap first, and worked the greenhouse out round it.'

'Difficult?'

'I've got all day at it, now. Nobody's beck and call. Until this business.' Slowly, rubbing his hands cleaner on a rag, sitting on a chair with sawn-off back, he spoke of his wife. She frightened him with her quietness, bottling it inside herself. Her chapel friends had been, and the parson, pastor, whatever. Seemed decent. Wasn't an educated man, not in your sense, Mr. Mansfield. But knew his Bible backwards. He told her plain. On about David and Bathsheba. How everybody's put to trials. My grace is sufficient. 'She didn't listen, Mr. Mansfield. He could have been talking in Greek. I thought she'd got this religion serious, but it's all gone, rolled off her. It's her fault. She caused the lad's death. She should have kept him, not turned him over to that crew who'd neglect him while they went out boozing and going on. She won't hear sense. It's awful. She doesn't talk.'

They sat, on wall and chair, inside the glassless, spar-less greenhouse, unable to speak. In the end Mansfield said:

'What'll happen?'

'She might try,' words scorched slowly in constipation, 'again. Do herself in.'

'When's the funeral? Is she, are you . . .?'

'All over and done with. Before we knew anything about it.'

They went indoors.

'Is there a cup of tea going?' Hapgood shouted, false-jovial. They heard her fill the kettle, light the gas, waited. When she brought the tray in, her husband asked:

'Aren't you having one with us, then, Clara?'

'I don't want one.' Pause. Acid. 'Thank you.'

'Sit down, then. Make yourself sociable.'

She obeyed, folded her hands in her lap.

'I've been telling Mr. Mansfield about our bad news.'

She nodded, looked briefly, blankly in the visitor's direction.

'I'm very sorry, Mrs. Hapgood,' he said. 'It must have been a shock. Especially as you've done so much for the boy.'

Again, she acknowledged the words with a nondescript movement of the head.

'Made it worse,' Hapgood said, 'not knowing anything about it. You'd ha' thought Enid would have written at the time.' He angled for an answer from his wife, a phrase or two, however conventional, or self-incriminating, to in-dicate she heard, understood, made one of them.

Nothing.

'How did it happen, Mrs. Hapgood?' Mansfield joined.

The woman lifted a finger, pointed numbly at her hus-band, who answered.

'We don't know. That's the terrible thing. Like getting blood out of a stone. I've written twice, but, no, she don't care.' He stood, and from the back of the mantelpiece clock took an envelope, extracted the one cheap sheet of lined notepaper. Though he could easily have passed it to Mansfield, he stepped away, handed the letter to his wife who had to stir herself to reach the visitor. That appeared a small advance, an achievement in strategy.

He read the poverty-stricken note. They'd be sorry to hear Clive had died. Three weeks back. He'd caught the flu which had turned worse. Nobody had been invited to the funeral; it was all such a shock and over so quick. Love.

Enid and Eric.

Love? He refolded the paper, passed it to Mrs. Hapgood, who fumbled it into her lap. Her face sagged shapeless, putty-grey, eyes almost blind.

'Dreadful,' she said.

'They should have written before the funeral.' Hapgood.

'Perhaps she wasn't fit. Knocked over by it.'

'In these cases,' Hapgood looked at his wife, 'you've got to do your best. However you feel. However you are.'

She did not shift, seemed turned within herself, eyes unfocussed. If only, Mansfield's mind flitted hysterically, if only one could know where her eyes rested, what she saw, one might make contact, have expectation. Today, a cabbage could see further, understand more deeply.

'Does Tom know, Mrs. Hapgood?' He deliberately addressed her. 'Did she write to him?'

A shiver, some sort of movement, in her upper torso; she opened her mouth, but said nothing. After a time, she shook her head.

'We don't know that,' Hapgood replied.

'Well, you can say this,' Mansfield's voice seemed unnecessarily loud, strident, 'you did your best for him.'

The woman's eyes returned from nowhere, stared him out with a contempt that was savage. It was as if she had answered him with an obscenity, spat his commonplace kindness back in his face.

'You did your best for him,' he repeated. 'Nobody could have done more.'

He thrust the words at her. A quarrel. She must under-stand; he branded with this part-truth. Her attention drifted.

'You've nothing to reproach yourself with, Mrs. Hap-good.'

Again, the vegetable deafness.

'That's what I tell her.' Her husband joined forces. 'We did all we could for the poor little beggar. At our time of life, you couldn't expect more.'

Blank, a silence. Mansfield tried again.

'Are you going up to see Enid, Mrs. Hapgood?'

The suspicion of a shudder was all his answer. The hus-band clashed his false teeth, took hold of her chairback.

'Mr. Mansfield's asked you a question,' he snapped, voice squeaky with fear.

She smiled, uncertainly, crazily inappropriate, gulped.

He repeated his question. Much seemed to depend on it.

She puckered her lips, shook her head.

'You'd find out,' he said foolishly. 'See if there was any-thing you could do.'

She wasn't listening, and they fell to awkward silence, in obstinacy, on her part as if she were willing it. Hap-good poured his visitor another cup of tea, which cooled as they sat. He swigged it, made another effort.

'Can you bring your husband up to tea tomorrow?' he asked. 'That's if you're not doing anything special.'

Her front teeth scraped her lower lip paler.

'I've got my granddaughter, Sarah, staying with me. It'll be a bit of a change for you.'

Her expression did not soften, but a large tear squeezed from her left eye, divided into two on her cheek, dropped to her chest. The two struggled to ignore the manifesta-tion.

'What say, now, mother? Be a little outing?'

In the end she shook hands, and on the visit struggled to talk. This was specially so with Sarah, and after the meal she turned suddenly to the girl, with something like bad temper, unsluggish, said:

'Little Clive Hapgood died.'

'My grandpa told me.'

'Do you remember him? You played with him here. You and that other girl.'

'Daisy. Yes.'

'He died.'

'Was it unexpected?' The girl's voice was easy, with no overtones of distress.

'At four years old?'

Nothing more until Hapgood intervened to say the child had always been delicate. His wife returned to lethargy, sometimes trying politely to answer questions, now and then fidgeting. Mansfield felt exhausted, but when they stood at the door, said:

'Now come again, Mrs. Hapgood, won't you? I enjoy a bit of company.'

She smiled weakly, absent-mindedly. Her husband said:

'Come up and see us. Bring Sarah for tea.'

'We'd like to. Thanks very much.'

'When do you say then, mother? Tomorrow?'

She stared down the garden path, deaf. Sarah in the background eyed her grandfather.

'Will tomorrow do, then, mother?' Hapgood's big voice thumped a yard from her ear.

'Tomorrow?' A ready parody.

'For Mr. Mansfield and Sarah to come to tea?'

'When you like.'

The three words seemed chosen at random. Three blind mice. Doh, re, mi. Man at work. Touch me not. Stone a crow. Hapgood's face set blank as his wife's in depression.

'Give me a ring,' Mansfield said.

'You're coming.' Fiercely.

Next day he phoned to say his wife was in bed, under sedation. She had a mad crying jag when they got home, and again in the early hours. Now the doctor prescribed rest, no visitors. She had to be built up to fight herself. Dutifully Mansfield inquired each day, expected nothing, talked vaguely, ached himself with weakness, loathed the simple drill of asking.

Eleanor wrote to say she'd fetch Sarah, would stay overnight.

'This is an honour,' he said. The day spread bright over the valley, emphasising the square solidity of the houses, their craftsmanly finish. Sky was clear and the far woods blue. A huge tree could be clearly made out on the distant horizon.

'Magnificent.'

Eleanor waved at the panorama behind her, the valley with church-tower and chimney stacks, the coal-tips, the gentle hills scoured here and there to sandy earth where the builders were at work.

'Interesting,' he said, 'because nobody's made a fire. The dip there can smoke like a burning dustbin. They knew you were coming.'

Mother and daughter were friendly, equally talkative, but Sarah prepared to spend her last evening out at the ice-rink. Eleanor settled with a glass of gin, specially bought that morning, to congratulate him on his success with the child. After disclaimers, he mentioned her rapprochement with David.

'Oh, yes.' She smiled, on guard behind the raised glass.

'That doesn't sound too good.'

'I'm not given to enthusiasms, father, these days.'

'But are you pleased?'

She sipped, thinking.

'I suppose so. Yes. You could say that.' She gave nothing away, teased him. 'I was surprised when I had that letter from him. It told me to sit down and mull it over.' She grimaced. 'He was very attached at the time to some young woman in one of the companies, playing some part in the negotiations. I said to myself, "She's thrown him over." He told you all this, of course?'

'Not about this girl.'

'Remiss.' She furrowed her forehead. 'I wasn't jealous. She wasn't the first. It hurts but in a dim sort of way. We don't have normal conjugal relations.'

'I'm sorry.'

'I think I ought to cuckold him, to get my own back. But I've too low a temperature. I don't care for anybody. Perhaps when I grow older and sillier, I shall throw my cap over the windmill for some young boy, but not now.' Gin. 'I can see this is shocking you, but if we talk about it at all, we might as well be frank. When he said all this, I just asked myself, "What does he get out of this?" And to tell you the truth, I couldn't answer.'

'Take it on face-value, then. He's had a change of heart.'

'It's not likely. I could well imagine that he's argued himself into a position where he sees me as an asset, to be kept, but I don't think there's any emotional change. Once he'd taken up a line, he'd use all his charm. I know that.' She pushed her glass towards him. 'But apart from that . . .' She shook her head, almost brightly. 'He feels nothing for me.'

'Why did you take him back, then?'

'What else could I do?' She waved at the gin-bottle. 'It has its advantages.'

Mansfield poured. 'Do you like him?'

'Yes.' Socially, that, neatly, smartly. 'You don't make your way in the world as he's done without faults. If he wants something, he moves heaven, earth and almighty God until he's got it. That occupies him. He doesn't settle with his wife and rosy children round the fire.'

'That's what you wanted?'

'No, I didn't. I liked the excitements. I got something out of his victories. They were what I was after. Other wives looking enviously. I'd my own sort of power. I've changed in the last year or two. If he bought up I.C.I. now, it wouldn't mean much.'

'You loved him?' The question was necessary. 'When you married him?'

'That means so many things.'

'I'm not going to get any sense out of you, I can see that.' He meant that, jocular or no.

'I wish I was more satisfactory, father. Matters seem more black and white to you than they do to me. The generation gap.' She smiled broadly. 'We shall do well enough. He's genuinely fond of the children. In his way. He'll look after them. Any indiscretions we'll keep sensible. We have our position.' Her parody of a squiress shrieked. 'To maintain.'

'I hate it.'

'I know you do, father. That's why I put it to you like this. Inoculating you? It's genuinely unsatisfactory, I grant you, but I don't see us doing anything else. It's inevitable, but it could have been worse.'

'I wish . . .'

'Yes. It's no good. Wishing won't make it so. Let me tell you something now. I love my children, but they annoy me. Fortunately the burden of bringing them up isn't altogether mine; I've got professionals on the job. Of all the people in the world, the one I love most is, I think, I'm sure, you. I mean it.'

'No.' Gasp, in joy.

'You don't make too many demands on me, or only those I can cope with. That's my defect. I'm cold, lukewarm. I love somebody who's away in the distance.'

'What about your father?'

'Well now, that's just a bit complicated.'

From the next room the piano sounded. A fall of melody, and chords, rather naive, solemn, winsome. The piece was not marvellously played, but adequately. Sarah.

'I thought that child had gone skating,' Eleanor said. 'Just like her. Supposed to be out, and here she dawdles jingling at the piano.'

Tears massed, swilled from Mansfield's eyes, in an

equilibrium of sorrow and happiness. His throat was blocked, and for the moment he seemed parted from his body, from the crumpled face, the weeping, not standing aside, but incapable of grasping the fullness of feeling. The god possessed him so that he grew too large for his own self, too sensitive an instrument to register the modicum of emotion that was his normal lot. He loved. He was beloved. Such confessions were only for the young, the inexperienced. Next door, the plaintive chords followed, one on the other, a Victorian drawing-room lament, a parody of beauty, a passing tribute, *albumblat.*

Eleanor looked at him in alarm.

He waved to her, signalling that all was well, but managed only a feeble massage of empty air. She stood, came across, undecided. Now the power of his feelings receded and he saw, unclearly, the figure he cut. From his pocket he took a large handkerchief and wiped his eyes in a business-like way, trying to smile. The music sauntered on, over the steadily short arpeggios at the beginning of each bar. He nodded towards it.

'Sarah?' Eleanor said. 'Do you want her to stop?'

'No.' The swollen throat had cleared.

'What is it she's playing? I know it well enough.'

'November 4th, 1847,' he said, proud of the fact.

'What on earth are you talking about?' Relieved at the normality of his voice, she returned to her chair.

'That's the date of Mendelssohn's death. Schumann wrote that "Memory" in the style of his friend. It's a perfect "song without words".'

'I didn't connect them at all.'

The music broke off; Sarah poked her head in.

'I'm going now.'

'We've just been admiring your playing,' Mansfield said.

'You must be joking.'

'I don't think you should speak to your grandfather like that.'

'Sorry. I'm not used to compliments.' She was gone.

Mansfield laughed out loud.

'Brazen wi' it,' he said, broadly.

Eleanor questioned him closely about his health, argued about the theatre, 'pop' festivals which she hated, and then she outlined plans for her house. She and David had decided to keep the Hampshire place; in some way this seemed interlocked with their decision not to part, but she was demanding considerable alterations. He wondered, dared not ask, whether that was her reward, rake-off, for compliance.

At the same time he envied her drive, apparent ability to get what she wanted from builders, interior decorators, her servants, her husband. While she was talking, and he admired the hard, aristocratic voice, the crisp manner, he suddenly remembered that this woman, he savoured again her slimness, the quiet elegance of clothes, the fine pallor, the proud shape of features, had confessed she loved him above all other people. It meant little. A word in the right place cost nothing. Like her husband she was capable of any hypocrisy, or lie, to gain an end. He believed her; without compunction, he believed, in innocence.

With great clarity she explained why she needed a second larger rockery. It seemed a matter of life and death for the moment. He noticed, abstemiously, that she drank rather a lot, but her manner went unaltered. They were eating brown bread and Wensleydale cheese when Sarah returned, bored, wishing she'd stayed with the old folks.

The next morning as soon as they'd driven away Mansfield became restless. He went round the visitors' bedrooms, parcelled up the sheets and pillowcases for the laundry, not leaving the chore to his home-help. He prowled about the house and garden, looking for work. A single glass on the draining board, Sarah's last-minute drink of water, took on bogus significance. He wanted those two back, and the world stopped.

He sat in the shed and oiled his motor-mower.

While he was cutting grass, a small man entered the

garden, inquired for Mr. Mansfield.

'My name is Brown. I'm pastor of the Gaul Street Pentecostal Church.'

He looked like a workman out for a Sunday stroll. Grey hair grew thickly round the sides of his head, but the bald crown was fuzzed. The hand he held out had known manual labour, and recently.

'I've come about Mrs. Hapgood.' The voice lacked music. 'Her husband says you're the only person who can do anything with her.'

'What's happened?'

Proud of the compliment he invited Brown inside. They sat to coffee, and the pastor explained that Mrs. Hapgood seemed withdrawn, refused to stir, neglected her house and husband, did not rise at all yesterday from her bed.

'That's a case for medical treatment.'

'They've had the doctor.'

'What do you want me to do, Mr. Brown?'

'Her husband says that if you told her to get up, she'd very likely obey.'

'Hasn't he?'

'He's frightened. He fears she might attempt her life again.'

'So I do the dirty work?'

Brown looked mildly up, ran a hand over his weather-beaten pate.

'I shouldn't think it's like that at all. You're a man she listens to; always has, he says.'

'Have you tried, Mr. Brown?'

'Yes. She doesn't pay any attention, drifts away, you know. I've reasoned with her.'

'She's obviously become worse in the last day or two.' While he'd basked in Eleanor's beauty, this poor woman had lost her soul.

'She has. It's a dreadful thing. Guilt. She blames herself for that child's death. And now to see her staring upward at the ceiling, almost as if she's dead. My heart bleeds for her husband. He doesn't know which way to turn. He daren't leave her side for five minutes.'

'Can your church do nothing?'

While he asked the impertinent question, he was shocked at his own vulgarity.

'We arrange for people to sit up with her. To give him a good night's rest, at least. And some of the ladies see to the meals, the shopping. Somebody calls in every day without fail. We pray, Mr. Mansfield. I take it you're not a believer.'

'I wouldn't say that.'

'Neither is her husband. But he's a decent man. He knelt down with me today. He knows need. He won't call in vain.'

Mansfield disliked the words, felt a stir of superstitious awe. Now the texts would begin, the soapy rhetoric. Already the man's voice was changing, to anoint holy words.

'You'll go, Mr. Mansfield?' Brown was matter-of-fact.

'When?'

'As soon as you can. Her husband said, "If only Mr. Mansfield would come, but he's got relatives staying with him." I got your address. I came straight up.'

'Today, then?'

'If it's possible.'

'Now?'

'Yes. If the Lord moves you. Now.'

Mansfield sighed, torn in himself. This manifested itself as a test, of his faith, or lack of it. He'd to go, order this poor woman up out of her bed and back to her chores. If the experiment failed, he'd take the blame; Hapgood and Brown would walk scot free. He did not mind that, for he'd no desire to try this matter. What part of his business was it to go commanding the devils in and out of people? And yet. Yet. A probe of pride, a tempter nagged. 'You could do it, Mansfield. But speak the word.' Showbiz of sainthood.

'Do you mind if I offer a word of prayer, Mr. Mansfield?'

This man. Brown dropped to his knees on the carpet, began, hands clasped but speaking in a different voice. There was no rant about, nothing plangent; if anything his voice called softer, but seethed in intensity as if he needed to hiss his petitions into God's closed ears. The content of the prayer, the skeleton, was sensible: bless the woman and her dear ones; restore her if it is part of the heavenly will; help this Thy servant who was about to visit the bed of sickness; grant him the word in season, as from Thee. God bless and save Thy children the world over. Amen. But the superstructure galled Mansfield, reminding him of the prayer-meetings of his youth. God was constantly prompted about what He had said in His word. It was exactly like Eng. Lit. exams where frequent quotations from and close reference to the text carry high marks. If God knew both the Bible and Clara Hapgood's situation He did not need this pedantic nagging. Was that born of doubt, then? It seemed unlikely. Brown wrestled with his recalcitrant Deity because that was the accepted form. Didn't Jesus commend the importunate widow? Or Jacob hold and shake the angel in Peniel? Nothing shall come of nothing. Speak again.

Brown circled the subject.

Then Mansfield realised that neither God nor the sick woman was the target of his prayer. It was he. Sadly he listened, as if to an unsatisfactory theatrical performance. He recognised the sincerity, the truth of what the man did, but it meant nothing to the listener. The shape sagged wrong. The ordeal was smothered with verbiage. Clara was forgotten.

Brown rose, and they went outside where the visitor complimented the host on his garden. Reassured, Mansfield made him a present of a bag of windfall apples and a picking of runner beans. When they shook hands, both appeared cordial, like old friends.

After lunch Mansfield, who'd bathed, changed into sub-fusc, presented himself at the Hapgoods'. He'd no idea why he'd taken these precautions which, he joked with himself, were about as effective as bardic robes and mystic charms. But he shivered. Nothing here was unserious. He'd been pushed into something he neither wanted nor approved. Chest tight, blood thumping, he stood, feeling sick, forlorn, neglected, and without power.

'I'm glad you've come,' Hapgood said. 'Mr. Brown came in to say you would.'

'Seems a decent man.'

'Thrusts it down your throat too much for my liking, but he's put himself out. I'll say that for him. And his congregation.' Hand rubbing. 'Well, come on up and see Clara, Mr. Mansfield.'

He turned towards the stairs door.

'Just a minute.' Hapgood released the knob, reluctantly, almost in surliness. 'What is it exactly you want me to say to her?'

'Say? You say just what you like, just what's in your mind, Mr. Mansfield.'

Again he swung round swiftly, grasped the handle, but did not turn it, waited for the objection.

'That won't do.'

Now Mansfield sickened with fright; he crouched down, legs trembling, on the edge of a chair and leaned on his stick. Why should he bully this good man, who trusted him?

'I don't understand you, Mr. Mansfield.'

'You think I should tell your wife that there's nothing organically wrong with her, and that she should get up, get on with her life?'

'Well, no, not exactly like that . . .'

'What do you want, then?' Bolder than his weakling thighs, pinched calves.

'Yes. Yes. What you said. That's right. That's what I want you to say. You see the doctor . . .' Abject surrender behind a loud voice.

'Why doesn't he tell her so, then?'

'He has done. He spoke lovely to her. Explained it. Might have been our Fred putting it to his mother. And so's Mr. Brown. In his way.'

'Have you?'

'Times without number, Mr. Mansfield. I've pleaded with her.'

'You might have done better to smack her face and drag her out of bed.' A brief flash of irritation in the pain, the weakness.

'She's my wife.'

The rebuke rang for all its half-heartedness.

'What makes you think I shall do any better?'

'She's always looked up to you. When we didn't know what to do, about the boys, she'd say, "You ask that Mr. Mansfield." And lately she's ever so proud to know you, when you've invited us up to your house. Like friends. She often mentions you.'

'Has she done so since she's been in bed?'

'No.' Resignation blurred his expression. 'She's hardly spoken.'

Now, by the door, Hapgood waited, like a patient butler, the signal to admit his master upstairs.

'Suppose I say all this, and it has a bad effect?'

'You won't, Mr. Mansfield. You know how to put it.'

'What happens is utterly unpredictable.' Petulant, now, impressing the man, cruelly putting him in his place. 'Nobody knows what her reaction will be.'

'You wouldn't want to hurt her, Mr. Mansfield.'

'It's nothing to do with wanting. If I tell her to pull herself together, then she may do something dreadful.'

'You mean kill herself, try to kill herself again?'

'That, yes. Or withdraw completely. Or die, give life up.'

'The doctor didn't say anything like that.'

'The risk is always there. If we attempt to interfere with another human being's personality, then the consequences may be dire.' That sounded rotund, objective, grave. As long as he could sit here mouthing words, masking his cowardice with specious eloquence, he felt safe, began to revive.

'I don't know what to say, Mr. Mansfield.' The hesitancy contrasted miserably with the strength of his voice.

'I'll see her if you wish.'

It was almost incredible, but in the last minutes he had forgotten the woman upstairs, the man he was talking to, his own ordeal.

'All right.'

Hapgood had the door open. Sluggishly Mansfield pulled himself from the chair, stumped upwards. They halted on the landing in front of the bedroom door which was closed.

'Shall I look in, first?'

Mansfield nodded, shivered again in the chill. The wallpaper behind him felt smoothly damp to his hands. As Hapgood opened the door, the landing brightened garish with sunshine. The two men entered.

With a shock of surprise, Mansfield saw that the room had been freshly decorated. The woodwork, door, window, skirting-board and the old-fashioned metal fire-place were all painted a sober pink, salmon gloss, not unbecoming. The chimney-breast was papered in a striking pattern of massed stylised flower-clumps, in dark blue, with yellow and scarlet thickly outlined in black. The other walls gleamed nondescript white, silver wheat-ears. A navy carpet stretched wall to wall and the bed's coverlet, brand-new, was a striking green. A modern veneered dressing-table in a corner, the light oak of a bed, was the only other furniture. The whole effect startled, spoke of newness, a brash jazz of colour.

He needed to turn to see the invalid, whose head was by the passage wall. She was sitting up, a pale blue bedjacket over her nightgown, with an open copy of the *Guardian Journal* by her hand.

He asked how she was.

174

Her face was pale, and her hair untidy; she wasn't wearing her dentures, while her glasses, pearl-grey rims, straddled her nose crookedly. Quietly, but audibly, she replied, and attempted to tidy the sheets of newspaper. Her husband took up a position by the dressing-table, demanded, a sergeant-major, if she'd like a glass of lemonade. Her answer, that she would, was again perfectly clear.

As she drank her husband completed the folding of the paper, then replaced her glass. She ordered him to fetch Mansfield a chair in from the front room.

'He can sit on the bed. He's not a proud chap.'

She pursed her lips and obediently he left the room. Mansfield said he was glad she felt better, adding pleasantly she'd soon be downstairs and outside.

'I don't know about that.'

'What exactly is the trouble then?'

'I've no strength. If I try to walk my legs go from under me. The same with my arms. Well, you saw me with that newspaper.'

'Has the doctor,' Mansfield, standing, had confidence in himself, 'given you any indication why this should be so?'

Her husband blustered back with the chair, made the visitor sit, and then perched himself on the sill of the sash-window. The interruption, noisily hearty, precluded conversation, but immediately, on quiet, she said:

'He doesn't think there's anything wrong with me.'

'I see.'

'He doesn't know anything.' Aggressive whine.

'What does he put the trouble down to?'

'It's all in the mind.'

'And that isn't true, then?'

She did not answer, but plucked uncomfortably at the neck of her bed-jacket, as if to cover herself. After some moments, Hapgood, said, bullying:

'Mr. Mansfield has asked you a question, Clara.'

'What was that?'

Hapgood snorted disgust, seemed to bang his back on

a window pane. Patiently, Mansfield reworded his query. She considered, thrusting her bottom lip out, and answered:

'I don't know. Nobody does.'

'Well, then. You're probably right. Nobody does know. But are you going to do anything about it?'

'I could no more get out of this bed and get dressed than I could grow wings and fly.'

'The doctor doesn't think so.'

'He's only a young man. If our Fred came in with his black bag and told me I could walk, I wouldn't believe him. And he's older than this man, better qualified.'

'That's hardly a fair comparison, Mrs. Hapgood. But if you saw your husband about to jump out of the window, or you realised there was a rapidly spreading fire in the house, could you use your legs then?'

'I don't know.'

Hapgood rapped the pane behind him, said coarsely:

'I'll open up, and we'll see.'

The other two ignored him.

'Mrs. Hapgood,' Mansfield said, 'will you try to get up for tea?'

'I can't.'

'Will you try?'

'It isn't any use. I can't use my limbs.'

Mansfield turned about, brusquely, reassuring himself, so immersed in action that he paid no attention either to himself or the woman. Like a conjurer, a huckster, he lifted the small clock from the mantelpiece.

'What time do you have tea?' he asked Hapgood.

'Half past four to five.'

'It's within a few minutes of three now. This is what I suggest. You rest for an hour, and at four-thirty your husband will help you downstairs. You need only to put on your dressing-gown and slippers. We'll get the tea ready while you look at television. Will you do it?'

'It won't be any use.'

176

'Will you try?'

It was like these tussles he'd had as a schoolmaster, harassing pupil with a show of firmness, while the brunt of the struggle was borne elsewhere, by smaller boys or the parents.

Mrs. Hapgood burst into tears.

She cried in frenzy for a few seconds, then controlled herself as if emotional reserves were drained. She sniffed, felt blindly about the bed for a handkerchief, but made no attempt to turn her face away from the two men who were watching her. In the end Mansfield pulled a handkerchief from his pocket, and passed it to her. She mopped her face, and tried to hand it back. Ludicrously he waved it away. As she sat now, bony wrists crossed, she appeared so normal that he thought of offering her a comb, as to an unreasonable child in the hope that an everyday action would cure its tantrum. Suddenly she said, in anger:

'Leave me alone.'

'I'd like you to lie down, please. And forget us all till four-thirty. We'll lay the cream buns out downstairs, and then fetch you.'

'Lie down, then, Clara.' Hapgood came across, began to unbutton the bed-jacket, but she brushed him away, swivelled over on to her side. Solemnly, her husband pulled and smoothed the bed-clothes, looked for enlightenment from Mansfield.

When the two arrived downstairs, Mansfield instructed his host to rest in an arm-chair. Bossily he drew the curtains, and the pair settled. In a very few minutes, Hapgood had nodded off, but Mansfield nagged over in his mind what he had done that afternoon. Pride jostled uncertainty; he'd spoken his piece with firm reason, but he remembered the burst into tears, dreading an equivalent collapse when they tried to walk her downstairs. The curtains moved, letting in straggles of light. Hapgood snuffled.

David would have rested. He was used to control, knew that any one of four methods would work if he pushed it hard enough. But his father could not even employ a mode that was in itself perfect, because he'd haver, switch tactics, do nothing with certainty. He saw too many sides, and had lost the power to assume responsibility. Every sentence he used upstairs he now altered, in vocabulary, in tone; he tried other approaches, but inside a quarter of an hour, with his eyes shut, he merely repeated words, feverishly, threshing over not with any hope of improvement, but in a whirl of physical uncontrol. He did not accuse himself of acting fecklessly, but merely felt his tense body pump, heave him into hot discomfort. Sweat troubled his face; his chest tightened while all the time sentences clanged and re-echoed in his head: 'You realised there was a rapidly spreading fire; you, you there, realised that a rapidly spreading, spreading, fire, if it was borne on you, if you grasped, a conflagration, a burning fiery furnace, you, you, realised . . .' His brain reiterated words to pummel him. Hapgood snored, but, he, the outsider, the stranger, had his head beaten about by the madness of weakness.

As he walked to the kitchen to fetch a glass of water he noticed that the other man stirred, murmured to himself. As he looked into the sunshine of the yard with its green painted gate Mansfield wondered if she slept, upstairs. He opened the back door to September warmth, walked to the bottom of the garden, sat on the wall, stared at the nearly complete greenhouse and returned. Within five minutes the mad words wounded his skull again, until he ached for release. When he finally dozed, he jerked violently forward, and momentarily imagined that he had been thrown on to the carpet.

At five minutes to four he took a turn outside, making himself pause, naming the dahlias, chrysanthemums, the Michaelmas daisies. The leaves on the lime-tree at the far end were brown-edged, shrivelling. He sat watching a vapour trail in the blue-green sky, sneezed, went indoors, woke Hapgood, who mumbled, dazed, stumbling, out of his wits. Mansfield in panic thought the man must have had a stroke in his sleep.

They put the kettle on, slowly laid the cloth. Out in the scullery, Mansfield cut the bread into fancy triangles, spread them with butter, meat-paste, ham. The cake tins were full with bought confections which they arranged on dishes, moving one, another, this way, that, old children pottering with toys. When the kettle whistled Mansfield said, steadily:

'Go upstairs and wake her up. When you're sure she's wide awake, get her out of bed, put her dressing-gown and slippers on. Take her to the toilet. In ten minutes exactly I'll come up. If you want me before that time, then shout.'

Mansfield waited, mashed tea, cosied the pot.

The operation worked to perfection. Mrs. Hapgood groaned, dithered as the old men issued instructions, hampered, helped. When in front of the electric fire, she dropped into a chair and closed her eyes, her husband's elation was so great that he said:

'The dying duck.'

That wry phrase summed the victory. After a time, Mrs. Hapgood ate a little, smiled, watched television. The men vied in praising her and each other. At seven, she returned to bed, on her hands and knees, and Mansfield prepared to leave.

'I don't know how to thank you, Mr. Mansfield,' Hapgood said at the front door. 'Nobody else could have done it.'

Again they complimented each other in the evening sunshine, finally shaking hands. Mansfield drove home delighted, wondering why he'd been so tremulous this morning.

When the phone rang he expected Hapgood and a further bout of self-commendation. It was Eleanor.

'Is that you, father? I've been trying to get you all afternoon.'

He began an explanation, which she cut short.

'David's in hospital.'

'Is it serious?'

'An ulcer. He was very ill in the night. Passing blood. He went in this morning, early.'

'How long?'

'The consultant says it depends. They're carrying out tests, of course.'

'He didn't say anything when he was up here.'

'No. I don't suppose he would.'

'But wouldn't he be on a special diet? Or have to eat a little often?'

'He wouldn't make a fuss. You wouldn't notice.'

She spoke from weariness, and he, this afternoon's great physician, was put in his place. He hadn't noticed his son's pain. And David had taken care not to bother him, him the healer. He licked his lips, sat with dissatisfaction, defeat.

Eleanor talked on, neatly as always. 'He wouldn't say anything to you, because he's got odd ideas about illness. If you're sick, you're weak in some way. You let yourself down.'

'Hasn't he been under treatment then?'

'Yes. He's been off for some months. But he looks on the doctor as a fool. What's the use of prescribing rest, when there's work?'

'It's this American business?'

'It's his whole damned life. He drives himself as he drives everybody else. And his body gets its own back. But he's been strutting, dishing it out, and now he's paying.'

'It serves him right?'

'His illness is the exact result of his way of life, if that's the same thing. He won't take advice, and now he's flat on his back.'

'You told him so?'

He heard her catch her breath, then she snapped:

'Why did you say that?'

'You sound angry, Eleanor. As if it's somebody's fault.'

'I'm sorry. I was up half the night, and now all this.'

'He'll have to go steady.'

'Can you see that happening?'

He kept her talking until she seemed easier, until she began to bully him gently about his own health. By the time they had finished, both were laughing, but ten minutes later he was shaking with weakness.

⚛ 14 ⚛

Mansfield found it difficult to sift the information about David's illness.

First there was talk of an operation, of treatment, then another set of specialists were summoned for consultation. In call after call, he nagged Eleanor, but she seemed always to offer slightly altered versions. In the end he spoke his fear.

'Look, Eleanor, are you being frank with me?'

'Yes.'

'Well, you're frightening me to death. Every day there's some new expert with some new line on the scene. Your local men can manage an ulcer, can't they?'

'That's the rich, father. The money. You can buy a dozen opinions.'

'I don't believe . . .'

'They think there might be something wrong with his heart. They don't honestly seem to know.'

'You mean,' Mansfield said, 'they won't tell you.'

'Of course they would. But they're not sure. They're testing him. And resting him.'

'Has he had anything wrong before, with his heart?'

'Not really.'

'What do you mean, Eleanor? "Not really"? It's not fair. I'm not a child.'

'There hasn't been much. What you'd call "a turn", apparently, in the office. I didn't know. I saw him the same day as the last one, and he never said a word.'

'The last?'

'It appears so. There may be some small defect. But they're absolutely optimistic. He won't be an invalid. The heart man swore that he'd be able to lead a normal life.'

'I don't like it, Eleanor.'

'I'm not exactly enjoying it.'

Immediately he apologised, and she promised that he could come down to set his mind at rest by seeing David. Now he was childishly afraid. Pessimism ordered his life; nothing could go right. He daren't embark on a small repair, or a shopping expedition. He dreaded the phone, but hated to be absent from it for more than an hour.

His only real pleasure was writing to Sarah.

They'd begun the correspondence as soon as she'd returned to school and had written to thank him for her stay. Her letter wasn't long, but it had sharp sketches of some of the staff, the local rector, one or two of the girls. He'd replied at length, giving his opinion of the weaknesses and strengths of the teaching profession, and in her answer she'd questioned some of his theorising. They went at it hammer and tongs for two letters, and by then the habit was fixed.

Sarah wrote twice a week, and he did not send a reply until he'd received a letter, though he wrote every day. They had an argument about the value of history, and he was delighted, recommending books to her. She reported which of these were in the school library and what the senior mistress said about his list. They even discussed if it were unhealthy for a girl and her grandfather to write in this way.

He loved the exchanges, especially now when the street seemed full of crying children, screams he could not bear.

Daisy's opinions were canvassed, and now and then a note from her was enclosed, precious, high-flying, but funny. The child was not only very clever, but she had no respect for any achievement or opinion; if she could make a verbal score she would. It seemed heartless to him, but she'd tear into an opponent as she'd knock down skittles, and he imagined she'd be as surprised at an expression of hurt or anger as if she heard the wood squeal.

Outside these sheets of paper, he lugged his pessimism glumly around. It seemed a physical matter, an aching of bones, a clutch in the bowels. He knew the cause.

The one standard in his life was his son's success.

For forty years now David had done magnificently, at home, school, college, work, management, directorships, finance. Physically he'd been magnificent, handing off, swooping along the boundary, hurling the javelin. He had married a beautiful woman, of the nobility, had fathered lively paragons of children. Behind him stood a series of houses, each larger than the last. The luxurious cars, capped chauffeurs, subserviently efficient office and domestic staff were tributes as eloquent as the press references, the magazine articles to the man's supremacy.

And the father had made his son into God.

When Annie Mansfield died, her husband was comforted by his son's brilliant degree, his exciting burst into research. That seemed ridiculous now, grossly tasteless, but could not be denied. The twenty-two years of marriage, the sudden onset of expected death, seemed less important than that B.Sc., that quickly following Ph.D. Whatever James Mansfield had done in the last four decades, there stood guaranteed the worldly success of his son, and the boy's constant statement of affection for the father who'd given him the opportunity.

Now Mansfield knew that David might die, might leave his children unprovided for, his wife in penury. That was unlikely; the man was thickly insured but the new uncertainty about his wealth drove the father to extremes of alarm.

As he thought this out, sifted fantasy from real fear, he knew that the end of his expectations counted most. David should grow, grab larger honours, ease his old man's death-bed with some solider show of world-astounding achievement.

Now he lay flat, fighting for his life, skin and bones in a physician's care.

Mansfield kept his terror to himself. When Hapgood appeared, for advice, with praise, he was well received.

'There's one thing I'd like to ask of you, Mr. Mansfield. A great favour.'

'Go on, then.'

'I don't really like . . . It's cheeky, like.'

'Oh, go on, man.'

'Well, if you're sure you don't mind. Now she's done a few steps up the garden and in the street I wonder if you'd ask her to come up and visit you here. I'd like that to be her first proper outing. It was you as got her up, Mr. Mansfield, and I'll never forget it. She wouldn't have done it for a no other man.'

'That's not true.'

But he believed it; in his depression, he longed to have done, even to be credited with, something valuable.

The pair came up in style to salmon and tinned fruit. Mrs. Hapgood made a show of walking about the garden, exhibiting her health. She did not act credibly, and as Mansfield mounted his pretence of watching her every step, he hated the lined face with its vacuous puritan pride. Why should this scarecrow walk while his son dared not move? A line from *Julius Caesar* branded itself in his mind:

' 'Tis true, this god did shake.'

His beautiful David cracked, uncertain, prey to death, while these two old caricatures hawked their smiles and gladrags round his paths. What life? What equity?

In his bitterness, he asked about Tom, to embarrass them.

Their faces turned sour; Hapgood blushed. The two looked at each other, guiltily, undecided whether they should hog their secret. In the end, the mother pulled herself together, said:

'He came over to see us, just yesterday.'

'Wanted money.'

'He'd moved jobs three or four times since we went that time to see him.' Her clayey face inclined backwards, mouth black for air. 'You tell Mr. Mansfield, Alf.' She sat on a garden seat blowing. Hapgood came nearer.

'He picked up with a woman.' Low voice, eyes suspiciously round the shrubs. 'And he's having to have treatment now.'

Mansfield was not listening; the god did shake; incomprehension showed on his face.

'At the venereal disease clinic. Perth House.'

'I'm sorry.'

'Picking up some filthy woman like that.'

'It's a disgrace,' she said. She, her husband, were slimy with his filth, sore with his pox. 'He can't seem to take a step right. But fancy catching that.'

'Even he looked down in the mouth. But he told us straight out and then asked for money.'

'Is he still living with her?'

'I don't know. I couldn't make out. I was that upset. And he never tells you anything if he can hide it. I asked him if she was having treatment and he says, "I don't know, I told her to."'

Like a sick girl.

Chemically, genetically there could hardly be a sniff of difference between the college principal, the consultant physician and this labourer, without the sense to wipe his arse. He'd stayed behind to batten on his parents.

'What did you do?' Mansfield asked. He did not want the answer.

'What could I do? I gave him five pounds and he had his tea with us. He couldn't even say thank you, not properly. Broke down. Sat in front of the fire and cried like a child, didn't he, Clara?'

'As if he'd break his heart.'

'He knew, Mr. Mansfield. He knew what we thought. But it was awful to see him with a hole in the knee of his trousers. A cigarette burn. I gave him an old pair of flannels of mine, and his mother patched his. She shouldn't.'

The mother sighed, creaking the seat.

'And yet I wanted him out of the house. I hated Clara touching his trousers. As if he'd contaminate us with his filth.'

'He's our son, Alf. '

'And I wish to God he wasn't.'

'You shouldn't say that.'

'I'll say what I think. He's dirty . . .' He broke off, acquiescing with his wife's expression.

'You've not seen anything of his wife, have you?' Mansfield to the rescue.

'Enid? No, nor likely to. She's gone off somewhere. I saw her sister in the street the other day. She could do with a good wash.'

Mansfield weighed his ill against theirs, but found no comfort. David must die, in a clean bed, under care he'd paid for; this other son would shamefacedly take his shot or two of penicillin, and slouch off to his next misdemeanour. He should die and then his parents could remember him as a child, could look on old photographs with pleasure again. All that was unlikely; accident-prone, he'd manage to outlive them and then waste the few hundred pounds they left him.

The visit passed heavily; they had difficulty getting Mrs. Hapgood back into the car.

Mansfield took a train to Hampshire.

These days he hated travelling, fussed, pestered railway officials for information, could not settle, read desultorily.

186

He remembered journeys in crowded trains in two wars, and to his recollection he'd enjoyed himself. Now as he humped in a first-class compartment, he fell into conversation with the only other occupant, a white-haired woman with stork legs, who complained about the rise in the cost of living. Her northern voice was blurred as if her nostrils were pinched in, and from moment to moment she flashed her glasses at him, her baby-blue eyes, as she licked at the lipstick on her thin mouth.

Once encouraged, she crackled on. She was seventy-six years of age, a widow. She'd invested in a house or two, had an annuity, a son and daughter were 'very good to her'. But one could not get repairs done, nor expect either civility or service at the shops. The government wasn't interested in her, Tory or not. And yet there were people drawing National Assistance to idle about on. The roads in the subsidised housing estates were cluttered with brand-new cars. Black men were buying up decent property to convert it to slums.

Oddly, he thought, and he did not attempt to argue, there was no mention of the young, students, drugs, permissive sex. Her complaints put simply seemed to claim that everybody, black and white, had much the same income, and the servility her own previous advantage had been able to buy was now at nobody's or anybody's beck. She'd had money, and used it. Those days were done. He wondered what she'd pawned to buy a first-class ticket. The witch's jaw waggled. 'I couldn't afford to travel in here if my son had not sent me the fare. He won't have me go second. They make no attempt to look after you.' And yet two minutes later she mentioned her broker, and some sort of investment her solicitor was suggesting. 'He's a friend, you know. Realises how I am placed.'

Fascinated at the thin lips, the crooked flailing jaw, the five rings on one finger, the painted nails, Mansfield was repelled, then in the stuffy carriage, suddenly wretchedly ill. He staggered to the toilet, washed dizzily, sat on the seat in the lurch and racket, before he pulled himself together.

No sooner was he back in the compartment than she drove at him again. He hated her. She should be investigating death not unit trusts. She flailed a gold propelling pencil at him, scavenged through her hand-bag, consulted a magnificently flashing watch to conclude, not without satisfaction, that the train was late again. He mentioned David's illness.

Immediately her interest was caught, and she described her time in a private ward. She had been paying insurance for years, the surgeons and nurses were admirable, but she had her grievances. Nobody had understood the extent of her pain; they neglected her, if briefly, when she needed attention; the meals were skimped; they sent her home too soon.

Mansfield decided she liked to complain. The revelation cooled him; he felt almost well. His own condition must be odd when a snap conclusion, however accurate, about a fellow-human-being could improve his health so radically, and rapidly. He listened all the way to London, so that by the time he stepped off, raising his hat, at St. Pancras he knew how much her dentist husband had left, her son earned as a dental surgeon, her daughter's husband had paid for the last house. Everything was priced; he expected to be slipped a bill. To conversation in train, say, five guineas. That would cover expenses. To listening. To doing oneself good making guesses. He pitied the porter swinging her bags; ten new pence.

Eleanor met him at Alton, informed him that David was out of hospital.

The sun shone warmly yellow; flower beds reflected the vivid light. David in a pullover, with an open-necked shirt, was sitting behind glass in an armchair with his feet up. His appearance was normal; perhaps he remained still longer than he did usually, but his smile was as broad, his handshake as strong.

'Well, young man, what have you been up to?'

'You can't have all the heart-attacks to yourself.'

'Jealous?'

'Hot favourite for the grave stakes. Sit down, dad.'

At once, he'd spotted that the trivial exchange upset his father, but he did not apologise. After a short silence, he straightened his face and explained his illness. He was a few pounds overweight; he could smoke less; he'd got to cut down his hours of work, and increase his exercise time. Yes, it was true that there seemed to be a slight organic defect, but none of the consultants wanted to be dogmatic about this. It might be important; he'd better take it steady.

David delivered this affably, in his deep, board-room voice The reasonable tone, choice of language, settled his father, who liked to think himself a man capable of hearing the truth, but the look of concern, slight amusement on the son's face took away the seriousness. They were not speaking of death, now, but of some matter like, oh, a common cold, unpleasant, unavoidable, but transient. When the pair walked round the garden before five o'clock tea and scones, they chaffed each other, enjoyed catechism, exposition.

The American business looked even more promising than expected. A couple of his young men had now taken up a series of inventions that would mean enormous profits inside two or three years. David's voice warmed.

'They were superb. They noticed and then grabbed.'

'I always thought nothing in industry could be trusted. Mightn't somebody come up with a better process to supersede yours?'

With clarity David explained why he thought not. The technical details, and David spared him nothing, baffled, but it appeared that once Uniflex had cornered the market, new lines would of necessity be brought first to them, even with foreign concerns.

'Industrial espionage?' Mansfield sounded knowledgeable.

Another fascinating parenthesis. David would have made a remarkable teacher. Even when he puzzled with technicalities, he never allowed attention to fade unduly. But the marvellous thing was the life of the man. He lived; he dazzled with a bursting intelligence; even in this quiet invalid's voice there promised another hundred years of power, of command. Mansfield himself felt livelier, younger on the impact of his son's personality. Now he could argue his son's mortality, face it, because death had nothing to do with this big man, this brain, this quiet explosion of life.

'David, you do me good.'

The son's smile broke, river in spate, clouds dropping fatness.

'For a schoolmaster, you're a marvellous listener. I like nothing better than explaining a process, or putting a case to you. You hear me, project yourself onto what I mean.'

His father loved him, then.

Whenever Eleanor joined them, all three succeeded. They talked about the children, especially Sarah, and after Mansfield had given an account of the correspondence David expanded.

'That's marvellous, dad. She's a clever girl and if you manage to make her appreciate what she's about, she'll be top-rate.'

'Why don't you?'

'I'm a non-believer now. I've just lost all taste for academic knowledge.'

'Don't you believe him, father,' Eleanor said. 'He's trying to get you into an argument. He still reads scientific journals. He's not just on the look-out for industrial tips.'

'That's true.' David spread wide fingers, ran them neatly through thick hair. 'But it's as if dad here were working some desperate little croft in Scotland, all rock and sweat. Now and then he'd read a poem, for relief, for rest, a touch of colour. He wouldn't have time, or energy, to do it often. In fact, it'd be a marvel if he did it at all, but being himself, he would. But if it was a case of choosing between next year's crops and a poem, I know what even you'd do, dad.'

'Surely, both are important . . .'

'I'm talking about a desperate situation. Barren ground, twenty-four hours' slog a day to raise a pittance.'

'Is that how you are?'

'Exactly.'

'Raising a pittance?' They all laughed.

'No. But as fully occupied. That's one thing schoolmasters don't understand. Long hours, no holidays, killing worry.'

'It's easy to see you've never been at the front of a class. You can't disguise the fact that teaching's hard work. When I knocked off at four o'clock . . .'

'You finished at four.'

'Reading, marking.'

'If you didn't do it, nobody'd be the wiser.'

'My conscience . . .'

'I'm not denying some schoolmasters slave. But I've been working a fifteen hour day regularly week in, week out for the past six months.'

'You couldn't do a fifteen hour day teaching for one week. You'd soon be dead.'

'That's what he very nearly is,' Eleanor interrupted.

'Thanks.'

They loved to needle. Mansfield imagined that this son was so far advanced in the hierachy that no one argued with him now, except when he paid lawyers or engineers to offer mild criticisms of his schemes.

'When you've stopped boasting,' Eleanor chaffed them, 'perhaps you'll help me think about tomorrow's dinner.'

'We retired men . . .' David.

'Senior citizens.'

Mansfield revelled in this hour, with its cups of weak Indian tea, and buttered scones. They'd sit, talk, plan, obey Eleanor and then the youngest child would bounce in, flop on to her mother's feet, and charm or ignore them. Sometimes they'd stay so long that they'd barely time to prepare themselves for dinner.

Once, mischeviously, Mansfield asked David:

'Can Eleanor cook?'

'Of course.'

'She could manage a meal?'

'If she had to. Yes.'

'She never does, though.'

'There's no need. You might see her in the kitchen. Now and again. Trying something out. I shall tell her what you've asked me.'

'How are the pair of you getting on?'

'Well.' The son never exaggerated on serious matters.

'What about all this talk of riling each other? If I remember you rightly, you couldn't watch her eating an apple or reading a book without being driven wild.'

'That's what I thought.'

'But,' said Mansfield, 'it's not so now?'

'It's not so now. I know. We could have divorced and never found out we'd get over it.'

'Is there any love, David?'

'I'm fond. We'll leave it there.' He'd seemed extraordinarily gentle. 'Or better. You go and ask her.'

'Do I have to report the answer?'

'I think I know what it is.'

David's attractiveness sounded there. A man who knew his mind was not afraid to speak it.

'We're not doing too badly,' Eleanor said to his enquiry.

'A modest claim.'

They crossed a wide road, Eleanor primly driving, into a hedged lane. She pulled into the grass verge.

'It's shaken him up.'

'Of course. He's more dependent on you now.'

'I don't know about that. We've money . . . No, we're right enough, father.'

'He won't leave you?'

'Oh? Once he's better. I've been surprised how well we've got on since he's been home. Honestly. That's all.'

'But it's not love.'

'No. I shouldn't think so. Can you have love between man and wife without the sex thing? I suppose you can. Lots of people claim . . . Mutual respect. Care. Protectiveness. Comfort.' She tapped the wheel as she listed the words. 'They don't appeal to me much.'

'What do you want, then? A shattering affair?'

'To be left alone,' she said.

'I'm sorry.'

'I didn't mean by you.' She spoke to his corner of the huge windscreen. 'I'm frightened. He seemed fit, and then down he goes. It might be one of the children next. Sarah. Oh, I don't know. Nothing's stable. Anything could, will happen.'

'This has taken it out of you, Eleanor.'

'Has it?'

They sat in awkward silence on the cushioned seats. She tried, he thought, to escape, to skim amongst the trees, the hawthorn bushes, but only with her eyes, to project herself out of the comfortable warm reality of the car, into the air, the branches, before metal and leather disintegrated, rusting her, tangling her in their ruin.

'I'm lucky,' she said, distantly still. 'He recovered. Your wife died.'

'She wasn't much older than David.'

'Were you . . . ?' she began. 'Were you . . .?'

'I can't remember. I've one or two little memories. Like verses on scent-cards. They've been fixed. Somebody fetched me out of the classroom. I knew she was going to die, but it shouldn't have been then. It churned me. Her heart packed in. But it was a shock, even though I'd prepared myself.'

Eleanor had placed a hand on his arm.

'But I'd David. It was as if I could switch off from my loss at home, and concentrate on him. I was lucky. My sort of personality must have allowed that.'

'I never knew David's mother.'

'No. He is like her in some things. Go-getter. Wanted

her way. But there wasn't much opportunty when she was housebound. She blossomed in the war. W.V.S. Evacuees. Oh, she could run them around.'

'And you?'

'Me?'

'Chase you about. Make you fly.' Eleanor's voice laughed.

'I suppose so. She never interfered with school. But I grant you things were done her way in the house.'

'So it was a relief?' Why must she pry?

'Not in that sense.' He'd answer honestly. 'She'd been so ill for some months that I had to look after domestic arrangements. It meant less work and worry for me, not more. Annie was a brave woman. Nobody wants to die at forty-five, but she sat still under it, didn't give way very often.'

'Sometimes?'

'Yes.' He sucked breath in. 'She had pain, heavy discomfort and no chance of a cure. One of these is enough to depress most of us.'

'What will happen to me if David dies?'

'Financially?' He was glad her importunity gave him the chance to probe.

'Partly. Though we should be able to live. The children would go to exactly the same schools. No. He's alive. Even when I hated him, he was there, a big somebody. It probably sounds ridiculous to say this, but even if we had been divorced, I'd have been comforted to know that somewhere, married to somebody else, starting a new family, David Mansfield existed, threw his weight about.'

'Why do you say that, now?'

'I was very young when we first met. I haven't been attracted to anybody else. I thought I had, but this is my only serious love. I don't know whether that's good or not.' She sounded genuinely amused.

'D'you know, Eleanor, I think of you as experienced, knowing all about everything.'

'I was eighteen when I saw him first. I'm not any wiser, now.'

'You cover it very efficiently.'

'It's true. I've children. I sit on committees and give orders, but I'm no more stable or mature than I was when I left school.'

'Except you don't love David?'

'He wasn't in our firm, even, then. My mother was dead, and I used to go with daddy to conferences. He was with Line Halstead, then, pretty well straight out of university. He drew attention to himself, somehow. Just stood up and proved somebody's basic mathematics was wrong. Some real big wig. And he upped and said so, off the cuff. Of course, Gervase Ford was after him like a shot. You must have heard all this?'

He had; he could not hear it often enough.

All gleamed gold behind the hedges; the distant farm-house on its plough-land, the bungalows in fir-trees shone richly under a high sky, scarred with cloud-wisps. Life had value; Mansfield sat proud.

'I would say,' his voice at the beginning of the sentence already sounded to him like those pulpit-pundits of his youth, oily with certainty, 'that you've exactly described middle-aged love. That was superb, describing your excitement at knowing he was chucking his weight about somewhere.'

'Perhaps you're right.' Weary?

'You don't sound convinced.'

'I don't sound anything.'

She'd had enough, and he, rebuffed, did not press her. In time she drove on, but stopped twice for the view, once making him get out, and walk a little way into a field past a copse to look across the valley, though now, in the late after-noon, mist dulled the bright edges.

When they arrived home, he was almost asleep, and she showed her concern, insisting that he put his feet up.

'I'm not good for you,' she said.

'I've thoroughly enjoyed myself.'

'You're the only person I can really talk to. Do you know, David told me once, when we first married, and he was away from home in a hotel, he got squiffy on whisky and spilt all his troubles to some man he'd just met. I thought that was good. I was a bit jealous, at the time. But when I talk to you I say the wrong things, don't I? You like plain black-and-white. Perhaps it's because you had to deal with boys all the time.'

He bridled. Insulted.

'And you're more subtle.'

'And awkward, and cruel, and capricious. I wish I weren't when I'm talking to you.'

'Isn't everybody?'

'I don't think so. Some, yes. But not everybody. Now you have a sleep until I bring tea in.'

That was true. At the end of an interview with Eleanor he might glow with love, or hate in deflation. At least, she lived, matched David in brightness, in superior unexpected élan; a goddess, godless high queen, she did not inhabit his world, obey its limiting statutes, but moved elsewhere, accepted or spurned his humdrum sacrifices. To see her walk from the room was to recognise her quality.

As he questioned his judgement, he remembered Annie.

Her father had been rector of Colston, in the valley of the Trent, a still place with a great Victorian church towering over the road and the trees. She'd never worked, except for her father, but had spent her holidays on the Mediterranean or the Near East from her childhood. She read widely, spoke her mind, refused him at the first proposal. He did not remember that too often, but she'd said as they sat in the rectory garden, flushed with kissing, 'No, James, I couldn't think of leaving my father.' That summed him; a poor exchange for a handsome widowed clergyman. In his mortification, he'd dug the lawn with his heels, stood, half-strangled, wished her good-bye and hared off, his eyes prickling with tears. He could hear her reproachful sentence, now. 'But daddy's expecting you to tea.'

It was only later he'd realised how she had schemed for the invitation, for the rector, like most selfish people, ignored or charmed rivals out of existence. The suitor had blundered in too soon with his proposal, before she'd made her mind up, and so she'd spoken out, turned him down, without thought for consequence. That girl, hair untidy, cheeks bright, bore no relationship to the woman he'd married, who'd run his home like clockwork and yet had time to take a bus twice a week to organise her father. It was odd that he thought of her as a solemn, middle-aged woman, ruling the roost, not averse to correcting him on a point of scholarship, reading his paper more carefully than he, choosing his books, telling him what he should think. Only when the war came, and she worked outside, was he left to decide for himself, though he found he had lost the taste for mastery. When she was finally taken ill, he nursed her carefully, found he could sometimes contradict her, slaved meticulously at her bed. Now and then she looked at him, as if to make some demand over and above the trivialities of illness, but it came to little. He kissed her, without affection, because it was his duty, as he cleaned up after her incontinence. The discipline he enjoyed; it wrote a manageable timetable, and though he could see people were sorry for him, he thought they misjudged his plight. Fatigue brought him near despair sometimes, but he was healthy, hated illness, but not aggrieved at the chores with which her illness saddled him. But he did not remember her now in her sickness. The strong woman who'd dominated the home, could take the high-spirited David on, who'd made her forces' canteen the most efficient in the Midlands, remained but only vaguely in his head, as a sort of trance, a dark smear.

What he knew now was that he had chosen the right mother for his son. She liked her own way, and argued to get it. Intelligent, she'd make fun of some enthusiasm until the youngster learned to come to her with a perfectly prepared case, and even then she'd niggle, and retire disappointed when he beat her. She could praise because she could discriminate. David had won his scholarships for his mother, to earn that dry word of commendation which was hardly softened, qualified by a motherly hug or kiss. She never commented on his degree result, but both her men knew what she would have said. 'You've beaten them all, David. I'll say this for you, you're never satisfied with second best. Good boy.'

She'd be getting on, now, not so old as the woman in the train, but near the age of complaint. If she'd have lived she would not have shared her husband's slight disapointment, unease, about David's apostasy from academic work. Professor Sir David Mansfield, F.R.S? Not today, baker. Power fretted in her veins; she knew what counted. But oldish, sixty-five, she'd have been slower, smouldering against Eleanor, comparing her son's progress with his father's, that potterer about seed-beds. He tried to think of her again, hair awry, in the garden, beautiful because she'd refused him, because she'd confidence she would be asked again, because she was embarrassed, excited, caught off guard. That recall, his only memory of her beauty, hands flying to the tousle of her hair, seemed precious to him, but a fiction he'd made up. At one time he could not bear to remember the rebuff; now it seemed unique, like an anecdote in a sermon, larger than life, the power of God let loose in make-believe.

That pleased him, to sit in the warmth with a glass of dry sherry, light glinting on the ornate frames of mirrors, the two Allan Ramsays, the unfashionable green-grey Paul Nash. He could think kindly of death, as a pageant, a stately procession. 'And so beside the silent sea, I wait the muffled oar.' He remembered colleagues of his youth, heavy men born in the eighteen-sixties with walrus moustaches and waistcoats, not unlike the young men today. He attended their funerals; it seemed these solid mathematicians and classicists all spent their Sundays in small independent ugly chapels which dazzled now not in scrubbed drabness but by great surges of flowers on the coffin, the bellying white rawness of the wood, the opulent gold handles and plaques. Young Peter Vryenhoef, his exact contemporary who'd died of consumption at the age of twenty-five. His own baby sister Agnes. There seemed something monumental about his memory; people were all good, rogues and idlers, because they had died; he could even remember the corpses of France without rancour. Death seemed in these hours of sitting as the climax of living, a final examination, without class-lists, or prizes. He had no belief in after-life, merely in the supreme validity of death, a great act, a marvel, a miracle that every one brought off. He recalled Allan Ramsay painting at the bedside of his dead child; grief dissipated by technique.

He enjoyed his fantasy, but dismissed it as emanating from a foolish man, who, frightened out of his wits, reassured himself by naming his enemy as a friend. Let pain split his chest again, or David's, this would be seen for what it was worth, the embroidered relief of a helpless and recently terrified victim. Mansfield was no fool, but he pampered himself, indulged his imagination, sniffing the wine, eyeing the richness.

A letter from Sarah dashed him. It was forwarded from his house by a neighbour, and said that she wouldn't write while he was staying with her parents. She sent them a duty letter weekly. If this seemed unreasonable to him, then she couldn't justify her decision. 'I just don't want to send off long letters to their,' underlined, 'house.' She didn't dislike them, wasn't unhappy there in the holidays, but did not want to write our sort of letters to that place. Perhaps, she continued, she had written the vein out; it was done. One thing made her uncertain. They were doing *Twelfth Night* for 'A' Level. 'I know it's your favourite play, but really it is crummy rubbish.' They said as much to old Fothergill, and she'd partly agreed, but had said something like, 'Ibsen would certainly have made a fine problem play out of the marriage of Orsino and Viola.' But, Sarah continued, there was nothing in it for her. All those speeches 'Build me a willow-cabin' that he'd recited, and she could remember exactly, could bear his voice still, in fact he made one misquotation, but they meant nothing to her, were rhetoric, pantomime froth. It was worse because Shakespeare had so much talent; he ought to have concentrated on his Lears, not these puff-balls.

He swallowed his disappointment, answered her briefly telling her she must do as she thought fit but promising her unflinching argument about T.N. as soon as he was back home. But the tone of the letter riled and saddened him. Sarah wrote heartlessly, as if their former relationship had not existed. She had turned about for no reason except perhaps to show she could, had pushed him off as ruthlessly as if he'd rejected her in the first place. And so perhaps he had; the letter relied so little on reason that he could well believe a visit to her parents constituted betrayal in her mind. Or perhaps she'd had enough of the correspondence, and seized the least excuse to end it, but she was the adolescent, uncertain of herself, immature, a chaos of conflict. But it was he crept about the house, avoiding conversation, hurt to the quick.

When the following morning he received a letter from Alfred Hapgood he, sore still, dreaded opening the envelope.

'Dear Mr. Mansfield,' (the script was a fair copperplate), 'I write with sorrow to tell you that my dear wife died yesterday. Last week, just after you left she was walking downstairs. I don't know why she had gone up. She was supposed to be resting in her chair. Any road, I was out in the garden as I usually am after three-thirty finishing the greenhouse and she must have fallen. I didn't hear anything at all and I don't know how long she lay there. She was unconscious when I got in and partly wedging the stairs door. I phoned for an ambulance after I'd struggled to get her free. Both her arms were broken and a leg beside other injury. They put her in plaster, but pneumonia set in, and she died. It was as if she didn't want to live any more. She never really came round.'

The writer told him he was not to think of trying to return for the funeral, and begged his pardon for inflicting these troubles on him when he'd enough of his own. 'But I thought you'd want to know. Excuse more as I am very upset. It's terrible. I can't think she's gone. Everybody's very kind, you'd be surprised, but I haven't grasped it yet. Yours sincerely, Alfred Hapgood.'

The words hustled through his mind, like a gale in withered leaves. Turmoil, skirmishes, a sky black with wild shapes, noise-bitten. That decent old man using the hand he'd learnt sixty years back in the elementary school thrusting down this consummation, his pen uncouth and noble. Mansfield felt the pathos, but the schoolmaster in him, saving him from the full assault of meaning, improvised an exercise: Write the following in a more connected style. While my wife was coming downstairs last week, subordinate adverbial clause of time, she fell, main cause, though, etc., etc., concession. Oh God, these words, these grammatical counters, were all Hapgood had at the end of his marriage. Now the style seemed heroic, wrought iron against invading grief, but that metaphor misled. Style was the man. Hapgood at his kitchen table, pen on paper or in mouth, churning out information of death to the relatives, the friends. Cable to Africa, to New Zealand. Regret mother died Monday. Letter following. Love.

What would Shakespeare have said? Absent thee from felicity awhile. Is this the promised end? I took by the throat the circumcised dog. Doth thou not see the baby at my breast/That sucks the nurse asleep?

He stumbled up from the breakfast table in tears, watched by a wide-eyed grandson. Thrusting the letter in Eleanor's hand, he made for his room where he found himself breathless in a chair thinking of nothing but the pattern on the wallpaper, the position of the shoes he'd worn last night. Dost thou not see the baby? Words tumbled nonsensically in his head, acrobats in weakness. Clara, beloved wife, who'd tried to kill herself, who did not want to live. Shaking his head, aghast at himself, he realised this death was a matter of no importance. In three months' time Hapgood would have established a more comfortable routine, and the principal, the doctor, would have recited through the correct, expected incantations. As for Tom? He'd need an extra pint, or argument, or trip up a dark alley? Poor Tom's a-cold. But Clara herself, waiting for the fire? He thought of the wardrobe with its line of ugly frocks. The presses with neat-laid clothes. The tokens Hapgood would bruise his heart on, dropped hairpins, old newspapers she'd spread in drawers, opened packets of almonds, ranks of jam-jars.

David pushed the door open. He wore a dressing-gown for he'd been breakfasting in bed. He sat, crossed his legs, his arms.

'I'm sorry, dad. Eleanor's just told me.'

And by the expression of your face, my lad, you think she exaggerated. Sobbing. Feeling his way out like a blind man. Robert was terrified. Here he sits, calm and collected.

Mansfield nodded, business-like.

'There it is, David.'

'How old was she?'

'Sixty-six, perhaps.'

'Not a big age, these days.'

The exchange steadied him because it was unexpected from David. You could hear exactly these sentences in any pub, club, church any day of the week. He wanted to laugh, to giggle rather, as his body expressed its self-contempt. Crossing his outstretched legs, he massaged his thighs, pleased to read the relief in David's expression. The old man put a good face on it. Under the calm, grief seared like fire. He'd not master it. That woman he'd fetched up from her bed with a word, so that she could walk again, help her husband, enjoy the rich autumn. In one unthinking minute, she trips, and is dead.

As he sat quietly answering David's questions he felt part of his body die with him. His mind registered gratitude to his son for keeping him company, for hauling the subject into the open, but alongside, deeper, more serious, his vitality froze so that he was uncertain whether he could put one foot after another. Why should this death loom so important? He had not felt so unalive when Annie had died. Mrs. Hapgood meant little, he supposed, to him. He did not like her, find her interesting. But his body grudged her death, paralysed itself icily because he'd never exchange trivialities of speech with her again. Nor did sympathy for Hapgood have a first rôle. He'd be better off without her. But she had died, at the snap of a finger, for no reason, when she ought to have survived. He shifted furiously in his aching chair, barely able to suppress the squeals that seemed to force themselves through arms, back-bone, to his clenched teeth.

David was asking about flowers. They would phone. Had he any ideas? Mansfield mumbled, shifting his head backwards, then downwards into his collar to reassure himself that he could. Again he willed himself to sit still, to inquire about David's health.

They'd had a bad night.

Neither had been able to sleep, and at three o'clock Eleanor had made tea.

'You shouldn't be down here, then.'

'It's set me up. I'm not getting well quick enough. That's the top and bottom of it. I don't want to spend the rest of my life in an arm-chair. I'd rather die. Off quick, like your Mrs. Hapgood. Pitch downstairs and out like a light.'

Though David's voice was crisp, unslurred, he looked away from his father. The old man hutched up straighter, spoke out.

'When I had my heart attack, I was convinced I was going to die. That was the worst. Not the pain, the struggle, but the depression, the absolute certainty that this was the end of it all, the humiliating end. I was a rigid box of agony, but at the bottom was this weakness, this emptiness, this conviction I'd done nothing worthwhile. My past life didn't come back; I could barely remember who and what I was now, though I could see, the room, the ambulance men, the number on the garden gate, the children gawping. Nothing told me that I'd had a good innings, hadn't done so badly. I couldn't hope. I couldn't even look forward to the end of the pressure and the pain. I knew I was done for, and that I was nothing, and worse than nothing. I wasn't worth saving.'

'You know that's not true, dad.'

'That was my death. I'm not saying it was anybody else's. Hopeless and inhuman. And the horror was that I was quite different from myself. I'm optimistic. Even sentimental. I look forward, and back. A holiday in North Wales when I was fourteen. When I first heard Fritz Kreisler. But nothing that had happened, or could, made any difference to that pain and that sense that I was done for, and that life hadn't been worth anything. I'm agnostic in religion. I didn't look forward to an after-life, but at least I thought that what I'd done had its bit of significance. It hadn't. The painful end of nothing.'

'We went to see Eleanor's old nanny,' David said. 'She'd nearly died. Kidney infection or something. Eleanor pressed me to go. "She likes men." I'm glad I did, because we seemed to be doing something together. Couldn't have happened a year back. Anyway, the old dear said, "I shall never be frightened of dying again. I knew I was going. But it was peaceful. Like sleep. All the discomforts were forgotten and I was nodding off." '

'Might be so in her case.'

'When I had my little turn, I was annoyed, and frightened, but I didn't lose hope. I was confident they'd get me on my feet again.'

'You're comparatively speaking a young man.'

'The old dear could give you a year or two.'

'It's this sort of heart attack. The pain was awful,

staggering, but I could just about manage that. It was this fearful feeling that there was no bottom in the world, that my bag of skin and bones had split apart at the seams. Perhaps I'm like Mrs. Hapgood, tested beyond strength. She couldn't look after a backward grandson, and she put her head in the oven. I couldn't stand this.'

'Isn't it a usual symptom?'

'Isn't what?'

'Acute depression. Presumably it's part of your body's fight for life.'

'I'm nobody; I'm doing nothing. That's what it did to me.'

'But you've been chasing about after these Hapgoods,' David said, 'and coming down here to see me, and writing those letters to Sarah and making a fuss of Eleanor.'

'Out of habit. I've been doing these things so long as I do them without thinking. If this had happened to me when I was young, if this conviction had been branded into me, my life would have been different. You'd say worse.'

'But you fought in the trenches. Wasn't that . . . ?'

'Perhaps, perhaps.' His will to argument had gone. Nothing mattered. 'I'm less resilient now.' The word trilled ridiculous.

'That's it, then. You'll recover.'

Mansfield leaned down, caressed ankle bone, wax smoothness of shoe.

'My time had come,' he said. 'I should have died then. My body was just strong enough to win.'

'But you feel well, don't you?'

'I'm living on borrowed time.'

'We're all doing that. But your health . . . ?'

'For an old man. Yes. Fine. I'm not grumbling. Anyhow, I'm supposed to be doing you good, not putting years on your back.'

'So you do. So you do.'

'Put years on . . . ?'

David grinned, raised a large policeman's palm in the

air. 'I seem to be talking to you for the first time.' He was making an effort. 'I could always ask advice, and you're a marvellous man to explain things to, but we are exchanging now.'

'You sound like some old Methodist class-leader.'

'Inheritance. I don't know whether you're saying anything sensible with this Lord Snow stuff, "we die alone". In fact, it's not my experience, and I guess modern medicine is so good that people die more easily now than at any time in history. But at least, you're saying something. You're making me sit up.'

'What's that mean?'

'I felt down in the mouth till you started. And now I'm chirping. It's marvellous. There's this man explaining, no mock modesty, never mind shame, how death did for him. In truth.'

'Cod. Once anybody starts on illness or dying, faces lengthen and we think we're hearing something. And because it frightened me, you . . .'

'Hold it, hold it. The medico at the hospital said how little fuss you'd made. The pain's hell and the depression's awful, but you grinned and abode. So don't give me how you went to pieces, because you didn't.'

The two sat silent.

'I was just wondering if comedy doesn't demand a greater concentration of wit than tragedy. That's everything in its favour.'

'There's the old schoolmaster for you. Bit of classification. Couple of ideas to occupy your minds with till tomorrow, boys. Even if we're certain to die in despair, dad, what you've just said about comedy makes life worth something.'

'It was a commonplace.'

'We have to make do.'

'What about the great advances in science? The little, for that matter? Or poems? Business coups? Political progress? Battles?'

'Life.' David sounded vague.

'Death doesn't matter. Death shall have no dominion.' Mansfield caught a glimpse of himself in a mirror leaning forward. He leered wickedly, a devil, an imp of life. 'I'm afraid we're talking nonsense, David. As if we're drunk.'

'Is that so?'

'There's not much in it. We're saying words to each other, but the effect's nil.'

'When I was a boy,' David grimaced, as if he were used to confession or seriousness, had to cover it with clowning, 'you said something to me. I don't suppose you'd remember. I'd run a quarter-mile at Newark that I thought I could win, and I'd come in second. I was really down, showed it, told you so. And you, out of character, said, "It'll harden you." That was more like mother, that bit vinegary. But it was you. Perhaps you were exasperated by something else, or by my sorrows, but you came out with it, shook me. Now I'll hand your advice back. What's happened will harden you, father.'

'I shall die easier?'

'Something of the sort. And don't tell me. I know what you're going to say. There are those who never recover from the toughening process, who are driven to neurosis, or worse. I've seen 'em. And you're not one. Now?'

They sat again, lacking conviction, casting round in their minds for clinching arguments. Both knew there wasn't over-much truth, but both loved the other, for the attempt, this flounder in muddy water. In the end Mansfield spoke first, at a tangent, poking a finger into his shoe:

'I didn't think you'd bear a grudge so long.'

'No grudge. It surprised me, and I remembered it. By and large it's true. Nothing succeeds like success, except success with two or three per cent failure.'

'Yes.'

'Don't be like that.' There was something of Sarah's insouciance.

'No. If we went away and wrote down what we've said here this morning, it would read pretty stupidly. But it's done your trick for you. It's pushed Mrs. Hapgood out of my mind for ten minutes.'

'Fine.'

'She's back now. I feel a bit sick.'

'I know.'

Eleanor rapped on the door, scrutinised the pair.

'Would you two like a cup of tea?'

Both refused, to her chagrin, but she sat, if only on the arm of a chair. 'Awkward with it?' she said. 'Is there anything you do want?'

'Love,' David answered.

His father burst into a laugh, a dry hack of surprise, which thumped him into coughing. Eleanor patted his back.

'Choke up, chicken,' David called.

The fit subsided; they sorted themselves out.

'Touch of the graveyard there,' David said.

'How mean.' Eleanor. 'I need a drink if you don't.' She left, hurrying.

'A good lass, that.'

'Yes.' David blew his nose noisily. 'She's like my mother. Needles you into work.'

'I thought how sympathetic she was. She can sit still, David, which is more than your mother ever could. If it had been left to me, I think I would have called you "Dave". You're still "David". That's a tribute.'

'A confession.'

'Perhaps I'm wrong. I never could bear to be off target. I'm blaming her for my own superior shoolmaster's scruples. They don't matter now I'm a scruffy old man, do they?'

☙ 15 ❧

Mansfield fired off his letter to Sarah, explaining Shakespeare's supremacy.

He stared at the blank paper, shivering, uncertain of his means, but as soon as he began, he lost, indulged, himself. The hour and a half spent here tired and warmed him. Not until he'd finished it, personally handed it to the postman, did he realise that this was the day of Clara Hapgood's funeral.

Not without irony, he allowed the expected sadness to wash over him. He saw the slow walk, imagined the solemn words, the hymns, pews trembling with the wooden bourdon. Glad that he could not attend, he immediately turned his mind to the funeral meal, ham and tongue, strong tea in best china, but most to the jovial cackle of conversation, a resurgence of life. Perhaps this chatter, these grins and nods, were merely self-congratulation; we hung on a bit longer than she managed. The heartiness covered weeks and months of heartache, but there was about a funeral, as he never found, oddly, with a wedding, a statement of life, of resurrection, of vivid joy. Escape the noose and sing. At this time they'd be back from the cold chapel and bleaker cemetery, warming their backsides, warning their cronies, pleased to be there, aware of it all.

Eleanor called in.

She entered daintily, not throwing her weight about. When he mentioned the funeral, he realised she expected this, had prepared herself. Cheerfully firm, she spoke appropriately, encouraged him to say his piece, then switched the subject. Would he like to hear the local choral society?

'Depends what they're doing.'

'Well, that's it, really.'

'What's that mean?' He liked gentlemanly bullying.

'It's Mozart's "Requiem". I didn't know whether you'd want to go.'

'A funny choice.'

'The president died and left a lot of money for a big performance. They're doing Purcell for the first half.'

'I'll go, then.'

'Are you sure? It won't upset you?'

'Not in the way you think. I need up-ending.' His voice trailed into the nonsense that packed his brain. The industrial Midlands swirled with the autumn leaves round the coach in the Prater. Beloved of God.

Eleanor sat down, eyed the room. In the movement he was returned to his own childhood, to his mother who'd look thus before she flicked the duster from her apron pocket and set about the furniture. Sixty years. Only the last week as the Salvation Army played 'Sovereignty' in the street, the collector at the door had smelled of Lifebuoy, red bars in the scullery, boyhood's knees and neck pummelled by the soaped flannel.

'Everything all right?' he asked, pleased with himself, a man again.

'Yes.'

How beautifully she sat there, gently, like sun on alabaster.

'David still in bed?'

'Yes.' She smiled.

'That's good. Make him do as he's told.'

She passed, ran a finger down the ridge of her nose so that he wondered, mischievously, if she was going to thumb it at him.

'Every minute I hold him there, keeps him alive another second.'

The words meant nothing to him, like a tune to which he had not listened. When it was over, he knew what she had said, feared it.

'Yes.'

'Yes. That's it,' she said. 'It makes a difference.'

'Will he be . . . all right?'

'That's entirely up to him.' Voice steady.

'And you, Eleanor.'

'I wish it were.'

Again she smiled, naturally, convincingly projecting herself like an actress.

'How long is he to stay at home?'

'Three months at least.'

'That's not long. Really. Is it?'

She narrowed her eyes.

'In their sort of world, yes, it is. But he'll stick it out, because he's himself and because he knows people will wait for him.'

'That's good.'

'For the next two months. We shall have Christmas together. He'll be marvellous.'

She chilled him; a shivering combed his back.

'You mean . . . ?' He dared not go on.

'What happens is that they're warned, but back they go, do as they've always done, and die within a year or two.'

'Does he know?'

'Enough people have told him. Consultants. Friends. Me. Every damned day.'

'He'll take notice.'

'Yes, when it's too late. He's acquired habits of work. He ricochets about the world. He pushes this, clobbers that. That's what he is. That's what he'll do.'

'But he's sensible now.'

'It coincides with a lull in work. A small mercy. But his pot will boil again. And if it doesn't he'll pump the bellows. He'll never learn.'

'Why do you tell me this, Eleanor?'

'I've got to tell somebody.'

'Can I speak to him about it? I mean do you want me to?'

'Yes. And he'll laugh, and clap you on the shoulder and

tell you he's never felt so well in his life, and ask you if you think he's cracked enough to hound himself to death.'

'I see.'

'He'll be reasonable, and you will, and go away cheered. And inside a couple of years he'll be dead. That's the pattern. He's lucky to have been warned, but he'll disregard it.'

'Eleanor, I'm sorry.'

'It may seen unfeeling, father, but what I'm trying to do is to enjoy what bit of his life's left. That's not much. But it's something for the children. These months and months of estrangement have done for me, in their way.'

'Done?'

'We were serious, convinced that nothing could go right with our marriage. Just think of it. We'd all we wanted, money-wise, but there was David's racketing round the world with his jobs and his women. When he came back to see the children I suppose I was reproachful and sulky and surly. I hated, and I took no pains to hide it. I didn't quite realise that David felt like that about me. Loathing. I've told you before the sight of him just there buttoning his coat up made me retch. This physical antipathy's unbelievable. When I describe it to you now I can't really believe that I, we, suffered. It's inhuman. But it's true, father.'

Her face whitened, seemed to thin, hollow itself, as she spoke. She held her knuckles bloodlessly tight.

'Then it righted itself. I didn't believe that either. But I came to see, slowly, slowly, that I wasn't deceiving myself. I'm not telling you it was what we felt when we first married. You know he's the only man I've loved. But it was calm.'

The sun suddenly brightened at the windows, theatrically.

'Like an unexpected half-holiday. You wouldn't have them at your schools where everything went to plan. But sometimes they let us out, oh, because somebody had won a scholarship, and we'd get a sausage for tea.'

He remembered fish on Good Friday, and then four-thirty for the railwayman's bunfight, cream horns and éclairs, a clown, men decked up as women. And on that day a bonus of sunshine, as today, great sheets of spring light.

'I know,' he said, 'what you mean.'

'I don't want to exaggerate. Everything wasn't perfect. But it was viable. Do you know, father, I seem to be putting words on what barely exists. It's disappeared.'

'I'll halve it,' he said gruffly.

'Then. Then this. You never expect it to happen to you.'

'He was too fit, looked after himself. Dieted. Walked, didn't he, every day?'

'Not recently. There's no time. The other evening I sat in my room with my head in my hands, and do you know what I thought? It seems so mean that I hardly dare say it. I will because it'll show I've got some sort of nasty wits about me. Suddenly, it presented itself to me, almost as if my own voice called it out. "It was probably his adulteries which kept him alive. That's the only exercise he's had recently." What do you think of that?'

'I don't, I don't know . . .'

'It's rubbish perhaps.'

'To me, Eleanor, it's a shocking thing. He's had more success than anybody I heard of, and yet there he is chasing these dirty madams . . .'

Her laugh shrilled, was checked.

'I'll say what I mean. I don't care what rank or status they hold, dirty madams is what they are.'

'He's a very attractive man.'

'I'm ashamed it's a son of mine. Alfred Hapgood's youngest, Tom, caught syphilis. But he's only a labourer.'

'You're not to say anything about this. Not to David.'

'Somebody ought to.' She grimaced. 'What's wrong with him? Beautiful wife and home and family.'

'That doesn't make a satisfying sex-life, father,' she said.

He stopped, amazed, mouth wide.

'Do you mean to say you can forget it all, then?' His vulgarity burst out.

'I hate it. And when I sometimes met one of his . . . his madams,' she giggled on the word, tense, despicably, 'I shivered with hate. My skin crawled. But I suppose it was my fault. I didn't give him what he wanted.'

'That's no way to talk.'

'Nothing's any way to talk. There's nothing to be said. Words don't sort this problem out. I'd spit and cry, and plead, and rail, at first, but he went off to his conferences, and his mistresses. And now I think they kept him alive.'

'You've no proof of that.'

'Neither way. That's worse. Suspicion. The only unusual thing is that I got my punishment before my prize.'

'You don't make much fuss, Eleanor. I can't fathom you, really.'

'I think David's going to die, father. I don't think anybody or anything can prevent it.'

'That's his punishment, then.'

Now she in turn gaped, near incoherence.

'That's wrong. His death's got nothing to do with sexual morality, and you know it. It's to do with the way he flogs his body, and fumes, and chases about the world. And that is the way he's built. If he didn't, he'd think he was below standard, not doing justice to himself. And you and I are to blame for that, aren't we? We've expected it, demanded it from him. In part. In some measure we've helped make him a self-destroying machine.' She stopped, actually clapping her hand to her mouth like an infant. 'I've got to get after somebody,' she said. 'It's pathetic.'

'I know,' Mansfield began, 'the most pathetic phrase in the language.'

'Yes?' She did not want to hear.

'When people are standing half-seas-over in pubs, and somebody's mentioned, or arrives unexpectedly, then they say, "One of the best." That's it. "One of the besht." '

'Why's that, father?'

'That's the only way they can come to terms with the world. Half-kali-ed. And when they'd had a few all standards of reason and judgement go, and any tomfool who turns up is one of the best. That's pathetic.'

'I wish I was like that. Then nothing would matter only goodwill . . .'

'Spurious goodwill.'

'If you like.' She screwed her face at him. 'Vinous bonhomie. You don't go in the pubs, do you?'

'Have you heard of hangovers?' Aggression. He must beat her.

'And when ordinary life's worse than a hangover?'

'Is yours, then?'

She switched her attention away from him, concentrated on a piece of carpet behind him, to his right. Now the pair had finished speaking they seemed in no way connected or concerned with each other. Mansfield stood up, testily, hobbled across the room, picked down a book from the shelves. He opened it, stared at the print and after some minutes discovered to his surprise that he had not even read the title. He snapped it shut, eyed the spine: *The Princess Casamassima*. Returned, it resumed dignified anonymity.

'Look, Eleanor,' he said.

'I'm looking.' She was.

'Why don't we talk sense to one another? There's no certainty whatsoever about David's death. It's just your pessimistic frame of mind. He'll be careful. He's more sense than you give him credit for.'

She waited, inviting him to argue his case with her silence. When he had finished. she paused, then stood, her long skirt ends whirling, and made for the marble mantelpiece and its ornate mirror.

'The best medical evidence suggests that he'll live two years if he goes on as he has been doing.' Her voice was small, in hate, precise, wounding. 'Doctors can be wrong. They often are. You can please yourself, but I feel bound to believe them. In two years' time, I shall be thirty-seven, and a widow. I don't look forward to it.' She stopped, back to him, head down, fingers out, thumbs under. 'That's the only sense I can talk. I'm sorry.'

She spoke apologetically, but immediately burst from the room. He considered moving after her, to dry tears, but almost immediately heard her outside, issuing an order, or outlining a request. Calm. Imperious. Distant. Splendidly at home. Still in the spell of that sentence or two, he looked at his hands, the scrubbed nails, the writing corn on the middle finger, the gold wedding ring, the folded-back sleeve of his pullover. The veins humped high, in faded grey ugliness, while the neatness of the knitted wool was new, perfect. Sighing, he pushed towards the mirror, noted his rumpled white hair, its schoolboy crop, the small moustache, the moist, moping eyes.

Still hesitating, tapping at his leg with a fist, he went upstairs to David's bedroom, was admitted.

'Well, dad?'

David lowered the *Financial Times*.

'I've come to ask you a serious question.'

'Have you, by God.' Folded the paper. 'Ask on then.'

'How long have they given you to live, David?'

'They?' Ironical, scoffing.

'Your doctors.'

'What's got into you this morning, dad?'

'I'm not fooling, David.'

'Obviously. But every question suggests its answer, doesn't it? And I'd guess you want me to name some short period, two weeks, three months.' Lightly, but he smiled, sat up straighter. 'We are in a tizzy this morning.'

'Come on.'

David rasped his whiskers; he had not yet shaved.

'I'll come on.' He sucked his finger, eyes sharp with mischief. 'The most sensible medicos I talked to said that if I worked as I had been doing, I might drop dead at any time. At the outside they'd give me two, three, four years.'

'Two years.'

'The figure varied.'

'They told Eleanor . . .'

'I see. And softened the blow here. And now you want to know what I propose doing?'

'That's about it.'

David lay flat, pulling the sheets up to his chin, closing his eyes. The foolery both riled and shocked his father.

'You see me, dad, don't you?' he began. 'In bed. At ten minutes to twelve in the morning.'

'Yes, now. Now. You feel ill.'

'I feel fit. Mirror, mirror on the wall, who's the fittest twit of all? David.'

'You wouldn't be carrying on like this if you weren't embarrassed.'

'Embarrassed? About death? That's not the word. Terrified.' Again he sat up, powerful, his pyjamas open wide at the broad, gold-haired chest. 'I am doing as I'm told. I'm acquiring habits of lounging. When I go back to Tennant Towers, I shall try my newly learnt way of life.'

'And?'

'That's it. I've tried to be an obedient patient. It came easier than I thought. But when I get back, on the old hue and cry, I don't know. You're probably right. I'll kill myself at the desk.'

'What about your family?'

'They're provided for.'

'With a father? Where's your sense, David. I'm not talking about money. You'd leave Eleanor . . .'

'People like Eleanor and myself aren't in the close touch with their children that you were with me. If mother had died, and you, both, when I was small, I should have landed up in a Children's Home. Rich people farm their youngsters out, to schools, to servants of one sort or another. My influence, you're going to ask, are you? My example? Advice? My pull? Well, yes. But what can I tell Sarah? Your friend? I don't talk to her much, but in a year or two she'll think that I'm not only preying on the human race, but polluting the environment even for myself. And there's truth in it.'

'But, David . . .'

His son slapped the rumpled bedclothes.

'And she'll go and live with a garage-hand who pushes drugs or plinks an electronic guitar on the side. I've no advice to give my brood, except, Eat, drink and be merry, for in two years we die.'

Now he tapped his handsome, cleft chin with the rolled truncheon of the *Financial Times*.

Mansfield, on the edge of his chair, reeling forward, forced himself to sit straight but could not hide or master his trembling. David, now on one elbow, disdained to notice him. Lost, stolen, strayed. Mansfield's boots were bright, his trousers creased, but he barely lived inside a small area of pain, nausea, lacerating grief. He did not know, could not name, himself.

'There's nothing for it, dad. I don't want to snuff it. My life's too interesting. But if I do it's no use making a song about it. I remember as a boy . . . You've had more influence than you think, my man . . . your leading off how Mozart had died at thirty-five. You were obviously moved. The tears in your eye worried me. "The waste, the waste. If he'd lived another twenty or thirty years . . ." '

'Uh?' All he could manage.

'I thought to myself, "Look what he did with the thirty-five he had." '

'That's . . .'

'He lived as if he knew that was all he'd got.'

'David.'

'It crossed my mind. That's all. And the thing to do is not to sit groaning over his premature death but to get off and play and listen to his music. While you're sobbing your socks off you could be hearing Jupiter or the G Minor.'

Like a potholer, coming up from clayey darkness, James Mansfield peered about, tested his battered heart.

'Life's not so cut and dried,' he said, choking on his husks of words.

David buttoned his pyjamas, cocked his head in mock-interest.

'Sometimes you're driven into a corner,' his father croaked. 'All you can do is weep. You're incapable of walking out, deliberately choosing to sit in the concert hall.'

'I agree.' Creamy pride. 'But at the time, I thought, callously perhaps, that you were enjoying your gush of emotion, were deliberately wallowing in it, and that if Mozart's music meant all you said it did you'd have done better to put "Dove Sono" on the gramophone or practise an hour on the Sonate Facile. He died early, but nothing we can do will alter that. All we can change is our knowledge of his music. So.'

'I am as I am, David.' Pitiful. Thin gruel.

'This argument's running mad. But I've got your message. Two years' life if I don't behave. I'll repeat it, if you wish. I understand it. It aches in my bones every time I look out of the window.'

'And you've a wife and family.'

'I have. And a father, who can't make up his mind whether I'm a bloody fool or a rock-hard, stony, thick-as-two-planks, electro-plated sod. Well, I'll tell you. Just as sometimes your life, your failures, your inadequacies led you to indentify with a great genius who died young, and read your regrets for missed opportunities in sorrow for masterpieces he never had chance to write . . .' He stopped to look at his father. For the first time he saw the old man pinched and constipated on his chair, icy and shrivelled, a pale, gulping, grey-skinned bag of piss-and-wind. Waiting he dismissed his pity, politely waiting. 'In the same way, dad, I'm suffering. I don't want to die. I want to live as I did before, taking jobs and men on . . .'

'And women.'

'Yes, if the truth be told.'

'Tom Hapgood caught the pox.'

The sentence acted like a password. David frowned, moved irritably about, tugging the bedclothes, but he did not speak. He acted an awkward, clumsy, sulking child.

'I needn't have said that. I'm sorry.' Mansfield.

'No, nothing, nothing. It happens. And you think I deserve it, something of the sort. You're shocked. Let's leave it.'

'Eleanor?'

'Go on, then. Say your piece. Read the lesson.'

'There's no need, David. You could bring the words out as well as I could. It's Eleanor I think of.'

'Yes, but you do your thinking inside the limits of your prejudices. So all, so all.'

Mansfield felt a collapse within himself, then the tears on his cheeks, sudden, noisy sniffling and sobs. His son, straight now, watched him, tongue moving about his mouth as if to shift some apple-peel from between his teeth. The father strained, at nothing, in solitary self-confinement. It was not that his son had abandoned moral principles; the old man knew himself cut off, dependent on his own resources in some murderous inhospitable prison. Chance of survival, nil; span of life, short. Comfort, none. He wept in degradation, without passion, in despair. This morning's presentation: filial success.

David made no attempt to move.

He did not speak, or touch his newspaper, or make an overture towards the croucher. Tongue investigating teeth, he withdrew until the old man got up, and shambled towards the window.

Humbly Mansfield willed himself to see. Paved courtyard, paddock, fields' dark hedges, three tablecloths in violence on a clothes-line. Inside his chest sobs retched, but mechanically, uncontrollable as hiccoughs. Fumbling for his handkerchief, he saw two black kittens in a field, dashing, tangling, at some little object on the ground, dead mouse, fir-cone, acorn. He'd no interest, but he looked to put off the time when he'd turn, walk out, prepare to go home to die.

A huge sob of self-pity wrecked his breathing.

'Come and sit down, dad.'

He heard, did not budge. Why should he?

'Dad.'

Exhibit his shame? Bastard.

'Are you coming to sit down, dad? I should.'

He blew his nose hard, wiped his face. His teeth clacked, as he gulped, but he was not crying. Now he could face faceless. Where were the kittens? Black with white shirt-fronts at rolling speed. Nothing there, either.

Deliberately, in weakness, legs witless, he crossed four yards to stand at the foot of the bed, exactly in the centre. To himself he still lacked identity; the pyjamaed trunk of his son loomed unclear one moment, perfectly defined the next.

'Yes,' he said.

The word spat, cost blood.

'No,' said David. Mansfield had no idea what the exchange meant, but he felt steadier.

'I'll go and get ready for lunch.'

'Just like that?'

'Like what?'

David slapped his left breast.

'Aren't you going to say anything, then?'

'No, thanks.'

'You're going to walk out, are you? Leave me?'

Seconds crystallised in silence round the jocularity.

'I wish I could say something to you. And mean something.'

'You have, dad. You've done me good. In your own way.' Grinning now.

'We haven't a shred of religion between us, to hang on to, David.'

'No. Afraid not.' David pulled his legs muscularly out of bed. 'We don't regret it, do we?'

'Sometimes.'

'You want an after-life, dad?'

'I'm lonely. Now and then.'

Eleanor knocked, entered, at her ease.

'Oh, you are getting up? Good. John Belvoir rang to ask if he could call to see you this afternoon. I didn't put the call through to you.'

'What's he want?'

'He thinks something of you, David.'

'I doubt it.'

'He's not a bad man, for a duke. So get bathed and shaved, will you?'

'Yes, darling.'

Eleanor looked hard at her father-in-law as they walked downstairs together, but she did not speak until she had opened the study door.

'He's well, isn't he?'

'Full of himself.'

After lunch, David was sent to nurse the library fire, and punctually at two-thirty the Duke of Belvoir arrived. He seemed more powerfully built than Mansfield remembered, of middle-height, but lumbering. His dark hair was oiled. Eleanor opened the door for him herself, brought him first where Mansfield sat, *The Times* crossword on his knee.

'You've met David's father, haven't you?'

'Yes. Of course.'

The duke proffered a large, cool hand.

'Beautiful weather,' he said. Mansfield remembered he lived in South Africa. 'It's the light. Liquid, if you know what I mean.'

Mansfield could think of no reply, but found himself delighted at the visitor's assumption of equality.

'Your young man improving?'

'Yes. Very much so. Eleanor and I were saying . . .'

'Eleanor will know how to look after him.'

'I wish I did.'

'She's perfect,' Mansfield said, gushing. Belvoir rewarded him with a smile that slit deep trenches by his mouth.

'And practical. Is he a good patient?'

'He's surprised me,' Mansfield said.

'Oh? How's that?'

'He's done as he's told.'

The ducal right hand patted a saturnine face.

'I think that's difficult, Mr. Mansfield.' He appeared genuinely engaged with the question. 'We all like our own way, even if we don't get it.'

Mansfield knew that he ought not to be taking such an abundance of pleasure from such banal stuff. But he was. Snob or not, he could not deny it. The sun swung momentarily through the three great windows of the stair, so that the hall was washed with a purity of white sunlight. This is my beloved son.

'His father's keeping a sharp eye on him,' Eleanor said.

'I'm sure he is.'

'I hint. Father puts it into words of one syllable.'

The duke nodded, solemn as a mandarin. Behind, Mansfield heard a knob turn and turned to see David, enormous, filling the doorway.

'Hello, John.'

'David.'

The men shook hands, but Belvoir turned immediately to Eleanor and her father-in-law.

'He looks well. I thought he'd be pale, thin.' Genuine relief.

'One puts weight on lying in bed,' David answered.

'Not a pound.' Eleanor.

David towered above his visitor, fair to dark, dynamic to static.

'He's a big boy,' the duke said to Mansfield. The sentence complimented him, rejoiced, braced, rejuvenated him. He remembered it three days later when he'd arrived back home, and found Hapgood at the station to meet him, and hanging greyly, sheepishly back his son, Tom. Then when that shabby, shoddy figure preceded the older men up the stairs, a case in each lumpy hand, Mansfield recalled the duke's cordial, playful words. In his relief at being greeted, Mansfield repeated the remark:

'He's a big boy.'

Hapgood had not understood, but nodded, and shifted his golfing trilby.

'Ay. They all grow up,' he said. 'Worst luck.'

That hall, white with unexpected sunshine, and the broad uprightness of David, against the duke's heavy-shouldered elegance, with Eleanor unseen, admired, and he himself, the plebeian everyman amongst the heroes fixed itself on his mind. Belvoir spoke affably to him and he did not forget.

Bitterly, with a cringe, humiliated in self-hate, he made himself remember this scene, this light when three days before Christmas a thrombosis flattened David, burst his heart, killed him in minutes. His father saw him once more, in his coffin, handsome as on his wedding day, the dead face proud enough to outface death, last judgement, hell's legions, God Almighty. Eyes closed. This flesh. And his father, deader than the son, had neither answer nor question, a mere twist in the bowel, a dribble at eye and nostril, craw throttled.

Light sank in the hall.

'Come on in, John,' David called. 'Ellie?'

'Not just now. Later.'

'What about you, dad? Coming in to set us right?'

'No, thanks, David. Old man's siesta time.'

David frowned jovially.

'Don't waste your life in sleep,' he pronounced. 'Mozart didn't.'

The door closed.

Eleanor laughed, shook her head, seemed not to know which way to run.

'Great,' she said, from the first step.

'Great.'